Blood Descent

Book Two

H. Leigh Cornwell

H. Leigh Cornwell, Publisher, USA

Printed in the United States of America.

ISBN: 978-0-9837490-2-8

www.blooddescent.com

Cover Design by Berni Stevens
Cover Photo by Caleb Cornwell
Edited by Kristin Burns

For those that share my love for the immortals.

Prologue

Spain 1253

"Ouch!"

"Filipe, stop acting like a child," Marco chided his little brother. "I was running father's vineyard by your age. Yet, he has allowed you to become soft."

"But it hurts! Is this your revenge for me not being able to help you today?" accused Filipe. The words were spiteful, but his soft brown eyes relayed the pain and guilt overpowering him.

"Be still. I need to make sure it is not dislocated, the amount of swelling is cause for concern," said Marco.

He attempted to manipulate the ankle gingerly but it seemed any amount of pressure applied only served to hurt his brother.

"I am sure whatever it is you think you are doing to help is only adding to it. Owww! Such cruelty! You wonder why God has not blessed you with a child?"

Marco abruptly let go of Filipe's foot, turning to make sure his wife was not in earshot. He caught a glimpse of his beloved Brianda through the window. She was outside tending to her garden, her sun-kissed golden brown ringlets partially obscuring her exquisite face.

"Filipe! Learn how to control your tongue!" Marco spat. "Your thoughtless comments can wound as easily as a knife."

"Father says he is disappointed that two years passed without a grandchild," said Filipe. "He wonders how such a healthy woman has yet to give you a child."

"It seems father has enough sense to keep his opinions to himself, you should learn from his silence," chided Marco.

His glare let Filipe know it marked the end of their discussion. He loved his little brother dearly but he often spoke before thinking.

The subject would not lie dormant forever. Eventually someone would inquire as to why there were no children. Marco's eyes returned to Brianda. She stared off absently toward the vineyard as if their thoughts were on the same bleak subject.

It had been weeks since she allowed him to touch her. Her inability to bear children became obvious months ago. The condition tainted her belief that he still desired her as a woman. Nothing he said seemed to change her feeling on the matter.

With a defeated sigh, he turned back to Filipe. He looked so helpless laying there in the bed.

"I am going out into the vineyard. There is much that needs to be done before Brianda's father and brother arrive tomorrow," Marco said. "I will make sure Brianda checks in on you while I am gone."

"I am sorry I was not more careful. You should not have to do all the work alone."

"These things happen, Filipe. It is impossible to always be aware of your footing." Marco turned back to his brother when he reached the doorway, speaking in a low voice. "Please, do not mention children to Brianda."

Marco and Brianda entered the hearth room at the same time. She placed her basket on the table and set about putting together some food for Marco to take to the vineyard.

"How is he today?" Brianda asked.

"He is alright, but he will not be able to walk very much for a few weeks. I cannot feel any evidence of a break, although it is double the size today."

"Poor thing, you know he will spend the day moping because he cannot be with you. He absolutely idolizes you."

"He will be fine. Could you check in on him every so often to make sure he has anything he may need?" Marco asked, taking the meal of bread and cheese his wife put together for him.

"I will take good care of him."

Her words were followed by an awkward silence. There was a time not long ago she would give him a tender kiss before he would leave her for the day. She made no move toward him but lowered her gaze to the space between them. Unable to find the words to comfort her, Marco left in silence.

The shadows were lengthening when Marco realized he was becoming hungry again. He took is meal too early. It seemed to be as good a time as any to take a break. Finding a shady spot beneath a small tree, he sat, taking a drink of water. His eyes absently scanned the vines before him while his mind wandered.

Brianda came to the forefront of his thoughts, as she did so often lately. Eventually she would return to her normal self, he thought hopefully. Sure, he was heartbroken as well but it did not change the fact that she was his wife and he loved her more than he could ever express.

He became aware that, subconsciously, his eyes came to rest on a leaning support post. With a sigh, he got up to resume the maintenance he was out to do. It did not take much to prop the post back in place, the true exertion came in forcing it back into the ground. Bracing himself to thrust the post back in place, Marco shoved with all his strength. The post barely budged but the energy behind his attempt caused his hand to slide down the weathered wood, forcing a splinter as thick as a finger into the webbing between his thumb and forefinger. Pain almost dropped him to his knees. What kept him upright was the fear of the sliver tearing the skin completely through. Mentally preparing himself for the agony he now faced, he quickly slid his hand up the way it came.

Blood seeped from between his fingers as he clutched the wounded hand to his chest. He headed home. Brianda would have to help him tend to his injury. For the first time since Filipe hurt himself, Marco silently cursed his carelessness. If his brother would have been with him he would not have attempted such feat on his own.

When he finally made it to the house Brianda was nowhere to be seen. He walked to Filipe's room. The door was ajar. His first instinct was that the blood loss altered his perception. But no amount of wishful thinking could change the scene that transpired before his eyes.

Brianda was naked astride his brother, leaning forward to kiss him hungrily. Her hips moved against his bare body while Filipe's fingers dug into the flesh of her buttocks, urging her on. Brianda's back was to the door. Neither of them was aware of his presence.

Within two strides, Marco seized Brianda by her hair, pulling her from Filipe. She shrieked, grabbing frantically at his hand to release her. He threw her aside, focusing his attention on Filipe, who was trying to cover himself with the blanket while, at the same time, trying to block the punches Marco was landing on him.

"Stop it!" Brianda screamed, her fists drumming on Marco's back.

Filipe's face was already covered in blood, no telling if any of it was really his. But Marco's brutal assault did not cease. Brianda jumped on his back, flinging her arms around his neck in an attempt to stop him.

"You are killing him! Stop!" Marco's assault did not waiver. "Be angry at me, I made him do it!" she pleaded.

Her words stopped his merciless attack. Marco grabbed her wrists, pulling her around to face him.

"Why? Why would you do this to me?" he snarled, hatred thick in his voice.

"You are hurting me," she sobbed. He gripped her arms tighter. She let out a scream before frantically trying to explain. "You assume I am barren...but what if it is you who cannot produce children?"

His eyes hardened. He released her wrists and grabbed her by her jaw.

"My manhood is now in question?"

She clawed at his grip, cowering under the accusation in his gaze, struggling against him to free herself. Terror filled her hazel eyes.

"You blame me for your adulterous ways? How dare you!" he roared, throwing her into the wall with all his might.

Her body met the wall with a disturbing crush of bone. Instantly she crumpled to the floor, her bare limbs twitching a few times before ceasing to move at all. Her eyes fixed on the doorway, unblinking.

Behind him he could hear Filipe struggling to get up. Marco rounded on him, bracing for attack. The boy flinched, cowering behind his raised hands.

"What have you done, Marco?" he whispered, his arms fell to his sides. Filipe was getting off the bed, trying to steady himself. His left eye already swelling shut, his right eye stared at Brianda's motionless body on the floor. His chin quivered as he spoke, "We only did it for you."

Marco laughed. It was a humorless, chilling sound. He struck Filipe with the back of his hand, sending him back sprawling across the bed.

"My brother would never have broken my heart," Marco spat.

He latched on to Filipe's swollen ankle, pulling him across the bed into his reach. Screaming in pain, Filipe groped in desperation for his only chance to defend himself. His hand found the hilt of the knife in Marco's belt, freeing it from the sheath. Marco pushed back from Filipe's slashing attack. The knife caught his forearm, splitting the skin open, but it was not enough to stop him. His brother's attack only spurred his anger further. Marco took hold of his brother's arm, turning the weapon against him. Filipe fought back but was no match for Marco's strength. The knife plunged into his brother's chest, Filipe's eye went wide with shock. A low, breathless moan emerged from is parted lips.

The pitiful noise snapped Marco from his blinding rage. He quickly reclaimed the knife from Filipe's body, easing numbly back from the bed. Blood poured from the vicious wound in his brother's chest.

"What have I done?" Marco gasped in horror. The knife fell from his clenched fingers, clattering to the floor as he watched Filipe's eye flicker partially shut and glaze over in death.

1

The limousine pulled up in front of a very posh looking high-rise apartment building complete with doorman. Its awning stretched almost to the curb. I suddenly felt extremely underdressed. Jeans and gray hoodie, under a worn denim jacket, did not quite fit the dress code here.

Nikos silently watched me in the rearview mirror as my door was opened by another large, muscle bound immortal wearing a suit. He offered his hand to me while his other hand held an umbrella. I allowed him to assist me from the car. He was blonde with baby blue eyes. If he looked tall from where I sat, standing made it apparent that my position was not lending to an optical illusion. In spite of my feeling I was headed to the principal's office, I couldn't help thinking that if he were shirtless, I would probably be getting an eye full of nipple. He closed the umbrella once we were under the awning, passing it off to the doorman as we walked into the lobby. My black Chuck Taylors squeaked on the marble floor from the rain. I did my best to ignore the noise.

When we reached the elevators, my escort pressed the button and turned to me.

"Good evening, Jacquelyn," the man finally spoke. "I am Von, Lattimer's personal assistant. Sorry for the delay in speaking but I was under the strictest of orders to not linger too long outside with you."

I attempted to speak when the elevator doors opened and he ushered me inside. Von was rugged but not as intimidating as Nikos. His clipper cut hair seemed a bit casual for the black pinstripe suit he wore. He pulled a key from his jacket pocket, inserted it with a twist into an unmarked keyhole and pressed the top button before returning the key to his pocket. With his hands folded in front of him, he stared straight ahead, reminiscent of a secret service agent in the movies.

"Can I ask what this is all about? Why he didn't want me outside too long?"

"I am not at liberty to discuss Lattimer's affairs in his absence," Von said. "I am sorry if you misunderstood, Lattimer did not want *me* outside long."

"Oh."

How presumptuous of me. Von picked up on my bewilderment and was kind enough to explain.

"If you have not noticed, Nikos and I stick out a little. Our presence means Lattimer is in the city. He is trying to keep this trip low key since he does not come to New York often." Von momentarily paused before continuing, "His presence is rarely a good sign."

With an apologetic shrug he resumed his face forward stance. I stared at the climbing numbers, trying to will them backward to no avail. The elevator stopped and the doors slid open. Von turned to me and spoke in a hushed tone.

CHAPTER ONE

"Jacquelyn, I was not trying to scare you. But you did ask," he said and stepped into the penthouse. "If you will, please follow me?"

I took a deep breath and did as he requested. The spacious entry was decadent, to say the least. Black and white marble made a checkerboard of the floor. Ancient statues occupied alcoves in the walls, surrounded by lush plants and potted trees. The room was capped off with a domed ceiling that could have been painted by Michelangelo and was supported by four massive pillars. In the center of the room was a seat that completely encircled a pedestal, displaying a life-size white marble statue of a naked woman. Her head tilted up with one hand reaching toward the sky.

We passed through the room to a pair of double doors, the clicking of Von's shoes finally louder than the squeaking of mine, thanks to the carpet in the elevator. He opened the doors, inviting me in.

"Please, have a seat. I will tell Lattimer you are here."

Von exited through a different doorway than we entered, quietly closing the door behind him. The light, airy feel of the prior room we came through stopped at the door. This room was dark and foreboding. Everything about it was heavy. Although the solid carved sixteenth century wood and dark velvet furniture was quite beautiful, it had such an oppressive feel. Long velvet curtains draped the tall windows. Rich oil paintings in gilded frames hung from the walls. One side of the room contained a substantial mahogany desk with two chairs facing it and a book shelf behind it. The other side had a sofa flanked by complementary chairs. Straight ahead, two wing backed chairs faced the fireplace. They had a less formal feel than the desk setting and were not as cozy as the sofa area.

I sat in the royal blue velvet chair straight ahead that sat next to its twin. A small carved table separated the chairs, equally angled to enjoy the regal fireplace. The mantle was adorned with priceless antique statuettes beneath a large oil painting of an exotic pale skinned man quartered away, yet staring directly at the observer. It was one of those paintings with the eyes that follow you throughout the room. He wore a black embroidered doublet with a white collar fanning out over the top of the high neck. His close trimmed beard was black like his glossy, slicked back hair, which made his silver gray eyes all the more eerie.

The fireplace lit with a whoosh of gas. I jumped. My hand went to my chest. I chuckled to myself, shaking my head. This place was starting to get to me.

"I did not mean to frighten you."

My head whipped around to look at the seat next to me. The abrupt appearance made me gasp in surprise. Sitting there with his legs crossed was the man from the painting. The only difference was his long, straight black hair hung free, almost to his elbows. His beard had been trimmed into an immaculate goatee and his clothes were modern. He wore an olive button down shirt and dark slacks. His eyes were just as mysterious as in the painting, yet so much more haunting than the artist could interpret.

"Which time?" I asked, trying to catch my breath.

The corner of his mouth turned up for a second in a quick grin. He didn't reply while he appraised me from the depths of his chair over steepled fingers. His expressive eyebrows and deep-set eyes gave him a sly appearance. While his straight bridged, narrow nose added a commanding edge to his face. His smooth ivory skin betrayed the wisdom of age in his eyes.

"So, you are the lady that has shaken the hive," the man said with a thoughtful grin. "I am Lattimer." The statement was punctuated with a slow, tilted nod.

What was I supposed to do? Curtsy? Bow? Shake his hand? My lack of response went unnoticed as he continued.

"Let me get straight to the point," Lattimer said, leaning in toward me. His expression turned serious. "You have killed an immortal in what could be taken as revenge for a human." I attempted to defend myself, until he raised his hand to stop me. "I am well aware of the circumstances. However, the only immortals that can kill without consequence are the maker, one who has the authority to pass judgment, or me. Normally when any other immortal destroys another, there is an inquiry to sort the details and discover the motivation. Punishment is then dealt as deemed necessary. With that in mind, my summons to you will not raise question."

"So...this has nothing to do with Violet?"

He settled back into his seat, "Would you like to talk about it? From what I was told, you were attacked. Self defense is an acceptable plea. Unless you feel there is something more to it that I should know?"

"No, that's what happened. Although I would be lying if I tried to say that her death didn't come with a sense of justice for Claire as well."

Surprise flashed across his face, "I appreciate your honesty. Most who are summoned to me are not so forthcoming. But then again, they usually have the luxury of many years and history under their belts before they find themselves under my scrutiny. The majority are not thrust into volatile situations from day one as you have been."

"At the risk of sounding disrespectful, if your summons wasn't because of Violet then why am I here?" I asked. My stomach sank as his brow rose at my question. I quickly tried to amend my inquiry. "It's just that Marco will be worried about me and I haven't called him because of the comment Nikos made about waiting until I spoke to you."

His jaw clenched while he stared at me. He stood and walked to the fireplace mantle. Even as he spanned the short distance, he moved with an air of authority. His spine was straight with his head held high but he still managed to move with grace.

The silence in the room was uncomfortable. The shadows felt like they were closing in. Lattimer turned to face me, his expression stern as he spoke.

"Jacquelyn, I am a very, very powerful man. The entire immortal population of the world would jump with a clap of my hands. But I am not one to abuse my power or bully those beneath me. The majority of the fear my followers have of me is often rumors blown out of proportion. Flights of fancy I chose not to extinguish. Through their own devices, they have saved me from playing the role of the heavy handed, fear inducing ruler. The type of leader one would imagine I would have to be to oversee such a massive group of predators."

He returned to his chair, collecting his thoughts. More than anything I was curious as to why he was telling me all of this, an immortal barely two weeks old.

"For the most part, the way I run our extensive community appears to be working. Those that report directly to me I trust to handle situations that arise in their areas. In the rare event that they cannot, I am notified and a solution is quickly found. Once in a while something occurs that slips through with no conceivable way to make amends. Even still, these events have never made me question my methods or prompt me to change my ways.

"One such situation that I could have handled differently has been brought to mind recently with your addition to our population. I believe it is a situation that I may finally be able to put to rest and not think on again, if you would be so inclined as to lend your assistance."

The explanation offered did little to put me at ease. When such a powerful man needs the assistance of one so novice, it cannot be a good sign, for the novice anyway. The more expendable one never tends to come out ahead, do they?

"I lost one of my children, that is, one that I made. Her name was Aloisia. It was around the mid thirteen hundreds that she simply disappeared. She fell for a mortal man that was being held captive and tortured by his father-in-law. The crime for which he was being detained was murder. He had killed his brother and his wife in a fit of rage. Aloisia followed his screams and the scent of his blood to an old shed. He had been tied to a post for two and a half weeks. His captor gave him enough sustenance to keep him alive but not enough to give him strength. Every morning he would be whipped and every night salt would be rubbed into the wounds. The torture he endured broke Aloisia's heart. Having been a slave girl, she knew the agony of a lashing. She did not believe him to be a bad man but a victim of his own anger. That very night she freed him and turned him before his severely infected wounds could kill him.

"I had never seen her so happy. She brought him to meet me, to receive my blessing and, by law. Back then, you see, I required all new immortals to be registered. I could see the possibility of overpopulation turning into our own sort of plague. Thankfully, so did the others. Eventually I put an end to the blatant practice and now keep my records in a discreet manner," Lattimer said, offering me a quick smile.

"The man she arrived with was a kind, handsome man. I could not tell if his weeks of torture had made him humble or if that was just his demeanor. But I liked him instantly. They were together for almost a century when Aloisia vanished."

Again he stood and walked to the mantle. When he faced me, grief clouded his eyes.

"Soon after, he came to me of his own free will. He relayed a tale that I was not quite sure I believed. Given his murderous past, I could never completely rid myself of suspicion of him. His version of the story was that they started to constantly fight about everything. This went on for almost a decade until he claimed he could no longer live in such a manner. He finally told Aloisia he wanted to leave. A depression took her, the likes of which he had never before witnessed. She refused to feed and spent her waking hours in bed staring out the window. The day she disappeared, he said it was almost sunrise when she told him she would always love him and ran off. Thinking she was being melodramatic, he did not go after her. He was convinced that as soon as the sun started to rise, she would return.

"I did not know what to think. He wore the appearance of a man who had lost everything. There was no one to contradict or confirm his story. The thing that always bothered me was the fact that she never came to me. My door has always been open to all immortals, especially my children.

"My concern for you right now is the fact that you still have no idea what I am talking about. You are the first he has allowed to get close to him since Aloisia," Lattimer said. He crossed his arms across his chest, tilted his head to the side and looked at me quizzically before continuing. "His past is common knowledge amongst his peers. Why would he not tell you when certainly you would find out eventually?"

CHAPTER ONE

All the blood drained from my face. I felt as if I was going to be sick. The lashings should have struck a chord in my mind. Even if they did follow a crime I could not imagine Marco capable of. Why wouldn't he have told me? My week that had been blessedly free of emotional torment was about to come to an end with the familiar sting filling my eyes. The fireplace became an undulating orange blur. A shape appeared between me and the fire. I blinked the tears away so I could see. Lattimer was crouching before me and took my hands in his.

"Jacquelyn, I need your help. I need to know what happened to the young woman I saved from a life of slavery and abuse." His timbre was strong but his eyes were troubled. "You have been my first ray of hope since I lost her. Aloisia was like a daughter to me."

The walls of my world were once again caving in on me as I stared into his pleading gaze. Eyes that I once found eerie were suddenly tearing at my heart.

"I realize you do not owe me anything but I need to be able to lay her to rest, once and for all."

2

The walk back to Marco's somehow didn't seem even close to long enough to put everything into perspective. Still, a much better option than having Nikos deliver me back that much quicker. If nothing else, at least it stopped raining.

Where to begin trying to sort it all out? I had no idea how to look Marco in the eye and pretend I knew nothing—much less how to go about getting him to tell me anything. He chose not to tell me these things as it was, so why would he confess to murder? I could only imagine how bringing it all up would go. *How was work tonight, honey? Not as tough as killing Aloisia, I'll bet.* Yeah...this was going to be pretty close to impossible.

Yet, every time I closed my eyes, I could see Lattimer crouched before me. The distraught look in his eyes begged me for help much more intensely than his words ever could. I would be lying if I tried to say I took no pleasure in having the most feared and influential immortal in the world kneeling before me. Fifteen seconds of power trip aside, could I really deny him? But then again, could I betray Marco? Plain and simple, that was what it all boiled down to. There would be no pleasing both parties. Someone was going to end up very unhappy with me.

The worst part about it all was the fact that I already knew who had the upper hand in this situation. Lattimer needed the same answers I did, if only for different reasons. Marco's duplicity had already decided for me.

The familiar sensation of an immortal close by tugged at my thoughts. Dread made my stomach sink. I didn't have to look up to see that Marco sat on the steps of his building waiting for me. Taking a deep breath, I told myself I could do this, because I had to. I knew if I looked for him, he would already be approaching me. In an attempt to remove any tell tale emotions from my face, I concentrated on the fact that he had no reason to suspect anything. Like Lattimer said, my summons would not raise question, right?

Sure enough, my prediction was correct. His almond eyes were locked onto mine as he moved toward me. The damp pieces of hair that hung in his face evidence he had stood vigil for a while. Uncertainty overshadowed his normal confident demeanor. The closer he got, the more I started to wonder if I was wrong and he did suspect something. I was being paranoid. Concern was the only thing that showed in his eyes. I felt fairly sure, anyway.

He stopped in front of me and said nothing before taking me into his arms, holding me tight. I embraced him in return, thankful I didn't have to lie to his face immediately. The feel of his body mingled with the familiarity of his scent, but something was different. It took me a second to put my finger on it. Although he held me close, the contact did nothing to comfort me. I had always felt a calm solace in his touch. It was gone. Reaching into the depths of my soul, I found the strength to not panic. Everything in me wanted to freak out. I pushed it aside, putting on a brave face. I could do this.

Marco finally pulled away, "Are you alright?"

"Yeah." *Breathe, you can do this.* "Just a bit freaked out." I managed a forced smile, which fit the situation anyway.

"With good reason, Lattimer is not the most objective among us, as I am sure you noticed. It was all I could do not to come after you. If it was not for Augustine, I just may have."

"I don't understand," I said.

"He blamed himself for your predicament and, having made Violet, he was accountable for her. How do you think Lattimer found out about what happened?"

The thought never even crossed my mind. Poor Augustine thought he got me in trouble with Lattimer for killing Violet. I really put Augustine in a bind. She was his responsibility. Of course, he had to tell Lattimer to keep me from looking like a cold blooded killer. I buried my head in my hands. He must be a wreck.

"I should go talk to him, let him know I'm fine," I said, looking up into Marco's tormented gaze.

"Well..."

"Well, what?" I asked, puzzled by his odd reaction.

"Maybe it would be best not to say anything about who said what to Lattimer. He feels bad enough about you being summonsed."

He had a point. Augustine was a friend. I didn't want him to think I was mad at him for honoring his obligations as Violet's creator.

"Oh, no. I understand," I said. "There's no need for finger pointing. I'm fine, and I suppose he's already aware that I'm back. So I guess it isn't even really necessary to address it if you think it's for the best."

CHAPTER TWO

Marco pulled me back into his arms and whispered in my ear, "You are a good soul, Jax. I really do not deserve you."

I pulled back first this time, "Come on, let's get inside."

Again I managed a smile not much less awkward than the first. The road to the truth was going to be a long one if I even possessed the endurance to travel it.

The next evening I found myself alone in bed. Marco had already left to open the bar. I breathed a sigh of relief. There would be a break in trying to act normal for a while. Unfortunately, the new day did not bring with it a plan of action. When we arrived at the apartment the prior night I turned in early. I hoped the solitude would give me time to think in peace. About the only thing I became aware of, without a doubt, in those wee hours before dawn, I was still at a complete loss on what to do.

One good thing, sleep came blessedly free of dreams. I could only imagine the awful directions that could have been explored by my subconscious mind. Maybe even the semi crazed playwright that dwells in the back of my mind, constructing my unconscious entertainment, even felt sorry for me and my task at hand.

It started to become obvious to me I would need to enlist some outside help on this one since, apparently, I was getting nowhere alone. Claire, my usual go to girl, oddly enough, didn't seem like the right choice. Even if I could steal her away from drooling over Augustine for five seconds, I wasn't sure her brand of advice would benefit my predicament. But another name came to mind and, at last, I felt the first step of progress. The thought of getting out of the city for the night only added new hope to my outlook.

I passed through the double doors into Marco's Place. He was next to the bar talking to one of his new employees, a human named Lori. I grabbed the stool closest to the door to give him privacy. Mid sentence, he looked up and signaled to give him a second.

Diana was bartending. Although I still questioned whether or not she was even old enough to be behind a bar, human rules didn't exactly apply there. She approached me, smiling, the long blonde ponytail pulled up on top of her head bouncing all the way. It would be easier to imagine her cheering on the high school home team than catering to the demands of the undead. But this was exactly where she wanted to be. She stopped in front of me, looking over at her boss talking to the new girl. Her face hinted at the disapproval she tried to conceal.

"Hey, Jax, what's up?" asked Diana. "Want a drink, or something in a glass?" She winked at me.

Apparently I would never live down the initiation prank she pulled on me thanks to Tatiana and Owen. Eager to change the subject as always, I went for the obvious.

"What's going on there?" I asked, nodding toward Marco and Lori. The girl's thick mane of brunette curls hid her face but, having met Lori, I knew how pretty she was. Not that I was bothered by it. I would just prefer to read a facial expression than to read her mind.

"Oh, new girl's just sucking up, as usual."

I found myself scrutinizing the situation a bit closer. No need to see her face if I opened my mind to her thoughts. Big mistake. She barely even heard the words Marco spoke, too busy imagining what she would do to him sexually. Marco knew this as well, the look he shot my way said it all. He shrugged. I knew he was right. Not much he could do about the feelings of a human. It was not unusual for immortals to have that effect on humans, even passively.

"Can you blame her? He is looking rather fine tonight," I said, admiring how his navy knit shirt clung to his physique. As if on cue, he ran his hand through his shaggy, shoulder length locks in an attempt to push the strays out of his face. What exactly did a murderer look like anyway? Like all the rest of us, I suppose.

My mind still open to human thoughts, I was not prepared for the memory that hit me. Diana had slept with Marco. Specific, graphic memories flooded my mind. I had to avoid looking at her for a moment. Looking down, I closed my eyes. However, one scene did grab my attention. Diana's hand tracing the scars on Marco's back. My own memories took over. Lattimer's pleading eyes flickered through my head, along with his request for my help. When I opened my eyes, Marco was staring at me. He excused himself from Lori, making a B line my way.

"Diana, could you go restock the cooler?" he asked.

She was off toward the back without a word. When she disappeared through the door marked 'employee's only', he turned back to me.

"Jax···I—" Marco started to explain.

"You had a life before me. There is no need to justify anything."

Even though deep down I believed what I said, it didn't mean I had to like it. I looked up to see Lori staring at us. The look on my face must have turned lethal, judging from her haste to leave my line of vision. Thankfully she had no memories of Marco I'd rather not view. Especially since she was only added to the staff after my addition to his bed.

"Ok," he said while trying to gage whether or not I meant what I said. "So, to what do I owe the pleasure of your visit?"

"I wanted to stop by to let you know I'm headed upstate today."

"Are you sure you are alright?" he asked skeptically.

"Yeah, I just want to get out of the city for the night. Besides, I've been meaning to check in with Olivia."

"Sounds like a plan, I am going to be stuck here all night, anyway. Here," he said, fishing his keys out of his pocket, "take the car."

"Oh, ok." I took the keys from his outstretched hand. "Thanks."

"Please drive carefully and call me when you get there."

"The demise of my Volvo was Silas's fault," I explained, trying not to sound irritated. "I am a very safe driver."

"Jax, that is not what I meant. You have not driven since your change. The way our minds process information is so much quicker than humans, it is easy to lose track of your speed. Remember discretion."

"Thanks for the heads up," I said as he kissed me goodbye.

The drive to the manor house was soothingly uneventful. I pulled into the circular driveway and cut the engine of Marco's BMW. My eyes slid shut, silence washed over me. The woods that surrounded the property dominated my sense of smell. Happily, I gave in to the serenity found in its pristine existence. A peace settled in on me that I hadn't felt since well before my transformation.

CHAPTER TWO

With my senses open to my surroundings, the faint click of the manor house's front door was easily audible. Reluctantly, I opened my eyes as Olivia passed through the door onto the porch. A gentle breeze rippled through her silken, caramel colored hair. Her pale green eyes emulated the smile that played on her lips. You always knew where you stood with Olivia, just one of the reasons I adored her. Exiting the car, I met her at the foot of the steps and she welcomed me with a hug.

"What an unexpected pleasure."

"I'm sorry, I guess I should have called first," I said, suddenly aware of my disregard for common courtesy.

"Nonsense! You know you are always welcome here." Her smile waivered and she eyed me suspiciously. "Why do I get the feeling all is not well?"

Olivia's knack for reading me was spot on once again. Her ability to accurately interpret my moods could only be rivaled by Claire's.

"Is it that obvious?" I asked, feeling like my visit seemed rather self serving. "I honestly didn't come by to burden you with my drama. More than anything I just wanted to get out of the city."

"Family, remember? I meant it when I said it, Jacquelyn," she affirmed with a sincere smile. "Regardless of what happened between you and Trinnian, you will always be welcome here. Even if he decides to return."

The mention of his name always brought mixed emotions with it. Not just because he was the one who sired me. He had been my friend and my lover. But he was also the one that abandoned me and condemned my best friend Claire into this eternal life against her wishes. Not that she's complaining now.

17

"Thank you. Speaking of family, where's that handsome man of yours?"

"Collin is out hunting–his second favorite pastime," Olivia said with a wink. She laughed at my stunned expression, "Let us go inside and you can tell me what is on your mind."

I followed her inside, all the while my mind sorted through all the things that occupied it, trying to decide what I would share with her and what I would keep to myself. It wasn't that I didn't trust her as much as I didn't see the need to give her more information than was necessary.

We passed through the foyer and settled into the front seating area of the massive living room.

"Is everything alright with Claire? Augustine seemed to think she was adjusting well last I spoke with him."

"Claire is fine. I don't know if she would have faired as well without Augustine, to be completely honest with you. He has been wonderful," I said.

"Good," Olivia responded with a content nod and quietly sat, watching me. "Are you going to make me drag it out of you?"

"No. I'm sorry...I just don't really know where to start."

"Ahhh. So it is Marco."

"How did you guess?"

"Because your reluctance to discuss this with Claire and Augustine and your need to get out of the city. But, most of all, you have his car. If you would have wanted to go for a run to think about something you would have had to tell him. He more than likely offered you his car when you said you wanted to come here to test that theory. Because you took his car he believes your motivation to come here is just a normal visit." My paranoia that he was on to me resurfaced with a vengeance. Olivia must have noticed me stiffen as she was quick to put me at ease. "Or he was just being a gentleman, knowing that you are without a means of your own transportation and offered you his," she said with a chuckle.

As quickly as it came, her amusement passed. When she spoke again it was all seriousness.

"How did you find out?" Olivia asked.

Lattimer's words echoed in my head. *His past is common knowledge amongst his peers. Why would he not tell you when certainly you would find out eventually?* Followed closely by Olivia's comments on my porch the night she and Collin came to my house. *It may not be any of my business but please use your gut instinct about the immortals you allow into your life. Just like in your human life, not everybody has your best interest at heart.*

"You knew." I could feel the confusion and hurt slide into place like a mask. "Why didn't you tell me?"

"What did I tell you when you asked me if there was something you should know about Marco?" Olivia asked.

"That you didn't know him well enough to pass judgment."

"And I still do not," she said. "All I know about Marco is what I have heard from others. I have never heard the account of his life first hand from his lips. Second hand information about someone, especially from people that were not present to bear witness, is not very useful to me. What also needs to be taken into account is the fact that these events occurred before I even existed. If Marco is a malicious killer, do you not think the urge would have forced his hand again at some point?" A tiny smile twitched at the corner of her mouth, "Besides, would you really have believed me if I said anything negative about him that night?"

19

I could recall the night in question with graphic clarity. It was the night I was attacked with a meat cleaver in my own home and Marco had selflessly come to my rescue. So she definitely had a point. I'm not entirely sure I would have taken any negative perspectives seriously about Marco that particular night. After all, he did gallantly drop everything that night just to help me, a perfect stranger at the time, I might add. Not exactly the actions of a cold hearted killer.

"Point taken."

"May I ask who told you?" Olivia asked.

With a sigh I told her about the events of the prior evening, sticking to the discussion about Marco and Aloisia exclusively. She listened intently without interrupting but I couldn't pick up on her assessment of the situation. When I finished relating my tale she finally seemed to reanimate. It took her a moment to speak as she collected her thoughts.

"Jacquelyn, I would suggest that you not take his request lightly. When Lattimer gets something in his head he tends to believe its importance takes on the same priority with everyone. Ignoring him is not an option," she stated firmly.

"But I don't even know where to begin trying to get answers from Marco."

"You are a smart woman, you will figure something out."

3

The manor house came into view through the trees. Fog had descended, thickening the air and adding a ghostly feel to the landscape. Trinnian stopped cold in his tracks. He could not help but feel hesitant to proceed, not having spoken to Olivia and Collin since the night he walked out on Jacquelyn. They were the only two in his existence that would not hate him for his choices. Still, he felt even they should have taken offence in his irrational behavior. In his heart he knew they would be happier to have him back than upset with his decisions.

Dead leaves cast off from the fall trees crunched under foot when he resumed his trek. The night creatures lurking nearby became silent. Undead had that effect on nature.

Just as he stepped out of the tree line, the front doors burst open. Olivia's peridot eyes locked on to his shape as it emerged from the trees. Her breathtaking smile adorned her exquisite face. The familiar twinge of dishonor muted the predictable flare up of desire he felt when he saw her after spending time away from her. He wished he could truly be the respectful man she thought him to be.

In the blink of an eye, she closed the distance between them. Her leap covered the remaining few feet. She latched herself onto him in a way that gave him difficulty ignoring his less than honorable thoughts. Luckily, he braced himself for the impact or they both would have tumbled to the ground. It took him a second to wrap his arms around her in return. His guilt prompted him to scan the house for Collin's presence. Collin was nowhere near them. This new found information should have allowed him to relax, but the result was the opposite. He pried Olivia off him and took a step back. Something about her expression found him momentarily taken aback. He spoke in an attempt to avoid an uncomfortable silence.

"I am not entirely sure what would be the proper words to use to ask for your forgiveness," he said. "The betrayal I have inflicted on everyone I have loved I do not expect to be forgiven, much less repaired. But I return home tonight fully prepared to be made accountable for my selfish actions."

"You sound like a melodramatic fool," Olivia mused, she stared a little too deeply into his eyes, causing him to look down. "There is nothing to forgive, Trinnian. You did what you needed to do at the time." He returned his gaze to hers, about to speak, but Olivia headed off his intentions with a shake of her head. "Oh no, I am not prepared to deal with brooding, self torturing Trinnian tonight." She grabbed his hand, giving it a slight squeeze, "Welcome home." Olivia turned with his hand in hers, leading him to the manor.

With morning still a couple hours away, Trinnian retired to his room. The familiar cold, empty space greeted him like an old friend. Maybe this was what eternity intended for him. He shrugged off the oppressive thought and sought out the warm comfort of the shower. Beads of hot water pelted his naked flesh while his mind rewound his conversation with Olivia.

He made a conscious effort to avoid the topic of Jacquelyn. She was a subject he had tortured himself over way too much recently and did not care to reexamine anytime soon. That whole fiasco was a closed chapter of his life, it seemed abundantly clear. Thankfully, Olivia did not bring it up either. The one thing that did pique Olivia's curiosity was Margaret and her fate following the night Owen removed her from the manor.

Trinnian went on to relay to her what Lattimer told him. The night Owen deposited Margaret on his doorstep, Lattimer simply suggested she try living another life. One where she explored who exactly she was instead of filling the role of being what others wanted or expected her to be. Lattimer then claimed he basically sat back and allowed her to evolve into the strong, independent woman she eventually became.

A smile formed on Trinnian's lips as he slipped into his robe, imagining who Margaret must be now. He knew the moment Lattimer told him about her complete transformation, he made the right decision in not disrupting her life with his self-centered intrusion.

Trinnian caught his reflection in the bathroom mirror in passing and paused to affirm what he saw. For the first time in weeks, his dark eyes did not look hollow and empty. Running his hands through his wet, dark hair he looked harder at his reflection. Did he really look...content?

A knock at the door disrupted his moment of introspect. He passed into the bedroom as Olivia poked her head in.

"Hey." The word was spoken softly, as if not to impose. Trinnian motioned her in and she continued, "I was going to turn in for the night but I just wanted to let you know how much it means to finally have you back home."

He almost regretted his decision to let her in as she appeared to float toward him in a plum nightgown that skimmed the floor. The way the delicate silken cloth clung to her as she approached brought back his earlier feeling of dishonor.

She wrapped her arms around him and whispered in his ear, "I missed you so much."

Her scent made it even more difficult to ignore his mounting desire. How many centuries had he been able keep his behavior admirable? The only difference now was his recent affair with Jacquelyn. Had her unleashing his decades of restrained needs and desires rendered him unable to keep them in check?

He slowly pulled back from her embrace, "I missed you, too."

Olivia's eyes locked intently onto his, her hands slid down the front of his robe. Delicate fingers found the belt, working to untie it. Trinnian's hands latched on to her wrists in an attempt to stop her.

"Olivia, what are you doing?" he asked, trying to keep his words firm yet gentle.

"Something I have always wanted to do."

She stood on her tiptoes, not letting her restrained wrists derail her plans, kissing Trinnian fully on his mouth. He pulled away, torn between longing and respect, the taste of her lingered fiendishly on his lips.

"Collin—"

CHAPTER THREE

"Collin knows," whispered Olivia. "He has always known."

Once again her lips found his, he made no attempt to stop her.

* * * * *

A couple days passed since my visit with Olivia. I started to feel better about Marco. Her logic prompted me to consider the possibility that he wasn't a murderer. Hell, even Lattimer wasn't sure. But when I was in Marco's presence, it just didn't feel right. I couldn't quite put the feeling in words. It was as if there was a tension that existed, if only one-sided. I knew there was no way Marco didn't suspect something was going on.

Collin came into the city to hunt with Augustine and Claire. They were kind enough to invite me, which gave me a break from my self-inflicted mental torture. Other than that, I spent the majority of my time holed up in Marco's apartment and he spent his time at work.

The onset of cabin fever pushed me to venture out. I headed for the bar, entering through the employee's only door. Diana was bartending again and Lori rushed past with a tray of drinks. Neither of them noticed me due to the bustling crowd. But, then again, neither did Marco, who was locked in a more than friendly embrace with an unfamiliar immortal female by the main entrance. She was hauntingly adorable. Her chestnut hair was cut short in a trendy fashion and her features had a youthful quality to them. Smoky eyes betrayed any assumption of innocence, yet they didn't interfere with her carefree smile.

She was the first to break their hold. There was a quick verbal exchange between them before she gave him a peck on the lips and disappeared through the main entrance. Marco watched her leave. When he turned back to head toward the bar, the smile he wore still lingered. That is until he saw my face. Apparently he was too busy to even notice my arrival. I could feel my jaw clench. By the time he reached me he was already in damage control mode.

"Jax, that was not what it looked like," Marco explained.

"Hum," I said, crossing my arms, "and what exactly did it look like?"

"Well...I am fairly certain it looked—" he stopped mid-sentence and shook his head. "That is my partner, Julia. She is part owner of Marco's. A few months ago she was feeling a bit burnt out so she left for an undetermined amount of time. This is the first time I have even spoke to her since she left. I actually thought she might not return."

I stood my ground as the wheels started turning. This was my chance, the break I needed to get to the bottom of everything once and for all. But I really didn't want to do it in the middle of the bar. He gave me a look that let me know I needed to say something. This was it.

"Kind of strange you haven't mentioned anything about this before tonight, don't you think?" My stony demeanor almost made *me* wince. This wasn't me but I couldn't pass up this opportunity.

"Like I said, I was not sure she was even coming back."

"Is it safe to assume there is more to it than what you're telling me?" I asked. "I have a strange feeling the bar wasn't the only thing she needed to get away from."

CHAPTER THREE

I turned to head up to the apartment where in privacy he just may be a bit more forthcoming. There I discovered Lori had been standing behind me. No telling how long she had been there but I caught the fact that she was pleased we didn't seem very happy at the moment. More specifically, she was hoping he'd 'dump my ass'.

"Don't forget I can read your mind, you stupid bitch," I snarled at her as I stormed by and back through the employee doors.

Marco caught up with me at the elevator just as the doors opened. He followed me inside. I stabbed the button for his apartment and stood there, staring a hole in the panel as the doors slid shut. Silence mingled with the tension in the confined space, triggering a feeling of claustrophobia. I was actually thankful when Marco finally spoke.

"Look, Jax, I am sorry. I did not realize it mattered."

"So there *is* more to this than you're telling me," I muttered.

He sighed audibly. The doors opened and we stepped into his apartment. I turned before we made it into the living room.

"Not even an attempt to defend yourself?" I planted my hands firmly on my hips in my irritation. "So then, I'm right? She left because of you?"

"She wanted me to commit to her but I was not interested."

"So you will be her partner in a business, and even sleep with her, but that was the most you were willing to offer?" I asked in a judgmental tone.

For some reason I was getting angry. Was it because I didn't want to be grilling him like this for Lattimer's sake, hoping he would reveal all he withheld from me? Maybe it was his cold treatment toward someone that loved him? Or was it the simple fact I was hurt by the things I was learning about him in general?

"Stop this!" he insisted. "Jacquelyn, you need to tell me what is going on."

Shit, shit, shit—he was on to me. Maybe I could still make this work, but I had to do it now.

"You tell me you love me but you won't let me in," I said, feeling like I was starting to choke up. "You can't expect me to love you when you keep things from me."

"No! Stop! Something else is going on here. You have been acting strange ever since you returned from meeting Lattimer," he said. His eyes scanned mine, looking for affirmation. "You flinch when I touch you. The way you look at me...it is like you see a stranger. I have been trying to give you space because I know what it is like to be under Lattimer's scrutiny, but it only seems to get worse."

Finally, there it was. He practically handed me the opening I needed on a platter.

"And how would you know what it's like to be under Lattimer's scrutiny?"

If he didn't tell me now I would never find out.

I could see understanding sink in, making Marco's gaze harden, "He put you up to this." My stomach sank as he continued. "He is using you to do his dirty work...and you are allowing him."

He tensed up, muttering a curse before punching his hand through the living room wall. I jumped back with a shriek. He turned to me with his jaw set in anger, but hurt owned his eyes.

"You want to know if I killed Aloisia? Is that all you need?" he snapped at me. "A part of me thinks maybe I did,

28

simply for the fact that I was not Lattimer. He used her and tossed her aside like all the rest. But she did not see it that way. She blamed herself that he pushed her away. Everything I did was compared to him. I never had a chance. But I loved her, she was my maker, and my love for her made me believe that, one day, she would see the man I was, not the man I could never be. When I finally accepted the fact that it was never going to happen, everything changed. She became angry with me that I would no longer act as her consolation prize. Since she created me, she believed I was hers to do with as she pleased. When she saw I had free will, she crumbled. She knew she had nothing left. The story ends exactly how I told him it did."

By the end of his tale, tears ran down my cheeks. I messed up. There was no doubt in my mind I should have just been straight up with him. But the damage had been done.

I reached for his hand. He retracted from my touch. The hurt that occupied his eyes now held his expression in sadness.

"The night I met you, I was not looking for anybody to share my life. I was content with the way things were, especially given the experience I did have with relationships. But you were thrust into it so suddenly, so completely, I could not help but take notice. That is when I realized that if I had been looking for someone it would have been you. You were everything I would have looked for." His eyes grew cold, considering me for a moment before he continued. "How I convinced myself you would have been different than the others..." He looked away, the muscles in his jaw twitched. When he returned his gaze to me it was empty. "I would prefer it if you were not here when I come home."

He turned his back on me and walked to the elevator. He stepped inside, turning to press the button, never making eye contact with me. When the doors shut, I did the only thing I could at that moment. I slid to the floor, buried my head in my hands and cried.

I could feel the driver's eyes on me as the car raced along the highway. As if being confined in a car with a mortal wasn't difficult enough, this one was dead set on annoying me. His attention once again flickered to my reflection in the rear view mirror. I made no attempt to hide my displeasure and his gaze quickly returned to the road.

Unfortunately there was no choice for me in the matter but to hire a car. Mine had still not been replaced since the accident and I was in no mood to run all the way to my house toting luggage. Specifically the two suitcases I had been living out of for the past week at Marco's. Not for the first time since Trinnian transformed me, I found myself mourning the passing of my boring mortal life. The very existence I once found mundane and predictable. Maybe routine wasn't so bad after all?

The car came to a halt. At last I was home. The driver opened my door before removing the suitcases from the trunk and hastily placing them on the sidewalk. He mumbled some sort of pleasantry, got back into the vehicle and sped off.

Lost in my own personal pity party, I didn't immediately notice the presence of an immortal. At first glance I could have sworn it was Trinnian. My heart froze and my breath caught for a moment. The deep brown eyes and short dark hair were similar, but the brawnier build and height told another story. It was Collin that stood in the doorway of my home.

On any other night, my normal reaction would have been to inquire what exactly he was doing in my house. The question itself would understandably be tinged with irritation, brought on by a mild feeling of violation. However, tonight he could have very well greeted me wearing my favorite lingerie and I wouldn't even question his motivation. At that point, I just wanted to be hidden away in the sanctuary of my home.

"Need help with those?" asked Collin.

"I got it, but thanks," I replied, climbing the steps with my suitcases in tow.

"You are probably wondering what I am doing in your house."

"The question did cross my mind now that you mention it."

I passed by him into my house, putting the suitcases down just inside the door, hanging my jacket and purse on the coat rack. Having rid myself of all burdens I plopped down on the couch, awaiting Collin's explanation since he was offering. The door shut and he came to join me on the couch.

"First off, I am sorry I did not ask your permission to use your home. I just needed somewhere to go where I could sort things out in private. Knowing you have been staying in the city I figured this was my best option."

Collin was probably the most difficult being to read I had ever met. Although he showed no signs of distress or sorrow his presence was enough to know something was seriously off. He was fine the other night when he came to the city. But again, like I really could have known the difference. I decided I wasn't going to pry, yet, in the same sense, if there was something he wanted to share with me I would gladly listen.

"Provided my presence doesn't bother you, feel free to stay as long as you like. It really makes no difference to me. As you know there is plenty of room." Then I thought maybe I should at least ask..."Are you ok?"

"I think so."

"Do you want to talk about it?"

"No, not really," he said before turning the tables on me. "Are you alright?"

"I've been worse."

"Do you want to talk about it?"

"No, not really," I answered.

In all actuality, I really didn't. Strange as it may sound, having him there in what I could only assume was a similar state of mind was somewhat comforting. My assumption based on the fact that Olivia was not with him and he was apparently going out of his way to avoid her.

We sat and talked about anything but what had brought us together in my home that night. It was the first time I actually sat and spoke with Collin one on one with no particular motivation except conversation. He was nothing like the cold, unreasonable man I once believed him to be. More than anything, he was an honorable man that understood the value of those that impact our lives for the better. It was those relationships he guarded viciously that could lead some to believe he was a suspicious, intolerant man. Which I had to admit I myself was guilty of in the beginning, that side being my first real impression of him.

With a new day encroaching on the night, I showed him to the guest room and made my way to my bedroom. I shut the door behind me and leaned against it. My bed didn't look as inviting and comforting as I remembered it to be. It actually looked a little stiff and sad. Nonetheless, it was exactly where I wanted to be right at that moment. I kicked off my shoes and crawled under the covers, not even bothering to undress. My mentally exhausting night easily lulled me to sleep.

A mob of people were cheering as a man on a crude wooden stage stirred them into a frenzy. His crowd was made up of peasants, poor folks that came into the medieval town square to see justice served. That much I gathered from the shouts and outbursts around me. I pushed my way through the onlookers toward the stage, trying to find out exactly what was going on. Off to the right of the man on the stage was the hooded figure of another man that appeared to have his hands bound behind his back. The man wearing the hood wore little more than a pair of ragged trousers. Dirt and blood caked his exposed flesh. A burly, cruel faced man clad in black held on to the bound, shirtless man as if to keep him from escaping his fate.

"Who amongst you would come forward to bear witness to this man's crimes?" Shouted the man pacing the stage, insuring the people got the show they came for.

The crowd became even more agitated as they shouted and pushed forward toward the stage. I broke through the front row when I was pushed from behind, my hands flailing out in front of me to catch myself on the edge of the stage.

CHAPTER FOUR

"We have a witness!" The man shouted triumphantly, motioning those around me to heft me up on the stage.

His enthusiasm brought earsplitting cheers from the throng of people surrounding me. I shook my head violently, pushing at the hands that tried to offer me up to the man on stage. My protests meant nothing as the man grabbed my hands and, with the assistance of those around me, pulled me to my feet on the stage with him. I now stood face to face with the man.

But this was a man I knew. This was Lattimer. His silver gray eyes glimmered with satisfaction that his request for justification had been so quickly filled. He grabbed me by my upper arm and turned me to face the crowd.

"Here is your witness! This poor girl has seen firsthand what this murderer is capable of! She has cast aside her fear to come forward and identify the monster that has lived amongst us!" he shouted, stabbing his finger theatrically in the direction of the hooded man.

The noise was deafening. My pleas could not be heard over the pandemonium that had overtaken the town. I turned to Lattimer, begging him to release me. A glimmer of hope came as he motioned his audience to quiet down. However, his actions were for his own benefit, not so that he or anyone else could hear what I had to say. I screamed at him to listen to me. It was as if he couldn't hear me.

"Remove the hood!"

The man in black ripped away the cloth that obscured the bloodied and broken man's identity. I knew this man as well. Even with his face battered and swollen, I could easily identify Marco. Gasps and murmurs rippled through the crowd.

"Is this the man you saw savagely murder the girl?" Lattimer posed the question, positioning me to better view Marco's face.

The people became still and quiet as a cemetery. I looked out at their faces, eagerly awaiting my confirmation. They were out for blood. A glance to my left confirmed my suspicions. An axe was propped against a chopping block. I turned to Lattimer to beg him to stop this. But when I spoke, the words were not what I intended.

"Yes, behead the animal!"

Once again the crowd was whipped into a frenzy, shouting for justice. I tried to pull away from Lattimer to go to Marco and protect him but Lattimer's grip tightened and, for the first time, he seemed to recognize me. The noise of the people distorted as if hearing them from under water. Lattimer's face filled my line of sight, obscuring all else.

"This is what you wanted, isn't it?" he asked with a self-righteous smirk. "Why else would you betray one that loved you so blatantly?"

My head shook back and forth slowly while the shouting of the crowd returned to full volume and recognition left Lattimer's eyes. The whole dreadful scene came back into view. Once again Lattimer became the ringmaster.

"You heard the lady, this man is guilty!" he exclaimed, turning to the executioner. "Remove his head!"

I tried once again to free myself from Lattimer's grip, to no avail. All I could do was stand by helplessly as the executioner shoved Marco down to his knees and bent him over the chopping block. With his foot firmly planted in the center of Marco's back, the executioner raised the axe over his head. Marco's defeated gaze came to rest on me as the axe came down.

CHAPTER FOUR

The door to my bedroom burst open and, almost before I could make sense of anything, Collin was by my side. My scream had alerted him to my distress that only existed in the realm of dreams, unbeknownst to him at the time. When he realized I was alright he sat on the edge of the bed next to me. He hung his head in relief before turning to me.

"Is this normally how you wake?" he asked. "Because I seem to recall being woken by your screams the night you and Marco stayed at the manor as well."

I sat up, rubbing my temples with quaking hands, "Sometimes. I tend to have pretty vivid dreams."

"Interesting. Some of us do not dream at all." He stood, looking down at me. "You look terrible."

"Thanks, just what a woman longs to hear from any man."

He gave me a quick, uncharacteristic smile, "I mean you obviously need to feed." He walked to the door, speaking without looking back. "Get yourself ready to leave for the night, we are going out," Collin stated, shutting the door behind him. His abrupt retreat leaving me no choice but to do as requested.

Our night began with a quick hunt in a seedier section of a nearby town. It was a place that was once a thriving community, abandoned by the very industry that built it, all but forgotten. Condemned buildings became refuge to criminals on the run and junkies, a virtual buffet for vampires looking for an easy meal.

When we returned to Collin's Range Rover, it became clear that we wouldn't be permitted to mope at my house tonight.

"What would you like to do tonight, Jacquelyn?"

"Oh...I hadn't really given it much thought." His look let me know I wasn't weaseling my way out of making a decision. "Fine...um, something normal. Dare I say human?"

"Like?"

I thought about it for a moment. It was Friday night. This would be so much easier if we were in the city. I tried to think about things I hadn't done in a while. Midnight bowling? Hmm, but that required bowling, something I was never any good at. We could go see a band. Nah, being in a bar would just remind me of Marco. Then it hit me.

"I got it. There is this really old theater a few blocks away that plays a random mix movie marathon on the weekends. If the lineup is good that could kill the whole night," I said.

"That actually sounds good. I haven't seen a movie in the theater since Olivia took me to see Jaws."

"Wow, you are old!" I chuckled.

Collin rolled his eyes and started the engine, "Which way?" he asked, ignoring my observation.

When we arrived at the theater the shows lined up for the evening were definitely random. We took our seats, catching the tail end of a 70's martial arts flick, complete with subtitles. Next was a B horror flick featuring zombies, much to my disappointment. For some reason I have always had an irrational fear of zombies. Thankfully this one was so bad it was almost a comedy. This was followed by a black and white gem containing actors neither of us recognized.

No movie was spared our sarcastic, scathing commentary, which actually made up for their own lack of ability to entertain. I was pleasantly surprised to discover Collin had a sense of humor just as dark and goofy at times as mine. Although there was more than once he did have to clarify his jokes due to the generation gap.

We barely made it home before sunrise. In the privacy of my bedroom, I lay on my bed and allowed my mind to meander through events of the evening. It seemed strange to me now that there was a point where I would have gone out of my way to avoid Collin. I could easily see him becoming a good friend. With a much needed feeling of being at ease, I gave in to sleep for the day.

The nightmare that ripped me from my slumber the prior night once again paid me a visit. This time when Collin came to my rescue I broke down in tears and confessed what had happened to me in the past week. I just assumed Olivia had told him. But, apparently, the tale I relayed came to him fresh from my lips. It wasn't until I finished what I had to say that I understood why he knew nothing of my meeting with Lattimer or the task that had been put to me.

He sat there on the edge of my bed for a moment in silence, staring absently at the floor. When he finally spoke, he relayed his own tale. One that explained how he came to be an immortal and how he believed Trinnian saved him in more ways than he could ever explain. But there was a trade off for him. He walked an eternal line between two beings that were in love with each other, knowing without a doubt that love would eventually come to fruition. That day had finally come. The love that he held for them both forced his decision. He decided to step aside and allow Trinnian and Olivia to finally act on the adoration they had for one another in the way it was meant to be.

My head was reeling. Collin's acceptance only made me angry. But what could I honestly say? It was his world. I was just the one looking in. Besides, I knew the majority of my anger stemmed from my already less than admirable feelings toward Trinnian. His bad judgment ceased to amaze me the night he turned Claire, claiming it was for my benefit. But Olivia? That was the part that left me feeling a bit blindsided.

With the grace of the worst timed interruption in the world, my cell phone rang. The number was unfamiliar.

"Are you going to answer that?" Collin asked, more than likely in an attempt to avoid discussing the matter any further.

I stared at the phone as the fourth ring sounded. Whatever, it was probably a wrong number, anyway. I hit accept.

"Hello?"

"Jacquelyn Livingston?"

"May I ask who is calling?" I inquired irritably. I mean, who really asks for people by their full name except telemarketers?

"This is Von, Lattimer's assistant." Oh, right, really old undead people. "Lattimer would like to meet with you at his place in Manhattan. Nikos can be at your house to pick you up in about an hour?"

Should it have bothered me more that they knew I was home or that they seemed to know where home was?

"Uh, that's alright, I know where it is," I said.

Running full out to the city was a much more appealing thought than being stuck in a car with Nikos again—much less having him in my house.

"Excellent. I am sure Lattimer will be pleased to hear you will be meeting him that much sooner."

With that, the call was ended. I tossed the phone on my night stand and exhaled loudly. The follow up meeting had not even been addressed in my mind. I was still dealing with the aftermath of the information acquisition.

"You need to go somewhere?" Collin asked, bringing me back to the here and now.

"Time to report to Lattimer. My presence has been requested at his place in the city."

"Take the Range Rover if you like, I do not plan on going anywhere tonight. The keys are on the kitchen counter."

"Thanks, Collin. I think I will."

Von met me in the lobby to escort me to Lattimer's place. He was even less chatty than before, which I wouldn't have even imagined possible. I followed him through the foyer past the marble statue toward the same doors we passed through last visit. He opened the door and motioned me in.

With a deep breath I passed into the room. I thought that if I actually took the time to look respectable, I would feel more confident. Being back in the heavy, oppressive space drove home the fact that it wasn't my prior rain soaked ensemble of a gray hoodie and Chuck Taylor's or even lack of makeup that made me feel self-conscious. It was the atmosphere. Struggling over potential outfits had been a waste of time. The black belted sweater dress I wore with knee-high boots suddenly felt ridiculous. Not to mention the time spent with the flat iron, smoothing my already straight auburn hair, section by section. Oh well, it was too late to turn back now.

Lattimer sat in the same chair that faced the fireplace as last time, which put his back to me. Of course he knew I was there but allowed me to take the chair next to his prior to acknowledging my presence. Before he spoke, he took a moment to consider my existence.

"Thank you for meeting with me on such short notice," Lattimer said. "I realize that this meeting was to take place in another week, but I have been made aware of the change in your..." he paused as if to conjure up the perfect word, "affiliation...with Marco. Regrettably I could only assume it had something to do with my task. I wish to make it known to you that this outcome was not my intention."

Perhaps his delicate choice of the word was his way of trying to show sensitivity to our breakup. Honestly, I didn't particularly care at the moment how he felt about my situation. The fact that he tried to show any sort of sympathy for something that was the direct result of his intrusion in my life began to make my blood boil. It was for the best that I simply pass on the information and be done with it all before my temper got the better of me. Returning home was all that I really wanted at the time.

"Marco stands by his story and I have found no reason not to believe him," my matter-of-fact delivery felt like proof, positive, I stood behind my words.

Lattimer once again appeared to be evaluating me from the depths of his chair. Finally, he slowly nodded to himself.

"Your cooperation in this matter will not be forgotten," he said as he stood, offering me his hand to assist me from my own chair, "I apologize if my request brought about the end of your involvement with Marco."

I stared at his hand, taking into account the implication of the gesture, mingled with his words. Really? That was it? He was officially dismissing me? The information offered to him was sufficient for his needs even though it was the exact same information he had of the incident prior to meeting me. I rose from the chair mechanically, without his assistance, and followed him to the door. Each step felt as numb as the one before it. I stopped in front of the door that led to the foyer while Lattimer opened it for me. He stood aside, politely waiting for me to exit.

For some reason I just couldn't walk away. I had to say something. My eyes locked on to his and I knew without a doubt the anger I felt flared within them.

"Relationship," I muttered petulantly.

In an instant his whole demeanor changed. His compassionate façade gave way to a cold, stone being that lurked beneath. My mind flashed to the segment in my nightmare where he taunted me. It was the same domineering look.

"Excuse me?" Lattimer requested in an irritated tone.

"The word you were looking for to describe my former connection to Marco. It was called a relationship," I stated coldly. It took all the self-control I could muster up not to flinch when his hand came up unexpectedly toward my face. His fingers touched my cheek tenderly for a split second until his thumb pressed into the flesh on the other side, firmly anchoring my chin in his hand. Tilting my face up to his, he spoke.

"Might I suggest you learn when to hold your tongue in the future?" he said in a calm, level manner that did not match the daggers that flashed in his eyes. "Nikos, will you show Ms. Livingston out?"

His hand left my face to motion toward the foyer. Sure enough, Nikos came into view, looking as menacing as ever. He followed me into the elevator while I did my best to walk with my head held high, putting forth the outward appearance of someone unfazed by petty threats. Turning to face forward,

CHAPTER FIVE

I caught one last glimpse of Lattimer before the doors slid shut. His aggravation remained obvious, a stark contrast to the man he portrayed when I first met him. Even an ancient vampire knows you can catch more flies with honey. He knew exactly what it would take to get me to do his bidding. Marco was right, Lattimer used me and I let him.

The doors opened to the lobby. I stepped out of the elevator, feeling as if I could finally breathe.

"Ms. Livingston?" Nikos said from inside, blocking the doors from closing with his hand. "I would consider the fact that Lattimer may have done you a favor in separating you from Marco. Personally, I would leave well enough alone."

"Meaning?"

"I would think twice before running back to Marco," Nikos suggested with a sneer.

Having said his piece, he allowed the doors to close. There was no way to understand the motivation for his comment. Nor did I care enough about his opinion to really worry about it. But my rebellious side decided Nikos had made my mind up for me. I was going to go see Marco and apologize. Not that I expected anything in return. More than anything, I had an overwhelming need to let him know I was wrong. Maybe that way my traitorous behavior may not totally ruin his faith in women.

Quite frankly, the fact that my code to get into Marco's building still worked did surprise me a bit. I'd be lying if I tried to say the trek to the doorstep of the bar wasn't occupied by an inner argument as to whether or not my functioning code would be a good thing.

I passed through the double doors, scanning the Saturday night immortal crowd, looking for Marco. His full staff was on tonight. Most of which I didn't personally know and not all were vampires. I could smell the humans in the room, and easily pick out where a few were, judging by the booths with the curtains closed.

Besides the usual wait staff duties, all humans that worked in Marco's bar were required to offer their blood to the patrons. For a fee, of course. The money wasn't the only incentive. Most believed if they complied with all of Marco's wishes, they would one day be rewarded with immortality.

One such human, Diana, was having her tray loaded down with drinks, courtesy of a male vampire I had seen bartending a couple times now. Diana's expression perked up when she saw me before taking on a sympathetic quality. Apparently she knew what had happened. To what extent I wasn't going to try to find out on my own. Last time I caught her train of thought, it was uncomfortable, to say the least.

"Jax!" she exclaimed, latching on to me. "I was worried I would never see you again."

Her scent churned in the air around us after she released me. My body tensed up at the memory of tasting her blood. The sudden surge of hunger accompanying the thought was instantly subdued by the fact that I liked Diana and the thought of hurting her bothered me. More than likely a lingering side effect of the night I drank from her.

"Actually, this may be the last night you see me here. I only came to see Marco for a second. Is he available?"

"He's in the office with his partner Julia. It's officially her first night back to work—crap!" Diana said, looking at one of the curtained booths off to our right. "I gotta get these drinks over there."

"And then some, looks like," I replied, knowing that the drawn curtain signified they were also paying to drink from her. "Diana, this place is going to kill you."

"God I hope so!" she said with a smile, carefully removing the full tray of drinks from the bar. "You may not remember but being human is exhausting."

"You think? Wait until you try immortality," I scoffed.

She laughed, turning for her table but having to pause for an opening in the flow of patrons. While waiting she added, "Don't you dare leave before giving me your number." Then she evaporated into the turbulent crowd.

In his office with Julia, huh? Only part of me hoped I wasn't about to interrupt something. Of course when I reached the door, it was closed. I was half tempted to turn around and head home. But that was probably only the part of me that didn't want to interrupt something. *Here goes nothing*, I thought and knocked on the door a tad louder than I intended. The force of the knock obviously controlled by the other part of me, the one that hoped I *was* about to interrupt something.

"It's open," Marco responded from within.

Marco sat at his desk while Julia was getting up from the chair across from him. He scanned me from head to toe before speaking.

"You can stay, Julia. I am sure whatever Jacquelyn has to say will only take a minute."

"Actually, I need to get back out there," Julia said. "It is really quite busy tonight."

Offering me a nod in passing, she left, closing the door behind her. I approached Marco's desk, the fact that he didn't offer the vacated seat was not lost on me. His lack of hospitality informed me he didn't want to give me any reason to hang around. I was more than willing to oblige by getting straight to the point.

"I'm sorry," I said, hoping my tone reflected the sincerity I honestly meant to convey in my words. "I should have told you that night what Lattimer requested of me."

"He can be very persuasive."

Marco's short dismissive response quickly put me on the defensive. Why couldn't he just accept the apology graciously and allow me to leave before I turned my own good intentions into a bitter standoff?

"I'm sure things might have gone much differently if you would have told me about it first," I pointed out, resisting the urge to plant my fists on my hips in a confrontational stance. Did the body language really matter? My comment was already enough to steer this conversation toward debate.

"You think I did not try? Remember the night Claire woke from her transformation, just before Augustine came to get us? I told you that I wanted to tell you something, but then Claire started to wake and I said it could wait so you could go to her. What do you think I was going to tell you? After that night I could not seem to find the right time. Your life was finally starting to calm down and I did not want to ruin that. I needed to choose the right time and words to explain it all to you. Do you know how difficult that is? How does one start a conversation like that?"

"I don't know, Marco, maybe by being honest?"

"Because being forthcoming worked so well for you?"

The validity of his question shot down any of the possible comments I could have childishly spat out. We had come full circle to the reason I was there in the first place. His sarcastic remark summed it up.

"I didn't come here for a fight."

"Then why did you come?"

"I wanted to tell you face to face I was sorry. You were right, Lattimer used me and I just let it happen."

Marco leaned back in his chair, arms crossing at his chest. His scrutinizing gaze examined me as if seeing me for the first time.

"I understand completely now," he said. A spiteful grin formed on his lips. "You went to see Lattimer tonight, and here I thought you got all sexy for me. I should have known *that* was for him, too."

"What the—"

"Just watch your back. Julia can tell you from experience how dreadful he treats his lovers."

"Oh please! You don't honestly think this was all over an attraction to Lattimer?" I asked, shocked he could even suggest such a thing.

"I do not know, although it certainly is a much more interesting explanation for your actions than you betrayed me, simply because he asked you to." Marco answered. "Why...do you have a better reason?"

"Because I was scared. There you have it, plain and simple. Why wouldn't you have told me about Aloisia? There had to be a reason. I was afraid of what exactly that reason may be."

"You want to know why?" He stood up so suddenly I flinched. "Because I was falling in love with someone for the first time in a very long time and I did not want to screw it up. I wanted to tell you but I knew it had to be done right or I would risk losing you. I should have seen from how easily you fall from one man to another that you did not take us as seriously as I did. I could have avoided all this heartache if I would have just opened my eyes. So actually, if you think about it, you running to Lattimer would at least keep you consistent."

"Fuck you, Marco."

I stormed out of the office, slamming the door so hard I heard something fall off the wall inside. Maybe I should have listened to Nikos after all.

When I emerged from the office back into the bar, all I could see was the front entrance. The anger responsible for my current state of tunnel vision showed no sign of letting up until I was as far away from Marco as physically possible. Halfway to my focal point, a voice sliced through my resolve.

"Bye-bye."

It wasn't necessarily the insincere sentiment as much as the snicker that followed it that stopped me in my path. Lacking the proper restraint of an adult that would empower me to walk away from such juvenile taunting, I rounded on Lori. My prompt reaction caused her to take an uncertain step back.

"You really don't know when to quit, do you?" I seethed.

In an attempt to regain her nerve, Lori stood straight and tried casually hugging her empty tray to her chest.

"If quitting were in my nature I wouldn't have known the pleasure I experienced last night, now would I?" Before I realized what I was doing, it was too late. My mind was flooded with images of her and Marco engaging in the sexual activities

51

she was obviously referring to in his office. Disgust got the better of me and was not lost on Lori, "Oh, you saw that? Maybe you shouldn't read people's minds, you stupid bitch."

I took a step toward her so fast her eyes got as round as the tray she brought up to protect herself. She watched me fearfully over the top of her quivering shield.

"Let me dump a little reality into your delusional world," I growled, jamming my finger into her tray. The impact smacked the hard flat surface into her face with a loud thud. Her hands grasped her nose as the tray hit the floor, rolling into the crowd. I could smell the blood before I saw it, determined not to let the scent distract me, I continued. "First and foremost, you do realize I can kill you with my bare hands and nobody would care. All you are here is a snack. All you are to anyone in your human life is a waste, a disappointment. Don't look so surprised, you should know you don't have the control to only display the thoughts you intend me to see. Trust me, I have seen enough to know what a pathetic, weak person you are." I took another step toward her, pinning her against the edge of the bar as she tried to back away from me. "And if you think last night meant anything to Marco you're fooling yourself. Didn't it occur to you that if he had any ounce of respect for you he'd have the decency to take you to his bed? Gosh, what am I thinking, after seeing the white trash you come from, maybe being bent over your boss's desk is the equivalent of a first date."

"Enough!" Marco shouted.

All noise and movement came to a halt. The interruption gave Lori the chance to slip away. She ran to Marco, still clutching her face.

"She broke my fuckin' nose!" Lori cried hysterically when she reached him.

It felt like the whole bar was staring at me...because they all pretty much were.

"Your ignorance could have cost you much more than that," he scowled. "Go clean yourself up."

She stomped off through the employee door to do as she was told. Marco strode toward me, ordering his employees to get back to work. The bar returned to its prior bustle.

"I think you need to leave," he stated firmly, glowering over me.

"*I* was the one that didn't take us seriously? My spot in your bed is probably still warm and you're already back to fucking your staff? Lucky for you sexual harassment in the work place is not an issue."

"Julia!" he called before turning his attention back to me. "I might take offence in your holier-than-thou attitude if I felt it suited you." Julia appeared by his side, "Could you please make sure Jacquelyn finds her way out? I have nothing further to discuss with her. She is officially banned, not only from this establishment, but the entire building. I am disabling her code, effective immediately."

I watched him walk away, heading for his office, never once looking back. That was it. It was officially over and completely unsalvageable.

"Jacquelyn?"

Julia was gesturing me toward the front doors. Her indifference a refreshing change from the more opinionated dispositions I endured all night. We exited the bar and stepped into the elevator.

"Can I ask you something?" asked Julia while we waited for the elevator to deliver us to the main hallway.

"Sure."

"If you really did not throw everything away to be with Lattimer, how did you do it?"

"I'm afraid I don't follow," I said, honestly unable to decipher her meaning. Maybe I could have been able to keep up if I wasn't so busy trying to decide whether or not it bothered me that she seemed to know so much about my affairs. I suppose even vampires are not beneath listening in doorways to private conversations.

"How did you deny Lattimer?" The doors opened and I made my way toward the outside with Julia on my heels. I felt no overwhelming need to answer her ridiculous question. Why would I? "So you did betray Marco for Lattimer. Do not get too comfortable, he is only using you like he uses everyone."

I stopped and stared at the final door, the one that would once and for all put this all behind me. But I couldn't bring myself to pass through just yet.

Was that honestly how they perceived my actions? I became so smitten with Lattimer after one meeting that I threw away everything that was evolving between Marco and me?

Julia planted herself between me and the exit, waiting for me to speak. Maybe I did need to set the record straight once and for all?

"Look, all Lattimer ever wanted from me was evidence against Marco. All I ever wanted after meeting Lattimer was the truth from Marco's lips. I knew nothing of Marco's past until Lattimer informed me. That was my motivation in the whole thing and that is way more than you need to even know. So if you'll excuse me, I need to get home," I explained, pushing by her and through the door.

The chilly nighttime air hit me, starting to release the tension that had me wound so tight. I stood on the steps of the building, enjoying my new found freedom. Even as bad as things got in the bar there was no denying the fact that a weight had been lifted off my shoulders. I didn't even notice Julia stood next to me until she spoke.

"In our world, things are not always so black and white as they may seem. You must always consider the fact that there are underlying motivations to any situation you encounter," said Julia.

She was seriously starting to ruin my moment. If she had a point, she really needed to make it and leave.

"Meaning?" I inquired, allowing my irritation to blatantly show.

"Do you honestly think Lattimer went to all that trouble just to affirm something he already knew?"

Her words resounded in my head, was I really that blind? So what the hell was it all about then?

The door to the building opened. Augustine and Claire joined us on the steps. Julia greeted them before going back inside.

"Hey," Claire said, trying to gauge my mood. "Diana called us. She said you were being thrown out?"

The light over the entry gave her golden blonde curls a luminous glow. But the concern for me that furrowed her brow and echoed in her big blue eyes seemed impervious to the light.

"Yep, watch this." I punched in my code. The keypad responded with a dull buzz of denial. Claire and Augustine exchanged a look reminiscent of those found at funerals. "I'm perfectly fine with it," I proclaimed.

My admission collectively changed their mood to relief. Was there anyone that didn't know the details of my love life?

"Claire and I were planning to hunt, then head to her place at some point if you would like to join us." Augustine offered in his endearing Italian accent.

He looked absolutely adorable, wearing a loose knit cap on his head. With his sandy brown curls poking out underneath, the effect only served to enforce his boyish image in my mind. Long lashes framed his hazel eyes, softening his intent stare, waiting patiently for my answer.

Thinking the distraction may do me some good I agreed and set out into the night with them. I did my best to steer conversation away from events of the night, which I actually found was easier than I would have thought. After all, Claire was distracted by Augustine's presence, snuggled up against him as we walked. Every time he opened his mouth to speak, she would beam up at him like a child in awe of a shooting star. But it was obvious Augustine was just as smitten, his arm around her shoulders held her securely to his side the whole time. Seeing Claire so happy helped me forget about my own misery.

We had walked for a while until at last Augustine stopped, bringing our attention to a car in a back alley. It contained two rather seedy individuals that were planning to rob a check cashing place down the street. They were armed and more than ready to use their weapons to establish control. This definitely wasn't their first time.

If Trinnian taught me anything, it was to look for these types of people to feed from. Not only were they less likely to be missed but you were actually doing society a favor. I suppose it was one way to keep from feeling like a cold blooded serial killer.

Claire thought it would be fun to pretend we were prostitutes. That would give us the ability to approach the car without raising suspicion. I had never played with my food, so to speak, but Collin told me how Trinnian and Olivia used to make quite a game of it. Trying to ignore the awkward feeling of it all, I agreed.

No sooner did I give in I found Claire's arm linked in mine, heading toward the vehicle. She was being loud, talking about some nonexistent loser she 'serviced' who was in town for a convention. I attempted to laugh and play along even though I was inexplicably nervous. I found myself wishing Augustine was with us, not waiting for us at the end of the alley. This just wasn't how I normally did things. Her method lacked the control I felt in the stalking method I typically used. I could see the driver's side window rolling down as we approached. The man called us over to the vehicle.

Thankfully, Claire did all the talking. I tried not to cringe as they discussed rates and services. Having complete access to their thoughts, I knew they had no money. The plan was to get us into the car and do what they liked before dumping us off somewhere. Then they would continue with the original plan involving the check cashing place. Claire suggested that if they were real men they would get out right here in the alley and let us make them beg for mercy. The offer was followed by a vulgar gesture I'd rather not describe.

Much to my surprise, it worked. The man got out of the driver's side and seized Claire, groping her shamelessly against the car. I turned just in time for the passenger to push me up onto the trunk of the car, yanking up my dress. My first reaction was to struggle against him. He punched me in the face with all his strength. I felt the sharp pain of impact between the back of my head and the window leaving me momentarily dazed. His attempt to rip my panties off triggered my basic survival instincts. No sooner did I think it, I had him pinned to the ground beneath me, savoring the smell of the adrenaline coursing through his veins. In that moment I understood the use of the game.

My teeth broke his skin. The familiar tingle of healing tickled my lip and the back of my head while I drank deeply from his throat. His adrenaline laced blood coursed through my body, leaving a champagne giddiness in its wake. I slowly stood up from his motionless corpse, having to steady myself against the car. A hand lightly gripped my elbow.

"Take your time."

Augustine held me firmly in place until I could do so on my own. I opened my eyes that had drifted closed to revel in the experience. Claire stood on the other side of me, watching me curiously.

"Sorry about that, I don't know what exactly happened," I mumbled, gradually coming out of my stupor.

"Adrenaline can be a bit much for newborns. You have to be careful until you get used to the effects," explained Augustine.

"But vodka doesn't touch me?" I noted.

"Alcohol can affect us the way adrenaline does. It depends on how often you feed and how old you are. It is one of those things that is different for all of us."

Claire broke into a huge smile, "Dammit! Next time I'm gonna scare the shit out of them first!"

I laughed, although I was still left feeling a bit foggy. Definitely something I would not have wanted to experience alone.

When we arrived at Claire's I realized this wasn't a simple visit. She was dragging out her travel luggage.

"Bumping up the daily clothing ration or are we going somewhere?" I asked.

"Well, since I was in no condition to go to Oktoberfest I had to cancel my trip. Somehow I managed to convince my boss that everybody does articles on Oktoberfest and that we should do one on what happens after everybody leaves. So, Augustine and I are going to Germany for a couple weeks."

Apparently she had no intentions of quitting her job. Could vampires hold down normal jobs? Not that being a writer for a travel magazine was a real job. Well, not in the sense that its nine to five and you have to punch a time card.

"You're going to keep working?" I asked.

"Some of us don't have a king's ransom in savings. Some of us also pay grotesque amounts of rent," Claire answered.

I knew her 'some of us' tirade specifically referred to me. This wasn't the first time she threw my financial situation in my face.

"I refuse to let you make me feel guilty because I am better at managing money than you are. My savings account is the byproduct of diligent budgeting, which, I might add, was made easier by moving out of the city. And you know that was my uncle's house. I bought it off my parents for exactly what they paid for it."

"Um, yeah, back in the seventies," Claire said, rolling her eyes. She turned to Augustine, "Her uncle was one of those crazy conspiracy theory types. The house has the ultimate man cave. He built his own bomb shelter without a city permit and hid it behind a wall in the basement. He was convinced that the government was in with the Russians and he didn't want them to know about it." She chuckled before catching my glare. Clearing her throat she added, "May he rest in peace."

"Besides, you are the one that has shrugged off my invitations to live with me for practically free in comparison to what you pay here," I said.

"But I love living in the city!"

"I have also offered for her to move in with me," Augustine said.

"Really?" I asked, smirking at Claire.

"I just don't want to rush into anything," she said dismissively, packing faster.

"With him or with me?" I asked, winking at Augustine. He laughed.

"You can both go to hell!" she hissed, vanishing into the bathroom, suddenly intent on packing toiletries. Talk of commitment always made her nervous.

I looked at Augustine, his smile lingered but didn't touch his eyes as he stared off toward the bathroom.

"She'll come around eventually," I whispered.

His attention turned to me, "I spent so long wishing Violet would just leave, I almost forgot what it was like to fear someone you adore might not stay."

"I don't think you have to worry about that. I have known that girl a long time and I have never seen her so happy."

His smile lit up his eyes, looking back toward the bathroom.

Claire finished up packing and eventually was speaking to us again. By the time they were ready to head back to Augustine's place my time frame to get back to my house was a bit snug. I decided to crash at Claire's since I wasn't allowed to stay at Augustine's with them in Marco's precious building. More than anything, I didn't want him giving them grief.

CHAPTER SIX

I called Collin to let him know what was going on since I did have his vehicle. He was more concerned with whether or not anyone knew where he was than with the location of his SUV. As before I left him at my house, I assured him I wouldn't rat him out. It was not my place to tell anyone anything if he chose to lay low for a while.

The first hint of sunrise started to make itself known. I was happy to discover Claire's bedroom had been prepped for immortal slumber. After a quick shower, all I'd have to do was crawl in bed.

*   *   *   *   *

A car came to a halt, parking cattycorner from Jacquelyn Livingston's upstate New York home. The late afternoon sun did little to warm the chilly October air. Lori looked around. The street was quieter than she would have expected on a Sunday. Not that she was complaining. It would seem the people that lived in these types of neighborhoods spent the majority of their time inside and kept to themselves...thankfully.

The house Jacquelyn lived in wasn't what she envisioned. It was a simple white wood frame house with a porch swing. Not exactly what one pictures in their head when they think of vampires. She laughed darkly to herself at the thought of them being listed in the phone book as well.

A quick check of her makeup in the rearview mirror reassured her that the bruising around her busted nose was concealed, it was go time. Grabbing the Avon sales bag from the passenger seat, she made her way to the front door. She knocked and pretended to wait what would be the appropriate amount of time. Comfortable no one was watching, she made her way around to the back door. If she weren't so intent on avoiding notice she would have squealed with delight. A small pane of glass next to the deadbolt was missing. She stuck her hand inside and unlocked the door. It almost seemed unfair this was going to be so easy...for her anyway. She gently touched the swollen, tender flesh around her broken nose. Like her daddy always said, payback is a bitch.

The feeling of being watched was never the way I would prefer to wake. However, when I opened my eyes, things went from bad to worse. Standing at the edge of Claire's bed was Nikos. His bored expression made me wonder exactly how long he had been there.

"She is awake, sir."

There was no need to question to whom he spoke. I sat up, cursing my post shower choice of sleepwear consisting of a snug fitting 'I (heart) NY' wife beater and 'Kiss Me I'm Irish' boxers. The self-conscious thought abruptly refocusing my irritation to myself, why should I care what Lattimer thought of me? While at the same time, my defiant stand point was unknowingly being undermined by the involuntary act of combing my fingers through my hair in an attempt to tame my bed head. I clasped my offending hands on my lap and scanned the room.

Sure enough, there was Lattimer, sitting casually in a chair surveying me from across the room the way he usually did. I would almost be willing to trade the ability to read human minds to be able to read the thoughts of immortals. If only to decipher his silent ogling and perhaps put an end to the discomfort I felt beneath his stare. It was all I could do not to pull the blanket up to my chin.

He stood and approached the bed, "Leave us, Nikos."

Nikos looked from Lattimer to me, not hiding his disapproval in the least before doing as he was told.

"How the hell did you find me?" I groaned after Nikos was on the other side of the door.

Lattimer gestured to the bed, "May I?"

I rolled my eyes, shrugging my shoulders, "Sure."

Instead of sitting he just stared down at me. Before I could even ask, I understood his hesitation. I snorted in disbelief before scooting over to give him more room. Finally content with the space allowed, he adjusted his black wool trench coat and sat facing me.

"I thought we had decided you needed to be mindful of your manners in the presence of your elders?"

"Really?" The incredulous comment spoken more to myself then out loud. I crossed my arms and reworded my offensive comment, "To what do I owe the pleasure of your company...sir?"

His jaw clenched and his gaze narrowed, "That." He flicked his hand in my direction. "That lack of respect," he growled. "Trinnian is lucky I do not destroy you and integrate him into the population of my dungeons. The very least he could have done was educate you in the significance of the immortal hierarchy or even how to interact appropriately with those of eminence."

"Well if it's any consolation, the only thing he actually took the time to personally teach me was how to hunt. And even that was just the one time. So judging from his lack of interest, I doubt he would care if you destroyed me. However, as far as incarcerating Trinnian, you may have to contend with Olivia," I snapped.

No sooner did I speak did I regret what I said. Lattimer may have a knack for knowing more than I would ever give him credit for but I was fairly certain even he didn't know about Trinnian and Olivia.

It took a moment before what I insinuated sunk in. When it did, his brow furrowed in thought. He stood, clasping his hands behind his back and paced away. When he turned to face me there was a sinister gleam in his eye.

"Trinnian has now completely turned his back on you. You no longer share a bed—or anything else with Marco," he stated, as if I needed a recap. "So basically you have no one?" He returned to the edge of the bed, staring down at me. "You do realize under my rule I retain the right to any and all orphan newborns?"

Dread seeped into my gut with the gravity of his words. From what little I did know about Lattimer, any truth to what he said wouldn't surprise me. In fact, the more I thought about it, the more I seemed to recall having heard something about him claiming newly made vampires for his own. The details as to his justification alluded me at the moment. Maybe that was it?

There seemed only one choice for me. I had to tell him about Collin. If he knew Collin was with me then there would be no question as to whether or not I was under the care of a guardian. Surely Collin wouldn't feel my telling Lattimer about him in this situation was a direct betrayal...would he? So why was I finding it so difficult to speak?

"Nikos!"

Lattimer barely raised his voice, yet in my ears it sounded like he shouted the name. I had to say something.

"Wait!"

I was off the bed, oblivious to the fact that I had latched on to his coat until his eyes left mine to stare down at my hands. Instantly releasing my grip on his lapels, I took a step back. He returned his gaze to mine. Nikos opened the door, awaiting instruction. Lattimer never took his eyes off me as he addressed Nikos.

"Could you please bring the car around, we are almost finished here," he informed his loyal subject.

As soon as the door shut behind him, I slumped back down on the bed. I could feel Lattimer's stare boring a hole in the top of my head. But I needed a moment to collect my thoughts and ask Collin's forgiveness—if only in my own mind. The bed shifted next to me under Lattimer's weight. Something about his position beside me stripped away a layer of his intimidation. Was it merely the fact that he was no longer looming over me? Whatever the case may have been, feeling more at ease I finally spoke.

"I'm not alone. Collin is staying with me at my house and expecting me to come home tonight."

Lattimer examined my expression, looking for any sign that I was bluffing. I fought the urge to look away, intent on proving to him he didn't scare me. But most of all, to prove to him I told the truth.

After what seemed an eternity, he appeared to accept what he had been told. But from the change in his demeanor you'd think he was surrendering to the enemy. His hand reached toward me and his fingertips brushed my cheek, "Fair enough," he said before tilting up my chin and kissing me tenderly.

A warm tingling wave passed through my lips, down my body, relaxing every muscle into jelly as it progressed. When it finally reached my toes I opened my eyes, never realizing they had even shut. I lay on my back in Claire's bed with the blanket pulled up to my chin. The room was void of any other immortals. Not even a scent lingered. I released the breath I had unintentionally been holding. It was a dream. At least I had no evidence to tell me otherwise.

I ran my fingertip across my lips, recalling the not so terrible sensation of his kiss. My touch making me fully aware that, although it was muted and dissipating, the feeling still lingered. Along with this discovery came another, I would be lying if I tried to deny the fact that I was slightly aroused...arousal being a concept that I hadn't really associated with Lattimer before. Julia's question from the prior night replayed in my head, *'How did you deny Lattimer?'* My determination to not share the mindset of one of his former mistresses suddenly made the thought of any attraction to him infuriating. Who could possibly want to feel any sort of sensuality toward a man that chewed people up and spit them out for his own amusement?

Forcing myself to think about something else, I sat up, looking for my phone. If nothing else, it always came in handy when there was need for a distraction. My phone blinked on the night stand, alerting me that I had a message. Before I even had it in hand, it rang. It was my mother. The time had finally come to surrender to the fact that I couldn't avoid speaking to her forever, I answered.

"Hey, Ma, what's up?"

"Oh thank God! Where are you?" she asked, audibly relieved.

"In the city, I stayed at Claire's last night. Why?"

"I always told your father you had a guardian angel, he never believed me."

"What are you talking about?" I asked. But I knew from experience when she started dragging divine intervention into things something bad had happened. Naturally, I started feeling uneasy.

"They said your Volvo wasn't there," her voice started to quiver with emotion. "So I knew you weren't even home. I knew you were safe. Even though we haven't spoken much over the past few weeks I just knew—"

"Mom!" I yelled, "Please tell me what is going on!"

"Jacquelyn, I am so sorry...your house burnt down this afternoon..."

She continued speaking but I barely heard her. If I had been standing, I'm not sure I still would be. My whole body went numb. All I could think about was Collin. I knew without a doubt he was in the house. We spoke shortly before I went to bed. He was digging through my movies looking for one to take to the guest room with him.

Tears welled up in my eyes as I tried to piece together what she told me. She said afternoon. So, even if he did escape the inferno, the sun would have gotten him. In the midst of her renewed babbling, she mentioned they had found no bodies. But I wasn't exactly sure what that meant in the immortal world. It never occurred to me to look into the fire pit when Collin was finished burning Silas's remains. I had to get home.

After assuring Mom I was fine and promising her I would have the Fire Chief meet me there, I got dressed and was en route to my house. Or at least whatever was left of it. A sickening feeling came over me as I realized the same could be said for Collin.

By the time I turned on to my street, the drive from the city was a distant memory. Every call I placed to Collin's cell phone went straight to voice mail, forcing me to face a possible reality I was not prepared for. I parked behind the Fire Chief's truck, avoiding looking at my house until I stood on the sidewalk in front of it.

The scene before me could have come from a Hollywood ghost film. Smoke and ash turned the once white house gray. It looked as if it had stood abandoned for years. Singed curtains stirred in the second floor windows that no longer held panes of glass. The acrid, charred smell that hung in the air relayed the story of what had happened here hours earlier. I could hear water dripping inside, lingering evidence of the fire fighters battle. Yellow caution tape corded off the front porch steps, tied from railing to railing.

A beam of a flashlight bounced its way toward the front door from the murky blackness within. The Fire Chief emerged through the doorway as I approached the porch steps. He held the caution tape up for me to duck beneath, introducing himself as we ascended the steps.

"I'm Chief Robertson. You must be Ms. Livingston," he said, handing me a flashlight.

"Yes, Jacquelyn, please."

"Well, Jacquelyn, you are quite lucky to not have been home for this. If this would have happened in the middle of the night while you were home sleeping..." The look on my face must have been pathetic enough to encourage him to rephrase his speech. "Suffice to say, the results could have been lethal. Let me show you what happened."

He walked into the house and stopped next to the staircase. The familiarity of the space ravaged by the flames that had only hours before consumed it. My refuge from the world had been destroyed. I took a second to look for any sign of Collin before returning my attention to the Chief. The beam

69

of his flashlight settled on an area where an art deco era wall sconce once hung.

"The wiring on this light shorted out, causing a fire inside the wall that spread into the living room and up the stairwell to the second floor." He used his flashlight to demonstrate the path. "These old wood frame houses tend to go up pretty quick. As you can pretty much tell from down here, the upper levels are more or less a total loss."

As if the news he gave me wasn't bad enough, my brain was able to identify the strange smell that mingled with the pungent smoke. It was the same scent that clung to the air the night Collin decapitated Silas. Immortal flesh had a very distinct odor when burnt. It was all I needed to confirm what I feared most, Collin did not make it out of the house. I walked to the bottom of the staircase. The door to the guestroom hung open. The scent filled the stairway.

I clamped my hands over my mouth to stifle the scream that grew within me. Tears streamed from my eyes as my body shuddered with the sobs that erupted. I wanted to go upstairs into the guest room to see for myself, if only to make sure he wasn't hiding in the back of the closet or under the bed. But I already knew it was futile, if he was there I would feel his presence. The sobs now bordered on hysteria. I felt the Chief's hands on my shoulders.

"Come, let's get you outside."

With no will left to refuse him, he gently ushered me back into the night.

Dorian made the familiar trip down the long hall that had been tunneled through the bedrock centuries ago. His journey took him toward the only apartments on this side of the underground colony. The setup of their community always reminded him of an ant mound. Limited access points from the outside fanned out into a maze of corridors on the inside. He had a love-hate relationship with their way of life. The security of their underground retreat stood at odds with his desire to dwell full time in the city. The pulsing life force of which currently throbbed at least four stories above his head, not that he could precisely tell from his current proximity.

When he finally reached the massive duel granite doors, he pulled the thick, crimson braided silk rope to his right. From outside the dwelling, no sound could be heard. But inside, the heavy copper bell would toll, announcing his presence. As the doors slowly crept open to admit him, a lone human male stood waiting to receive him. He gestured for Dorian to enter without speaking a word but Dorian could see the excitement that shone behind the young man's eyes.

"Good Evening, Alton. You are looking absolutely divine, if I may say," Dorian purred to the youth. His British accent lent a refined allure to his words.

"Thank you, Master Dorian," the young man beamed. "Acacius has been expecting you...if you will follow me."

Alton led the way through yet another labyrinth of hallways before stopping at an impressive set of wooden doors carved with serpents.

"He is having his evening snack but has requested I admit you right away," Alton said.

Safe refuge from the sun was not the only selling point to their way of life. They also maintained their own food source. Generations of humans had been bred here, ignorant to the fact that any other way of life existed. Essentially, their self sufficient community never even had to see street level.

Dorian stood aside to admire the young man as he exerted his strength to tug on the long brass door handle opening the hefty door. When it was finally open a respectful amount, Alton turned to Dorian, showing him inside.

"I will see if we can get you relieved early," Dorian said. He passed by Alton into a short hallway that ended at a pair of heavy silk curtains. His insinuation was not lost on the young man.

"I would be honored, Sir." Alton smiled, closing the door.

Dorian was about to proceed through the curtains into the chamber when something stopped him. It was the unmistakable sound of a female caught up in a moment of sexual pleasure. He should expect no less of Acacius. After all, he had a weakness for the ladies, especially those of the human variety.

CHAPTER EIGHT

Dorian waited patiently in the concealment of the curtains for the activity within the room to come to a conclusion. It didn't take long for the woman's moans to turn into howls and shortly taper off into silence. Dorian stepped out of hiding in time to see Acacius pull on a black silk robe, tying it securely at the waist. Acacius ran his hands through his shaggy, dirty blonde hair, not making much of an improvement to its disarray. A lusty grin twisted his mouth as he smacked the naked woman's buttocks and informed her she could go. She squealed and giggled, heading off through a door without a backward glance. He watched her leave and settled onto a sofa.

Dorian came to a halt at the top of the steps that led down into a sunken area bordered by deep scarlet colored sofas strewn with pillows. It brought to mind what one would envision a Sultan's tent to look like. The irony of the thought was not lost on Dorian.

"Tell me you have something of interest for me," Acacius said, offering the vacant space on the sofa next to him.

"Lattimer went to go see the redhead tonight," Dorian replied, descending the steps to sit as invited.

"Interesting," Acacius muttered, pondering the information. "How long was he there?"

"Not very."

"Not very?" Acacius asked, arching an eyebrow. "A lot can be accomplished in a 'not very' long amount of time. For example, when Gisele came into the room this evening to offer her blood to me, it was 'not very' long before I decided to ravish her as well. So, if you do not mind, I would appreciate it if you could elaborate?"

"Maybe a half hour, I am not entirely sure," grumbled Dorian.

"I see," Acacius said. "Do we know who she is yet?"

"Trinnian Talbott turned her about a month ago—"

"Trinnian...he is that pompous twit Owen Smith's protégé, correct?"

"Yes," Dorian answered. "A couple weeks ago she killed Violet, Augustine's lover." Noting the lack of recognition on Acacius, he elaborated. "Augustine, the artist?"

Acacius's brow rose in surprise, "The wicked little French tart?" Dorian nodded. "A newborn with the audacity to commit murder? I like her already."

"It was in self defense from what I understand. Violet's jealousy finally the product of her demise," said Dorian.

"So then I can only assume Lattimer's initial interest in her was his undying need to demonstrate his authority to the newly made female. After all, she did extinguish the life of an immortal. But that would only explain one visit. Since that first visit did not involve her being carted off to his dungeon, he should be through with her. I can only assume he wants her for something else," Acacius said.

"You know him too well," Dorian grinned. "It seems he was using her to gather evidence against Marco de Navarra."

"Marco? What ties does she have to Marco?"

"It would seem Trinnian abandoned her for an old flame and Marco was there to pick up the pieces."

"A good old fashioned love triangle...I really must get out more often!" Acacius commented cynically. "So what has Marco done now?"

"Nothing that I am aware of, this was to settle an old score."

CHAPTER EIGHT

"Oh God, Lattimer is still brooding over the death of his little slave girl, Elisa, is he?"

"Aloisia."

"Whatever," Acacius replied dismissively. "You would think he never shunned her in the first place. Is it not convenient how he only seems to try and lay claim to his former conquests when another male is involved? But even the consistency of his behavior even depends on which way the wind blows," he scoffed.

"There has to be more to it," Dorian observed.

"I agree," Acacius said. His gaze turned to the floor, absently tapping his finger on his lips. He appeared to be lost in all the possibilities that could be motivating Lattimer's behavior. Finally, his attention returned to Dorian, "You need to befriend this redheaded lady—"

"Jacquelyn," Dorian said. "That is her name, Jacquelyn Livingston."

"Whatever. Get to know her, pick her brain. Find out what she knows of Lattimer and what she thinks he wants from her. She is either very shrewd or completely worthless. Either way, I want to know what Lattimer is up to," Acacius paused. "It is safe to assume the sources you have gathered all this information from are good?"

"Actually, some of it came from Augustine. He has taken up with Jacquelyn's best friend, Claire."

"I see, so obviously no hard feelings over the loss of Violet. This Claire, is she human?" Acacius asked with renewed interest.

"No, also a product of Trinnian's making."

"Trinnian best watch the pace at which he makes immortals, Lattimer's paranoia will kick in and he will find himself locked away in a dungeon," Acacius sneered.

"Not too eager to have someone occupy your old quarters?"

The look Acacius shot Dorian demonstrated his lack of amusement towards the comment. Dorian knew he was one of the few close enough to Acacius that could get away with making jokes about his former incarceration.

"You said Augustine gave you some of the information, who gave you the rest?"

"Julia," replied Dorian. "Apparently Marco has been confiding in her about how Lattimer destroyed his relationship with Jacquelyn."

"Ah. This is a good thing," Acacius said. His eyes alight with hope. "Maybe she will finally gain Marco's affections, which will put him one step closer to joining us. The more that turn their back on Lattimer, the more that will turn to me." Suspicion invaded his expression. "You do not think Lattimer was simply using what he could to punish Marco for his involvement with Julia?"

"Perhaps. But she was here with us at the time he first met with this Jacquelyn."

"True." Acacius stood, adjusting his robe. "Now if you will excuse me, I believe I am ready for my second course of the evening." He strode across the room, stopping at the door Gisele exited through. "Please do take Alton with you. I have no desire to relive the highlights of his recent trysts with you yet another night."

"Your generosity is one of your most endearing traits," Dorian commented sarcastically with an inclination of his head.

"As is your sincerity," Acacius countered before closing the door between them.

*   *   *   *   *

CHAPTER EIGHT

It was the silence that bothered Olivia. Fresh out of the shower, she sat in her robe at her vanity combing through her wet hair. The stillness of the manor never really flaunted itself in her face until recently. She knew this bizarre way of thinking was her version of guilt. After all, when Collin left, he took with him any need for guilt. Or so he thought. He swore to them both he had only ever wanted their happiness. His leaving was for their benefit. At least that is what he said. It would only be through his absence that they could truly explore their love for one another. But she knew better. It was not that he lied to her completely. However, she knew him better than he knew himself and the sadness he withheld could not fully hide from her.

Placing her comb on the vanity, she caught Trinnian's reflection in the mirror standing in the doorway behind her. He approached, resting his hands on her shoulders.

"Remember how this place used to hum with activity?" she mused.

"It has become rather quiet over the decades," Trinnian replied.

"I swear sometimes when I am home alone I can still hear Marion singing softly to herself, strolling through the hallways."

"I miss that." He smiled to himself as his thoughts revisited the past. "Or Lawrence's wildly embellished stories of his nightly hunts. There was more than one occasion I laid down for the day only to be woken by him and one of his infamous tales. And they all started out the same way—"

They shared knowing looks, speaking in unison, "I would swear on my sweet Nana's grave...but you still would not believe me!"

The laughter of the shared memories tapered off. Trinnian pushed Olivia's hair over her left shoulder, affectionately kissing her neck.

"Are you ok?" he asked, studying her face in the mirror.

Placing her hands on his she responded with a gentle smile, "I am fine. I suppose I just got used to being surrounded by everyone I loved."

He knelt before her. Uncertainty tainted his eyes.

"Do you regret what we have done?"

Olivia looked down, gathering his hands in hers, kissing them. When she returned her gaze to Trinnian's, tears flowed down her cheeks. She shook her head ever so slightly, "No...and that is the part that hurts the most."

Trinnian's relief felt almost tangible. He wiped the tears from Olivia's cheeks and kissed her.

"I miss him, too. He was like a brother to me. But he is also a grown man, free to make his own decisions. It was his decision to leave. I for one take his blessing to heart. There is no doubt in my mind he truly wants us to be happy. Knowing him as well as I do, if not better, you know that is just his nature. He puts the ones he loves' needs ahead of his own. That is the way he has always approached his life. He will return when he is ready." Determined to put an end to Olivia's anguish, Trinnian came up with a plan to take her mind off things. "I say we go to the city to hunt like the good ole days."

She wiped away the remaining tears and smiled at him, "Can I play the girl who has had too much to drink in the wrong place at the wrong time?"

"You can be whoever you like," Trinnian smirked. "Although playing my sister may be a bit awkward now."

CHAPTER EIGHT

Olivia giggled, leaning forward to give him a quick kiss before rushing off to the closet to finish getting ready for the evening.

9

The charred shell of my home was no longer visible as I headed off for the twenty-four hour super store. I figured I could park Collin's SUV there and it would go unnoticed, leaving me free to return to my house when the fire chief left. As much as he felt sorry for me, he planned to stay until I was gone just to be certain I would not re-enter the dwelling alone in the dark.

Thankfully, he believed me when I told him I would be staying at a friend's tonight and had job interviews in the city all day tomorrow. I thought that would justify the inability to contact me during the day. He already had my mother's number in case he needed to be able to contact someone while I was unavailable.

The daytime cover story I used on the chief was not so easy to pass on to my mother. It wasn't the lack of being able to reach me in the aftermath of tragedy that bothered her. Oddly enough, it was the fact that this was the first she had heard of me looking for a job to begin with. However, I did manage to avoid lying flat out about where I sent resumes by saying I didn't want Dad tempted to use his connections to get me interviews. I wasn't sure if it was a demonstration of sympathy for my situation but she refrained from prying and let it go on that note.

With Collin's SUV parked in its less obvious spot amongst the other cars of the late night bargain shoppers, I headed back to my house. The initial shock of the fire was wearing off. But that sadness that came with thoughts of Collin wouldn't cease. I couldn't shake the guilt I felt over his death. Maybe I should have told him to go fight for Olivia? As much as he tried to deny it, I knew he wasn't completely fine with Trinnian stealing her away. But instead, I sat back and said nothing. The night that I found him in my house I should have told him I needed to be alone and he needed to find somewhere else to lay low. After all, it wasn't like we were old friends. I didn't owe him anything. But I allowed him to stay regardless.

The plain and simple truth of the matter, Collin was dead because I was too much of a coward to endure being alone. I used him to keep from stewing in an empty house in my own self pity. My inability to deal with the fallout resulting from the poor decisions I have made recently brought this on. Poor Collin was the innocent victim of my selfish actions.

I scrubbed the tears from my eyes with the heels of my hands. There I was, once again, wallowing in self pity when there were other things to consider. What was I going to tell Trinnian and Olivia? They had a right to know. It was not up to me to keep this from them. My opinion on the whole situation didn't matter in the grand scheme of things. The thought of facing them with this news wasn't something I was ready for.

Staying on the roads less traveled, I finally returned to my neighborhood. Eventually I ended up in my own backyard.

This view of the house wasn't much better than the front. The sharp, smoky odor was just as bad, too. I took a moment to prepare before entering the scorched remains of my home.

The back door opened with ease on squeaking hinges. So that was the secret to keeping the door from sticking? Set the house on fire. The insignificant moment brought a tiny smile to my lips and a stab of sadness to my heart. It was as if the house itself was telling me it would never be the same again.

I made my way through the ruined kitchen toward the living room. Once again the scent of burnt immortal flesh made itself known. If I hadn't been aware of my true motivation for returning initially, that scent made the reason all too clear. I didn't come back with delusions of salvaging my human life. I came back to find Collin. He deserved to be laid to rest properly.

The disturbing fragrance led me through the living room and up the stairs toward the guest room. Each step groaned louder the closer I got to the top until I finally stood in the second floor hallway. I glanced to the right, into my bedroom. It was complete devastation. Nothing had been spared. Taking a deep breath, I fought back a nauseating wave of fear and stepped into the guest room.

I don't exactly know what I expected to find but, whatever it was, wasn't there. Just to be sure, I peeked into the closet. Nothing. No corpse, no bones, no ashes in the shape of a body, not even that scent. Well, not like in the hall or downstairs, anyway.

That was when it occurred to me. Upon entering through the back of the house, I first caught the scent of burnt flesh when I was passing by the basement door into the living room. What if Collin made it into the basement? Could he still be alive?

Sure enough, as I made my way to the basement, the aroma was like following a trail. When I opened the basement door, the scent hit me like a wall. I stood frozen at the top of the steps, staring down into the dark. The familiar shapes found there quickly came into focus as my eyes adjusted to the pitch black. But my progress seemed forfeit to hesitation. Just because he sought refuge down there didn't necessarily mean he was still alive. He could have very well crawled his way down there and died. Surely I would have sensed him by now otherwise? There was only one sure way to find out.

With one last internal pep talk, I descended the stairs. My eyes scanned the space thoroughly, looking for any sign of Collin. The basement hadn't been spared from the day's destruction. When I stepped off the last step, a small splash confirmed the amount of water damage resulting from the fire extinguishing. Fortunately, for the efforts of the search, it was only a couple inches deep.

Sloshing deeper into the space, I found no sign of Collin. But this wasn't necessarily a bad thing. New hope actually arose from his absence. There was only one place left he could have sought cover. I mentioned its existence to him offhandedly in conversation but I never actually told him where it was or how to access it. The bomb shelter my uncle built—or 'the man cave' as Claire liked to refer to it.

I splashed my way across the basement to the false wall that obscured the entrance to the shelter with renewed optimism. Sliding the wall aside revealed what looked like an oval shaped submarine hatch situated about a foot off the floor. I turned the wheel until it stopped and pushed the hatch open. The very aroma that brought me to this point choked the air that drifted out from within the chamber. However, in its macabre wake came something glorious. Once again I could sense Collin.

Without further hesitation, I dashed down the carved spiraling stairway, a giddy feeling of excitement propelling me forward. The steps came to an end, opening into a spacious low ceilinged room. Everything was exactly as I remembered it, although I hadn't been down there in years. The one difference was the only thing that mattered at the moment. I could make out Collin's silhouette lying on a bed against the far wall of the room.

"Collin!" I gasped and ran toward him.

His condition became clearer the closer I got. Slowing my pace, I could tell he was alive, but that was only due to my immortal abilities. If I had to rely on visual cues, I would not be so convinced. Even with his back to me, the extent of his injuries was apparent. Most of his hair had been singed away. His clothes were blackened where they weren't burnt away completely.

I was a few feet away when he started to turn toward me. A heartbreaking moan filled the chamber when he finally succeeded at rolling on to his back. The sight of him stopped me dead in my tracks, dropping me to my knees before I could reach him. My face buried in my hands in an attempt to suppress the horrified gasp that tried to escape.

"Jac—"

The first syllable of my name was the only part he could say coherently. His left cheek and ear were gone. Teeth and bones were visible through the melted flesh on the left side of his face. His eyes were charred and black, rendering him blind.

"Shhh," I whispered, crawling toward him. Doing my best to sound calm, resisting the urge to give in to hysteria, I moved forward on quivering limbs. Collin needed me to remain calm, I was the only one he had right now. "Don't try to speak."

He complied and abandoned his attempt to turn his head fully toward me. I couldn't imagine the amount of pain even the simplest of movements caused him. There had to be something I could do to ease his hurting and jumpstart the healing process. My mind sifted through my available options, which, quite frankly, were insufficient. The first idea that came to mind was to let him feed from me. But I hadn't even fed tonight and me losing that amount of blood could be dangerous for both of us. Bringing a human to the house could risk our very existence. I could go feed and return to feed him, but was my blood even strong enough to really do anything? He had suffered long enough without me prolonging it with my stubborn and possibly futile attempt to heal him on my own.

Faced with the facts, we needed help. Our only option didn't thrill me in the least and I knew beyond a shadow of a doubt that Collin would be even less enthusiastic. But what choice did we really have?

"Collin, I'm sorry but I see no other alternative than to ask Trinnian and Olivia to come help us."

His reaction was worse than I expected. He tried to get up all the while gasping 'No!' repeatedly.

"Ok, ok, relax. Please, lay down," I delicately implored. My hands reacted to my first instinct to try to console him through contact but, instead, forced to hover over him uselessly for the lack of undamaged flesh to touch. He immediately lowered himself gingerly to the mattress and my hands returned to their ineffectual position on my lap. "You don't honestly believe I would even suggest they come if I had any other choice? Claire and Augustine left for Germany at sunset. Given the events of the past few weeks, honestly, those are my only choices."

My own admission brought on an overwhelming feeling of helplessness. To hear it from my own lips made the whole situation seem that much worse. How had things gotten to such a bleak point?

Collin spoke, releasing me from my pessimistic thoughts. At first I didn't understand what he said, but when he repeated himself I was able to make out a name I heard a few times before, 'Petrus'. Even with my limited knowledge of the man, having any other option than Trinnian was a relief. Collin carefully recited the cell number and I hit send with a renewed sense of optimism.

When I saw a car turn the corner and the headlights turn off, I knew this had to be Petrus. The sleek, pearl gray Jaguar that approached confirmed my suspicions as I signaled him into the detached garage behind my house. On the phone he said anything he could do for Collin would not take long, so the concealment of the garage should suffice. But it was definitely not an option for overnight parking. Not with any daytime post–fire activity that may occur. Petrus also assured me that judging from the state I described him in, Collin would survive his injuries. Trusting his assessment of the situation was the one thing that helped me hold it together. After all, Petrus did volunteer the fact that he had seen immortals recover from worse. I didn't feel the need to have him elaborate.

With the garage door shut, I waited by the side door while Petrus and his entourage exited the vehicle. When we spoke on the phone, he told me not to be concerned with anyone that may accompany him, reassuring me the situation would be handled with the utmost discretion. If Collin trusted him, so would I. At least that was the frame of mind I tried to adhere to as the unlikely trio drew near. They stopped before me, a massive bald man flanked by two women, one of which was human. I did my best to ignore the sweet perfume of the blood flowing through her veins. But her thoughts were another story. She was so excited about something she was consciously telling herself to act normal. The reason for her inner pandemonium I could not pin down. Petrus spoke, diverting my attention.

"Jacquelyn?" I nodded. "I am Petrus," he said, the introduction punctuated with his own nod. The gesture made his long black mustache touch the lapels of his black leather suit jacket. "This is Lisette." He motioned to a gorgeous platinum blonde in an ankle length sable coat. Her glossy pink, voluptuous lips slid into a friendly smile. But it was her smoky, gray eyes that captured my attention. The color reminded me of Lattimer's, minus the almost luminous silver quality his held. For a split second, my dream from earlier flashed through my mind. I shoved it from my thoughts, returning Lisette's warm smile. "And this is Kayla." He jabbed his thumb in the human girl's direction.

She gave me an awkward wave as her excitement teetered toward frenzy once again. Her hand absently pushed her blonde streaked brunette bangs from her eyes. A stray thought about forgetting her glasses flitted through her struggle for composure.

"Thank you so much for dropping everything to come help, we're working with limited options here," I said, in an attempt to ignore Kayla's thoughts.

"Collin is family, we look out for each other," Petrus replied.

His heartfelt response brought to mind the fact that Olivia told me that exact same thing once. The irony of her words seemed strangely insulting now.

"I do not mean to be rude," Lisette said to Petrus, "but we should really get to this. Tatiana is not the most hospitable one you could have left in charge."

The look on Petrus's face became thoughtful as he agreed with Lisette. Having met Tatiana myself, I knew exactly what she meant. I motioned them to follow me. The four of us quietly crossed the yard and through the back door into the house.

10

Petrus, Lisette, and Kayla followed as I led the way to the bomb shelter. When we reached the basement, Petrus hefted Kayla over his shoulder, muttering something about her being blind as a bat. He carried her like a sack until we reached the chamber that held Collin. There he set her down next to the wall, telling her not to move. She started to panic when he stepped away from her until her hand felt the wall. It was a small comfort to her to have something solid to hold on to in the disorienting pitch black. I found it comical that as a mortal, she feared the dark more than the company she kept.

Lisette and Petrus approached Collin. Neither seemed the least bit alarmed by what they saw. Collin's head tilted ever so slightly toward them, prompting Petrus to speak.

"Relax, old friend, it is me. I brought Lisette and Kayla along to help," Petrus said, turning to Lisette, "I will go first."

Petrus lifted his wrist to his mouth, his teeth sliced through the flesh as he leaned over Collin, letting the first trickle of blood drip onto his blackened eyes. When it started to flow free, he pressed his wrist to Collin's mouth, tilting his head to the right so blood would not seep through the flame ravaged flesh of his cheek. Collin drank until Petrus stopped him. Lisette stepped forward to repeat the process while Petrus went to retrieve Kayla.

The moment he touched her, the excited surge of thoughts returned to flood Kayla's mind, but this time I caught the theme that eluded me before. Petrus promised her immortality tonight in exchange for her help. He explained to her before they left the city that the amount of blood she would need to offer in order to be of assistance could kill her. However, he would not allow that to happen, assuring her she had proven herself to him and he would reward her finally.

Lisette finished donating her portion of blood and stepped back to allow Petrus and Kayla to come forward. Petrus turned to Kayla when they stood next to Collin.

"Do not be afraid, pain is only a temporary inconvenience," Petrus whispered to Kayla, tenderly kissing her forehead. She nodded and offered up her wrist. From where I stood I could smell the adrenaline leaden blood rushing beneath her skin. The enticing combination reminded me of the prior night's hunt. I could even taste it when I closed my eyes. When I opened my eyes, Collin was already drinking from Kayla. Her heart was slowing and Petrus now completely held her up.

Lisette took a step toward him, "Petrus?" Her tone part question part warning.

He ignored her but removed Kayla's wrist from Collin's mouth. Kayla slid down his shins to the floor, unable to stand on her own from the amount of blood loss. Petrus cradled her head in his hands, "Ungrateful bitch," he spat before breaking her neck with a twist of his hands.

I gasped, taking a step backward.

"What the hell, Petrus?!" Lisette exclaimed.

"What?! She was stealing from me!" he barked back.

"You could see no better way to handle the problem?"

Petrus shrugged, gesturing to the body laying at his feet, "Problem looks solved to me."

"You are such an ogre! Wake up, Petrus, the dark ages have long passed!"

"Sorry I am not as refined as Lattimer, feel free to run back to him any time if my archaic ways are becoming too offensive," Petrus said, grinning antagonistically at her insulted reaction. "I meant Owen—it is Owen this week, not Lattimer..." He trailed off as if trying to recall whether or not he had his facts straight.

"I have actually become accustomed to your unrefined methods, it is your lack of forethought that aggravates me," Lisette growled, ignoring his ribbing.

"Why do you care, anyway? You could not stand the girl."

"No, I did not like her but it sure was nice being able to have a bit of free time here and there," she said, storming off toward the steps. When she reached the first step, she turned back, "Some of us have lives, you know!" With that said, she gathered up her fur and stomped off toward the basement.

I gaped at the empty stairway in disbelief. A girl was just killed in front of her and all Lisette cared about was losing her time off?

"Once a thief, always a thief," Petrus was mumbling to himself, shaking his head, staring down at Kayla's lifeless body.

I was seriously starting to question Collin's judgment where his friends were concerned. The events that followed Kayla's death did little to sway my opinion for the better. I found myself jogging back to retrieve Collin's SUV, hoping Lisette wouldn't murder Petrus while I was gone. The need for the other vehicle arose from Petrus's explanation that Collin would heal faster in the city, having access to more blood. I suggested getting the SUV to transport him in, which came as welcome news to Lisette. Apparently she had enough of Petrus for one night and was refusing to ride back with him, insisting on riding with me. The only thing that would make my head stop hurting at that point would be to return to no more corpse in my home.

When I got back to the house, Petrus had just finished arranging Kayla's body in his trunk. He slammed it shut and turned to me.

"I did not mean to alarm you," he said, obviously in reference to Kayla, "but Collin needed human blood more than I needed her. The blood she gave toward his recovery will help boost the healing abilities of ours."

"How long will it take him to recover?"

"The time it takes to heal is different for all of us. He is not considered old in immortal terms, so it will not occur overnight. The fire on its own would not have been so bad, it was the daylight that accelerated the damage."

"But he will fully recover? Vision and all?" I asked.

He chuckled at the question, "It is our amazing ability to heal that defines us as immortals. I can only imagine what an ugly lot we would be if the scars of our existence plagued more than just our memories."

I laughed in return as he attempted to flutter his eyelashes in a coquettish manner. As far as first impressions go, I had Petrus pegged all wrong. When I first saw his hulking frame emerge from the car, his appearance brought to mind

Nikos. But more than anything, he seemed to be just a big teddy bear...ok, a big teddy bear that really hates thieves.

"Where is Lisette?" I asked, wondering if she just decided to head for the city on foot as opposed to spending another minute with Petrus.

"With Collin, she went in as soon as I came up with Kayla. She is pretty upset with me," he said, making his way toward the house. "So if I do not return with Collin in a few minutes, it may not be a bad idea to come looking for me."

It didn't take long before Petrus came through the back door carrying Collin. Lisette followed close behind with a couple of blankets she retrieved from the shelter in order to make Collin as comfortable as possible in the back of the SUV. Once we got him situated, we were off to the city.

Lisette and I rode for the first few miles in silence. I wanted so badly to inquire as to her relationship to Lattimer but I managed to refrain. The silence seemed to be testing my resolve when, at last, Lisette finally spoke.

"Sorry about that whole scene back there," she said. "Petrus just frustrates me so much sometimes. It is almost as if he lacks the ability to understand the impact of the decisions he makes. How he manages to run a business I will never know."

"I would be lying if I said I wasn't horrified by what occurred, but the more selfish side of me ultimately wants what's best for Collin. If it took her death to heal him quicker, I suppose I can't really object."

The admission reminded me of how much I changed in the past few weeks. My humanity was slipping away from me and I was powerless to prevent it. As much as I sat in judgment of their actions, I could see myself becoming as cold as Petrus and Lisette. How much longer would it take until I too held no respect for human life?

"That was the only thing that kept me from leaving. The fact that I know Petrus had the best of intentions. He was doing what he thought was best for Collin," Lisette said.

"What kind of business does Petrus have, anyway?"

I could feel Lisette looking at me as I watched the road, thinking about the question posed to her.

"He runs a gentleman's club."

"Oh," I said. My astonished reaction amused her. "Like a brothel?"

"No, not exactly, our customers rarely request sex. More or less fetish, role playing and fantasy type services."

"You provide these 'services'?" I asked.

"No, I am just the receptionist."

"And so was Kayla?"

Lisette sighed, "Yes."

"Tatiana?"

"She is much more suited toward the services side of things," she answered, returning her attention to me. "I will assume you have met her, so you know what I mean."

I nodded, mentally conjuring up a picture of the tattooed Russian cracking a whip. Yeah, that wasn't much of a stretch. Tatiana's look was reminiscent of Betty Paige's fetish pictures, the more I thought about it.

"How long have you worked for Petrus?"

"Since he first opened shop in New York. But I have known him for centuries," she answered. "We were both sired by Lattimer, which is actually how we met. Petrus used to be Lattimer's right hand man, as they say."

"Kind of like Von or Nikos?"

CHAPTER TEN

Lisette silently studied me before answering, "Yes, but more like Von," she replied. "You have met them?"

Why did I suddenly feel as if I had said too much? Would I ever get the knack of immortal conversation etiquette? Despite the feeling, I answered her anyway, "Yes."

"You have been to Canada?"

If we were closer to our destination I may have felt as though I could try to evade the subject. However, we still had quite a way to go. Besides, every other vampire in the city seemed to know my business, why not one more?

I gave her the cliff note version of my time as an immortal. She hung on my every word without interjection. For whatever reason, I even included the dream from this morning in my tale. Which, I might add, brought more of a reaction from her than the majority of what I relayed.

"You seem awfully sure this was a dream," she noted, unconvinced.

"And you don't?" I asked.

Surely anything she may suspect could hold no fact. I chewed absently on my lower lip while my mind ran through the first memory of my day.

"It would be wise of you not to underestimate him," she said, her tone almost conspiratorial. "He has a way of manipulating people to his will. If he wanted you to believe his presence was just a dream..." She broke off mid thought. "You have shared your story with me, let me share mine with you."

*   *   *   *   *

Lisette paced in the light of a single candle. Her parents sat at a table in their one room house avoiding her glare.

"We need to fight!" she boldly stated, staring down at them. "It is the Devil! We cannot trust it. How long has it stolen our people?"

"Lisette! Silence! What if it hears you?" her father chided in a hushed voice.

"It tells us to sacrifice one to save the rest? You believe that? The village drawing straws to decide who will lose their child? It is turning us all just as barbaric as it is!"

"You will not make trouble for this family!" he growled, slamming his fist on the table. The loud thump brought a fearful gasp from Lisette's mother.

"If you have not noticed, this is all that is left of our family! Three remain of five! How could I possibly make any more trouble—"

The back of her father's hand silenced her tirade.

"I told you to be quiet!" he fumed, hovering over her affronted stare.

She grabbed her cloak off the peg and unlatched the door. Her father attempted to obstruct her intentions.

"Step aside!" she demanded.

"I will not lose another child tonight."

"You are right, the devil feeds on its sacrifice from the village. It will have no use for me!" she spat as she pushed by her father into the night.

With no real plan in mind, she made her way to her father's wood pile to grab the axe. Prying it out of the stump took a little more effort than she anticipated. Bracing herself, she pulled, almost toppling over when it abruptly broke free. She turned in time to see her father closing the door. Whatever she planned to do, she was on her own.

Tears of frustration and anger spilled down her cheeks as Lisette ran for the tree line that bordered her village.

CHAPTER TEN

Concealed in the darkness of the woods, she slowed her pace to a cautious walk. Her ears strained for any sign that she was not alone. The woods were unnaturally quiet. Rasping breaths that came from her were the only sound she could hear.

She leaned against a tree, axe held ready to swing, trying her best to catch her breath while being quiet as possible. The darkness held on to the secrets of the night, revealing nothing to her searching eyes. She quietly sobbed. Her mind blur of emotions. How could her people have surrendered that poor girl so easily? Why would they trust such a beast? They all knew the fiend that dwelled in the night would not hold true to its promise. *Give me a sacrifice and no one else will be harmed*, it told the village elder from the cover of the shadows at sunset.

Something moved in the trees ahead. In a blink it was gone. Was her mind playing tricks on her? With a deep, unsteady breath, she proceeded deeper into the woods. When she got to the place she had seen movement, there was nothing. She exhaled and lowered the axe. The demon had what it wanted. Perhaps the monster was long gone?

A low moan from behind a fallen tree off to her left caught her attention. Try as she might, she was blind to whatever lurked on the other side. She had to get closer. Grabbing up her skirts to stalk forward, she silently crept toward the fallen tree. The closer she got, she could tell it was a female making the miserable sound. With one last scan of the woods, she peered over the tree.

Lying on the ground next to the tree trunk was the very girl that had been offered in exchange for the safety of the village.

11

Without a second thought, Lisette climbed over the fallen tree. Propping the axe against its trunk, she crouched down next to the girl and gently turned her on to her back to better assess her condition. The girl's eyelids flickered but never opened. Her lips were pale as death but Lisette instantly recognized her. The girl's name was Mary. She was the eldest daughter of a family that lived in the first house on the road into the village.

The only evidence of harm Lisette could see was smears of blood on her neck and shoulder. But there was no wound to account for it. Maybe she fought off the beast and this was not her blood at all? Regardless, Lisette had to get her back to the village before it returned.

"Mary," Lisette said in a hushed voice. The girl she tried to rouse gave no sign of acknowledgement. Lisette tried again, a bit louder, giving Mary a gentle shake. This time the girl's brow furrowed slightly and a weak groan came in response. "Mary, wake up!" Lisette pled. The whispered request filled with urgency. "I cannot carry you, you have to wake up!"

CHAPTER ELEVEN

Mary's head lolled back and forth while she grumbled incoherently. Lisette got to her knees thinking if she could sit Mary up, maybe it would be easier to revive her. As she reached down to grab Mary's arms, a voice from behind stopped her.

"A sacrifice by definition is to forfeit possession," growled the voice.

Terror tried to paralyze Lisette but she knew she was the only chance Mary had to survive. The axe leaned against the tree behind her, if she could just muster up the strength to face the demon, the weapon would be within her reach.

Slowly, she turned, unable to imagine the abomination she was about to face. What she saw betrayed every monstrosity her mind conjured up. The beast that ruled the darkness was not a two headed creature with sickle-like claws and glowing red eyes. Before her, just beyond the fallen tree, stood a man draped in a fur lined black cloak. His glossy black hair spilled over his shoulders, accentuating his pale complexion. This human form was not entirely without malice, his deep-set gray eyes held malevolence that made her breath catch in her throat.

Lisette was not a fool. She would not allow herself to underestimate this man. How many lives had he taken to become the feared being that stood in her path? She grabbed the axe, ready to defend herself and Mary.

"Not everybody agreed to your terms," said Lisette.

"By that you mean nobody cared enough about your opinion to stop the girl from being given up in the first place?"

"Who are you?" she asked, disregarding his question and the bitter truth it contained.

"My name is Lattimer," he replied, taking a step forward.

"Stay back! Or I swear I will cut you down," Lisette shouted, raising the axe as if to strike.

He put up his hands in mock surrender, "Fair enough."

"What have you done to her?" she asked, reluctantly lowering the heavy weapon.

"Nothing yet, really...if you must know, I was debating whether or not she would make a suitable companion when you barged in."

Lisette's expression turned appalled, "You think she could love such a devil? One that steals innocent women and children in the middle of the night?"

"Love? Who said anything about love?" chuckled Lattimer.

"You truly are a monster," she spat, trying to ignore the implications of his comment. "You do not even attempt to deny what you have done, much less try to justify the lives you have destroyed. Do you have any respect for human life?"

Any trace of amusement left his face as he took a step forward, stabbing his finger at Mary. "You think because she does not feed the worms, she lives? She is already dead! All of you are. It is just a matter of time before your rotting flesh alerts the others."

"Lies! You are trying to fill my head with your lies to confuse me! I am alive, just as she is. We all live until you come for us, one by one," she growled, clutching the axe tighter.

"If you only knew what it was like to truly be alive," Lattimer laughed. "You live...temporarily, I will give you that," he said, taking a step forward.

"I told you to stay back!"

"But as far as *living*? Look in the eyes of your fellow villagers then tell me that they are *alive*. Every inhabitant of your beloved village wakes in the morning and goes through the motions of their daily routine, content with the predictable nature of each passing day. There is no true passion for life to be found in any of them. No glimmer of hope for something more, no anticipation for what the future could hold. Each passing day is not seized as an opportunity," he stated, stepping over the fallen tree, "but merely a marking of time reminding them they are one step closer to the grave."

Lisette raised the axe, "Stop!"

The trembling axe poised to strike did little more than amuse her approaching tormentor. His smirk so brief it could have been imagined.

"I have roamed through cities that hunger for life more than any single inhabitant of your precious village could even dream of. I have seen ambition, lust and desire, first hand."

Without breaking stride, Lattimer grabbed the axe with one hand and encircled her waist with the other, forcing her backward until she found herself pinned between him and a tree. Her attempts to free herself were futile. When she gave up her pointless struggle, he once again spoke, his lips inches from hers.

"I have seen the rise and fall of empires. I have walked amongst kings," he whispered. Lisette attempted to speak but his narrowing gaze silenced her. He closed his eyes, deeply breathing in her scent. She shivered powerlessly in his grip. His eyes opened, revealing a hunger so intense her limbs went numb with fright. She heard the axe hit the ground with a thud. His cool cheek slid against hers until his lips brushed her ear, "I have lain with queens," he purred. "I have experienced pleasures you could not even imagine."

Lisette swallowed hard and tried to take a quivering breath. Lattimer's hands were pushing her dress up her thighs as his body pressed between her legs. She felt the rough fabric of his breeches rub against the soft flesh of her inner thighs.

"Please...I beg you," she said in a gasping whisper.

Once again, his eyes locked on to hers, his lips a breath away. It wasn't until his fingertips skimmed the flesh beneath her eyes that she realized she was crying.

"One day your begging will be for a different reason," he softly taunted, his lips brushing hers light as a feather. "You have decided for me—take her."

Lisette collapsed to the ground, gasping for air. Mary's unconscious body lay before her and Lattimer was nowhere to be seen.

When Lisette finally returned to the village, she received anything but a hero's welcome. Mary's parents reluctantly took her back, seemingly torn between their loyalty to her as family and their fear for what accepting her back would bring upon them.

Lisette's family took her in with the same mixed emotions Mary had been met with. Except her father was more than willing to vocalize his thoughts, informing her that whatever else happened to the village she would be directly responsible. The cruelty of his words hurt her more than his hands ever had. So when he asked her about what happened to her in the woods, she chose to lie. On their journey back to the village, Mary claimed she never saw the fiend and was unconscious the whole time. With this knowledge at hand, Lisette was free to tell whatever she chose.

The tale she chose to tell omitted Lattimer completely. She claimed there was no sign of anything but Mary when she happened upon the girl deep in the woods. Whether or not her parents believed her did not matter. The story she relayed was all they would ever get. Much to her relief, they did not press the subject. Having waited up for her return, they were almost as eager for sleep as she was.

But sleep alluded Lisette. She tossed and turned, irritated that exhaustion was not enough to induce slumber. Every time she closed her eyes she saw Lattimer's face. Even in her mind's eye, his piercing gaze brought with it the same intensity of emotions that existed in his presence. The overtone of fear was expected. But what lie beneath, colored her with shame.

Her train of thought started out innocent enough. Why were there only accounts of him at night? Where did he hide out during the day? What was he? He looked human. He felt human. That was the point where her thoughts strayed. With vivid detail, she could recall being locked in his arms, pinned helplessly between him and the tree. The feather light sensation of his lips touching her ear still had the power to raise gooseflesh on her arms. Her thighs trembled in memory of being forced apart by his body pressing in between them. A flush of heat spread through her flesh just as it had in that moment with him. It reminded her of how the contrasting chill of his fingertips sent a shock down her spine when he touched her face. The velvety soft way his lips grazed hers conjured up an ache so lucid, the origin of which could only be met with mortification.

Lisette's eyes shot open, she clenched her blankets so hard her hands hurt. The sheen of sweat that covered her flesh made her shift cling to her. She found herself having to concentrate to control her breathing for fear her gasping breaths would wake her parents. Luckily her humiliating state did not rouse them. She spent the remaining time until dawn thinking about anything but Lattimer and not once drifting off to sleep.

Morning chores behind her, Lisette set out to check on Mary. As she made her way through the village, she paid close attention to those around her. Even though she told herself it was to listen for any signs of trouble resulting from her rescue of Mary, she knew that was not entirely the motivation. Lisette found herself studying the faces of the people in her village just as Lattimer had suggested. Most avoided eye contact with her, no doubt having heard she had been the one that had stolen their sacrifice back from the devil. Nobody wanted to be seen having any sort of contact with the girl that would no doubt bring the end of days upon them. So far, their fears were unfounded. Nothing happened in retaliation for her actions. But it would take more than one night for the tension to lift from the population. The people of her village would not rest easy for a few days.

There was indeed something else that mingled with their unease and Lattimer knew exactly what she would find if she opened her eyes. Only one word could accurately describe the dull expression that lingered everywhere she looked. Resignation. It was not brought on by the events of the prior night. This disposition had taken root long ago. Lisette could easily recall Lattimer's request, *Look in the eyes of your fellow villagers then tell me that they are alive.* Much to her dismay, she had to admit, he was right.

"What do you want?" asked Mary's mother in a less than hospitable tone.

Lisette could not even recall knocking on the door, having arrived to her destination in a defeated haze. The stout woman in the doorway blocked her ability to see inside the dwelling.

"I just wanted to see how Mary was doing today."

CHAPTER ELEVEN

The woman's eyes were more intent on whether or not anybody was watching than to make contact with Lisette.

"She's resting now," the woman offered quickly before attempting to shut the door.

Lisette's hand shot out to stop it, finally securing the mother's attention. She scowled at the interfering hand before turning her irritated gaze to Lisette.

"Will you tell her I stopped by and will check on her again tomorrow?" Lisette asked. Her defiant tone was met with a cold, silent stare. No sooner did she remove her hand from the door, it slammed in her face.

That night, Lisette lay in her bed. Her mind meandered through the events of the day. Everywhere she turned she was shunned. As if being spurned by her fellow villagers was not bad enough, she may as well have been a ghost in her own home. Her parents barely acknowledged her presence, the fact that she was given supper almost felt like a blessing. She had never before experienced such loneliness in her life. The only thing that gave her hope was knowing it would all pass in a few days. Surely Lattimer would not have told her to take the girl then attack them. Once they saw there would not be revenge taken on them for what Lisette had done, they would have to forgive her.

Again, Lisette found herself battling sleep. As with the prior night, every time she closed her eyes, Lattimer was there. Unable to fight any longer, just before dawn, she drifted off to sleep. Her thoughts finally free of the miserable day. She became completely immersed in peaceful slumber. That was until a familiar voice disrupted her blissful rest.

"You have seen it?"

Lisette quickly discovered Lattimer sitting on the edge of her bed. She cautiously sat up, scanning the room to find her parents still sleeping in their bed.

"How did you get in?" she demanded in a low whisper, her fear at odds with the feeling of violation.

"I asked first," he responded, a provoking smirk played on his face. His eyes followed hers, "You do not have to whisper, they will not wake."

"What have you done to them?"

Not waiting for a response, she backed toward the wall in an attempt to be out of his immediate reach. Her former feeling of violation finally giving over to concern for her own safety.

"Nothing yet, would you like me to?"

"No!"

A sly grin spread across his face, he leaned on his elbow, essentially cornering her.

"You saw it."

"Saw what?"

"The empty look in their eyes."

"Maybe...perhaps what I saw was there because you stole their hope," she accused. "What could they possibly have to live for if it could all be taken from them any given night?"

"I am flattered you think so highly of me to be able to influence a whole community of people enough to lose hope...if I only had that much power."

"You do not believe fear can be that powerful?"

He stared at her as if to consider her words, "You do not seem to fear me."

Lisette sat up a bit straighter before speaking, "If you wanted to kill me, you would have done so in the woods."

CHAPTER ELEVEN

Lattimer slowly started to pull the blanket off Lisette. It was all she could do not to grab it as it slid away.

"Is that the extent of your fears?" he needled as the blanket no longer concealed Lisette. He reached forward. His icy fingers stroked the exposed skin of her calf. "There is nothing more I could possibly be capable of that scares you?"

Doing her best not to flinch, she crossed her arms in front of her, "You will not harm me."

In the blink of an eye, the fabric at the neck of her shift was balled up in his fist. She was no longer backed up against the corner of the room. Her face was inches from his when he spoke.

"Do not assume you know what I am capable of," he hissed.

Lisette woke with her shift twisted awkwardly around her and the blankets on the floor. Her hair clung to her face and neck, damp with sweat. Lattimer was nowhere to be seen.

12

The first light of dawn descended on the village by the time Lisette pulled herself together. Its gradual illumination did little to comfort her. Instead, it set a possible theory in motion. Her initial assumption was she had just woken from a vivid dream. But with the onset of the new day she wondered, could Lattimer really have been there? The approaching dawn would certainly account for his quick departure if he truly was bound to the night. Her hand absently smoothed the front of her wrinkled shift while her attention turned to the door. The latch was in place, just as it had been the night before. Her unease was self-inflicted, merely the result of an overactive imagination fed by the recent lack of sleep.

Lisette's day unfolded in the same manner as the prior day. Once again, her fellow villagers avoided her as she made her way to Mary's house. Though they tried their best to not make eye contact, a few people captured her momentarily in their bleak stare. Upon realizing the target of their focus, they quickly found something else to look at—some going as far as changing direction entirely. She tried her best to ignore them and the sadness resulting from their actions. But the rejection was starting to get to her, filling her with her own form of emptiness. Still, there was something to be thankful for, she heard no accounts of backlash from Mary's rescue. Her only hope still clung to the idea that, the more nights that passed incident free, they would have no reason to continue treating her like a leper.

One thing was different from the previous day. This Lisette discovered when she reached her destination. Once again, she found herself face to face with Mary's stout mother. But this time she was not simply going to shut Lisette out of her home, denying her visitation. This time she was going to give Lisette a piece of her mind. Before she could even request to see Mary, the girl's mother planted her fists on her hips and laid into her. She somehow managed a tone that got her point across without causing a scene.

"You cannot force your way into getting what you want with everyone. I know your stubborn, bullying ways work on most of the others, but they will not work on me. I will not give in to silence you nor do I fear you. You will not darken my doorstep again! The sight of you near my daughter will only serve to remind people of that night and I will not have my family shunned by the village. Maybe your family is used to being treated like outcasts because of your obstinate behavior and your crass tongue, but we are not. We get on well here. I will not remove my family from this village because of any assumed associations with the likes of you!"

Just before the door slammed in Lisette's face, she caught a glimpse of Mary over her mother's shoulder. Her color was better than last she saw her but that could have been attributed to her mother's tirade. At least her gaping expression certainly was.

The stout woman's words tormented Lisette. She wondered if there was any truth to what she said. The fact that Lisette really did not have any friends never bothered her before. Growing up, the other kids just seemed so dull and controlled they could not hold her interest. Other than playing with her own siblings, she preferred to be alone. Or had she just gotten so used to it? She always figured her solitude was her own doing. Lisette always had free will, which was what got her in more trouble with her father more often than not. When her older sister and younger brother got into trouble, she would always find a way to focus her father's attention on herself to spare them. After all, she had grown accustomed to his wrath. Maybe that was all the others saw? Her attempts to anger her father enough to spare her family?

Lisette did not like to think too much about her sister and brother. She missed them terribly. When Lattimer started taking villagers in the cover of darkness, Lisette and her mother hatched a plan to save her siblings from her father's abuse. One afternoon, they packed a ration of food and a change of clothes, sending them off through the woods. When night fell, they convinced her father that they must have gotten lost in the woods and the demon got them. Lisette and her mother never knew what truly became of them. Cutting all ties was the only way they could have escaped.

Having wandered to the edge of the village, Lisette stared into the forest, lost in her thoughts. Peering deep into the vast maze of trees, the peaceful escape it promised lured her in. Without a backward glance, she stepped into the shadowy serenity of the woods.

Away from the oppressive feel of the village, Lisette felt as if a weight had been lifted from her. She started to entertain the thought of leaving the place forever, reveling in the feel of her new found freedom. Stories of distant lands fueled her imagination. She found herself conjuring up scenarios of new lives in different places.

A familiar setting stole her away from her musing. She stood next to the fallen tree where she found Mary. Beside her, the tree that Lattimer pinned her against outshined all the rest. Moving forward, she reached toward its weathered veneer. Her fingertips traced the lateral pattern of the bark but her absent stare did not see the tree. All she could see was Lattimer. Again she found herself wondering where he was during the day. Somewhere not so deep within, a part of her wished he was there now. Any other day, the realization might have horrified her. But in that moment, it almost felt as if he was the only one she had left.

The golden late afternoon sunlight elongated the shadows as she sat at the base of the tree. It could have been defiance that cemented her decision to remain in the woods or maybe it was simply the dread that accompanied being under the gaze of the public eye. Regardless, she was not ready to abandon the liberating feeling of being in that moment.

Her surroundings melted away as she gave in to fantasies of silken gowns and lavish palaces. She had seen such things in images toted by merchants that passed through the village on occasion. Perhaps it was Lattimer's claims that brought to mind people bowing to her as she glided through gilded archways, nodding to them graciously. What would it be like to travel to faraway places and be somebody...anybody else?

She opened her eyes that had drifted closed to better accommodate her visions. Lattimer sat against the fallen tree staring back at her. Her heart skipped a beat but she would not allow him to see any sort of weakness in her. Darkness had fallen in the midst of her daydreaming. She became painfully aware she was unarmed and at his mercy.

"I had no idea you would come around so quickly," Lattimer said.

"I beg your pardon?"

"You did come to offer me your virginity in exchange for rescuing you from this hideous existence, did you not?" he asked, referring to their surroundings with an apathetic wave of his hand.

"Certainly not!" she gasped.

"Oh," he said, as if baffled by her response, getting to his feet. "Then I shall leave you to your regal indulgences." Lisette felt the heat of embarrassment rush into her face. "Although I must say, I personally imagined you on a bed of silks as opposed to wearing them."

Her jaw dropped open as she, too, stood, "Again with the tricks to try to confuse me. Is that how you win over your prey?"

"I need no 'tricks' to get what I want."

"Every girl dreams of silken gowns and palaces, your timing does not impress me," she stated, hoping he could not really read her mind.

"I was not trying to impress you at all. I rarely have to account for my abilities to anyone."

"I am still not impressed...I need to be getting home now."

Lisette turned to head to her house with the hope he would just let her walk away.

"Charles and Anna are fine," he said, stopping her dead in her tracks. "I followed them until dawn, making sure they had safe passage through the woods."

All the blood drained from Lisette's face. The names of her siblings brought tears to her eyes. She would not allow Lattimer to see her cry, instead she continued on, heading for home.

She ate supper in silence with her mother and father. Neither bothered to ask her where she had been. Nor did they say anything else. Their silence only added to the empty pit that was growing in her.

Lisette had almost finished cleaning up after their meal with her mother when a fist pounded on the door. Her parents exchanged a bewildered look before her father got up to answer the door. It was one of the village elders flanked by two other men she recognized.

"You and your family need to come with us," the elder informed her father. The man's eyes met Lisette's before quickly returning to her father.

"What is this about?" her father asked the man.

Lisette stepped back until she felt the edge of the table and slid a knife into her pocket.

"We will discuss the matter when we reach the church," the elder replied.

The elder led the way, followed by Lisette and her family who were, in turn, followed by the two men. Opening the doors to the village church, the elder stepped aside to allow them entry. All the residents of the village were already inside. A disturbing silence fell over the crowd as Lisette's family was led to the front middle pew, the only one that was vacant, and sat as requested. The elder took the podium, surveyed the audience and spoke.

"A situation has been made known to us that cannot be ignored," the man said.

His attention flickered to Lisette intermittently. Her stomach started to churn. Had someone seen her with Lattimer earlier in the woods? She tried not to fidget but her hand kept sliding toward the knife in her pocket.

"Mary, will you come forward?"

Lisette's eyes shot to the girl approaching the stage. Mary stared directly at the elder, unwilling to spare a glance at anything else. She looked terrified, as if her feet were moving without her permission. When she reached the podium the elder gently laid his hands on her shoulders.

"I am not going to make you retell the story you told me, but I need you here with me in case I omit anything. Can you do that for me?" he asked as if talking to an infant.

Mary nodded and looked down at her feet. A rumble passed through the crowd. Lisette looked around to find everyone looking in her direction, her head swum as if she would lose consciousness.

"This innocent child came to me this evening to warn us all of the demon that dwells among us," he said, pausing as the crowd murmured, reacting to his news.

"So you endanger us all, stealing us away from the safety of our homes to remind us of the devil that dwells in the woods?" asked a man.

The people were stirred into panic by the man's words, some rising to leave.

"Wait! Wait!" begged the elder. "We are safer here than in our homes, the devil has no power here. Not in the house of God!" The crowd reluctantly settled back in their seats, muttering amongst themselves. "There is more than one devil that lurks about this village. We never once questioned what lured the beast here in the first place. It came for a mate!"

CHAPTER TWELVE

Cries of disbelief and outrage rose from the people. Most were on their feet, ready to serve justice on the spot. Mary stood next to the speaker. She hugged herself, rocking back and forth. Tears dripped from her chin, her eyes never leaving her feet. The elder motioned for silence. It took a few minutes but his request was finally honored.

"Together, we will stop this abomination from obtaining its goal. In the meantime, I ask that everyone refrain from taking matters into their own hands."

The silence that followed his words did nothing to comfort Lisette. Nor did Mary seem at ease as she abruptly started mumbling the Lord's Prayer.

"Mary came to me earlier after suddenly being able to recall events from the night she had been offered to the beast." He glanced at Mary, who was now shaking uncontrollably and crying hysterically. Lisette felt bile rise in her throat, trying in vain to choke it down. "This poor girl witnessed the beast having consensual relations with Lisette," stabbing his finger in her direction "—and is even willing to show us the exact spot...in the light of day, of course."

The entire village was on its feet, pointing and shouting at Lisette. Her parents were backing away from her. Lisette stood shaking her head violently in denial, moving backward toward the pulpit, desperately thinking of a way out. Just then something hit her in the head, thrown from the crowd that now inched toward her. Another object struck her hip. This was about to turn ugly.

Lisette turned to run, finding herself face to face with the wide eyed Mary. She grabbed a hold of the girl, being pelted with things from behind and turned back to the crowd, holding the knife she had concealed to Mary's throat.

115

"Stay back!" Lisette shouted, "Or I will gut her like a pig!"

Mary wailed in horror, making a trickle of blood drip down her throat from her struggle against the knife. The onlookers gasped, frozen where they stood. Lisette knew she couldn't hold them off forever, frantically trying to figure a way out. Suddenly, the doors of the church flew open, splintering against the walls. Lattimer stood in the doorway. Ironically enough, relief surged through Lisette.

Lattimer stepped into the church, the villagers backed away as he advanced toward the pulpit. His fur lined cloak bellowing out behind him. When he reached Lisette, he stopped, gently taking the knife from her. He turned to Mary, slipping his hand into her hair, grabbing a fist full. The girl shrieked, clawing at his hand.

"I believe this belongs to me," he said, turning toward the crowd.

He held Mary at an arm's length, displaying her to his audience. Nobody took a step forward or even spoke as his glare took them all in one by one. Satisfied, he pulled her close and buried his teeth into her throat. The villagers shuffled uncomfortably as he drank from the girl until finally one tried to inch their way to the door.

"Halt!" Lattimer exclaimed. The offender stopped where he stood. Lattimer dropped Mary's limp body to the floor and held his hand out to his side. "Lisette..."

Hearing her name, Lisette's attention returned to Lattimer and away from Mary's motionless body. She nervously scanned the room before stepping forward to take his hand. He pulled her around to face him. She stared into his eyes, her body trembling with fear and excitement. Her breaths came in shallow, uneven gasps. He reached forward, his hand gripping her behind her neck. For a moment, Lisette could have sworn she saw vulnerability in his eyes, or maybe she just saw something she wanted to. He pulled her to him, his lips eagerly enveloping hers. She let go of any thoughts of hesitation, allowing herself to indulge her own desire. One she had denied even existed until that moment. She returned his kiss without restraint, the very act melting away everything else around them.

When he pulled away, she felt an ache that she had only felt in his memory. Again she also felt the shame that accompanied it. Lattimer's smirk confirmed her earlier suspicion. He could, without a doubt, read her mind.

"I am leaving," he whispered to her.

Lisette suddenly remembered where they were and the people surrounding them. Panic filled her. Unsure if it was the situation or Lattimer, she spoke.

"Take me—I beg you."

13

We sat at a traffic light in the heart of the city when I realized Lisette's silence was more than just a pause in her story. I looked over to find her smirking to herself, her platinum hair and ivory complexion taking on the red glow of the signal. The effect made her expression appear mischievous. She glanced my way, breaking fully into a smile.

"For all that has come to pass between us, my first years with Lattimer still hold happiness when I recall them," she said. "He was my first in many ways...friend...companion...lover...to this very day, the love I have for him remains intact."

"But..." I prompted, taking my cue from her tone.

She shrugged, "But, he is who he is—you know precisely what I am referring to. His controlling, arrogant disposition tends to clash with my rebellious, stubborn streak," she chuckled, but her amusement quickly dissipated as she continued. "Of course, there is more to it than just our individual quirks. The hurt we have inflicted upon each other over the years borders on unforgivable..." she confessed, her gaze narrowing, "you know, the spiteful kind of things we tend to reserve for those that only we can hurt the most. Sometimes I wonder how he and I manage to remain civil to one another when our paths do cross. Perhaps it is all loosely held in place by memories of how good we had once been together?"

Tempted as I was to pry, I managed to keep a lid on my curiosity. Even if she was willing to share, I was pretty sure we were close to our destination. However, there was something bothering me that needed clarification.

"How can you tell if it is just a dream or if Lattimer is really present?" I asked.

"At the time? I am not sure you can. But if it seems plausible when you are fully awake, the more likely it is that he was there. I know for a fact that it is almost impossible for humans to tell. Their minds are much more susceptible to immortal influence. So judging from that, I would assume that the longer you are an immortal, the more difficult it would be to fool you. Especially when you consider the fact that the older and stronger the vampire, the earlier they can rise."

It never really occurred to me that everyone else seemed to wake before I did. The more I thought about it the more apparent it became, which made me wonder what else went on around me that I was completely oblivious to.

"So how early can he wake?"

"Technically he can wake whenever he wants to, I suppose. It is possible for us to dwell during the day but it takes the right conditions," she explained. Noting my confusion she enlightened me. "In an environment void of sunlight, we can adapt in such a manner that the position of the sun becomes almost irrelevant. Of course, we will always be aware of it, but when it cannot touch us, what does it matter? The way most of us live, no matter how well we block out the light, there is merely a man-made barrier protecting us. For our own sakes, our bodies have evolved in such a way that we instinctively seek shelter, feeling tired when the sun starts to rise. We could ignore the urge to sleep but that would leave us feeling lethargic and not as well protected."

My train of thought must have been obvious. Without missing a beat, she answered my unspoken question.

"Well, maybe not you. Sleep still dominates your will in the daylight hours but its influence will pass with time. What I was referring to is the ability to abandon shelter for the night. Lattimer is so strong that he can withstand the last rays of sun as it sinks below the horizon. There not many still in existence that can."

"Oh, I get it. So while I'm still in a deep sleep, he can creep in without fear of me waking naturally."

"Precisely. Even if you do wake, you will not be alert enough to decipher conscious thoughts from subconscious ones," she said.

"Why do you think Lattimer uses the guise of dreams?"

"When he has his sights on someone, or something, he likes to keep tabs on them," Lisette replied. "What better way to get what he wants without raising suspicion?"

"Well, I have nothing he could possibly want."

Lisette smiled, "I would not be so sure about that. You are the kind of woman he likes."

"No, I'm pretty sure he would rather strangle me with his bare hands than invite me for a romantic stroll on the beach," I confessed.

Lisette laughed, "Fine, think what you will. But I have come to the conclusion long ago that as much as he would love everyone to bow to him, he prefers his women on the feisty side."

"Ok," I muttered sarcastically.

"Well, when the time comes, feel free...you will not be hurting my feelings," she said casually. "Trust me, a night with Lattimer is something every woman should experience."

Caught off guard by her candid train of thought, I looked to see if she was joking. Instead, she seemed to be lost in recollection, reliving a moment I'd rather not interrupt.

"Jacquelyn!" she exclaimed. I returned my attention to the road. We had been following Petrus, who now came to almost a complete stop to make a right hand turn. I had to slam on the breaks. Luckily, nobody was too close behind me. Lisette reached across me to lay on the horn, she was furious, "I swear he drives like an old lady!"

We continued to follow Petrus down the side street to an alley, turning into a narrow driveway behind a building that looked like every other one surrounding it. He came to a stop at a decrepit looking gate that lazily started to retract into the brick wall. We followed him down into a parking area, pulling into the vacant space next to him.

I popped the back door so Petrus could remove Collin from the SUV. Lisette got out, slamming her door. She crossed over to Petrus by the time I exited the vehicle.

"Jesus Christ, Petrus! I know ninety year old ladies that drive better than you! What if Jacquelyn would have hit you? You do recall you have a corpse in your trunk and she has a charred body in the back of the SUV..."

While she berated Petrus, I went to check on Collin. I had to admit the stale air of the garage was a pleasant change from being cooped up with the scent of burnt vampire. Upon first impression, Collin appeared to be sleeping in the same position as last I saw him. But when I sat on the edge of the bumper, his head turned in my direction.

"It's just me, Jacquelyn."

"I know," he said in a raspy whisper of a voice. His hand reached toward me, I gingerly took hold of it for fear of hurting him. "Thank you."

"You're welcome," I replied. "But I honestly didn't really do much...if anything I feel like it's my fault you're in this situation."

"You are a victim in this just as much as I am."

"You need to rest," I said. "No more talking. I'm going to get Petrus."

No sooner did I say it, Petrus appeared next to me.

"Lisette went to prepare her guest room," he said. "Ready?"

I nodded and Petrus leaned in to carefully extract Collin from the vehicle. Closing the hatch, I followed them to Lisette's apartment.

The door to the apartment was ajar when we arrived. Petrus headed straight for the guest room, where Lisette met him and helped get Collin situated comfortably in the bed. I waited just outside the door, trying my best to stay out of their way, yet close enough should they need me.

Lisette's apartment suited her. The décor was bold while the furnishings were inviting. Color played a key role in bringing the room together, objects that spanned an immortal lifetime cohabitated well together, courtesy of someone with the gift for attention to detail. But the focal point of the room was undoubtedly the nude painting of Lisette outstretched on the banister of a white marble staircase. Her body clung to the railing in such a manner as to keep the image from being obscene. With her cheek resting on the back of her hand, her sultry gaze drew the attention of the onlooker.

CHAPTER THIRTEEN

"Is it egotistical of me to say I love that painting?" Lisette asked from behind me.

"I don't think so," I replied. "It is very tastefully done, I love the way it almost looks like a black and white photo but at the same time it doesn't feel out of place in the colorful room," I replied.

"Thank you. When I originally asked Augustine to paint my portrait, this was not what I had in mind. But then Violet started being her crazy self so I insisted upon it." Lisette laughed, "Thanks for that too, by the way."

I gave her a quick smile in return—not exactly sure I was ready to joke about Violet. Especially with someone I just met. Petrus entered the room, sparing me the awkward moment.

"If you two want to go hunt, I will stay with Collin," he offered.

"Well, that is the smartest decision you made all night," Lisette grumbled.

"Jacquelyn, do not let her behavior make you uncomfortable. In the presence of other immortals, she is respectful and even addresses me as Sir—depending on the situation, of course," Petrus said.

"Well, as much as you infuriate me at times, you do have seniority. I would never dare disrespect you in front of anyone. But for all the decades we have shared, you are fair game in private," she informed him.

"Jacquelyn is not 'anyone'?" he asked.

"You know what I mean. She is not hung up on age and tradition yet." Lisette turned to me, "Not that there is anything wrong with that. It just gets a bit old sometimes."

Immediately, I recalled my fight with Owen and most of my interactions with Lattimer. I, for one, knew exactly what she meant.

Lisette and I set out to hunt in the city. Although, she did admit to me that lately she had been lazy and found that she fed more often than not from the clients that frequented Petrus's establishment. So it was almost a treat to 'eat out'. It didn't take long to stumble upon suitable prey. I was happy to discover the majority of immortals in our circle chose the same types of victims. One day, I would certainly find myself in the company of those that may not. But that would be a bridge to cross when I came to it.

When we returned, I curled up on Lisette's ultra-modern, crayon red couch. It was a bit firmer than it looked but, as tired as I was, it didn't even matter, sleep took me just a quick as if on a bed of feathers.

I wasn't sure if it was the warmth or the crackle of fire that I first became aware of, but I found myself laying on the floor in front of a raging fireplace. Looking up, Lattimer's portrait stared down at me. My mind scrambled to recall how I ended up here but was interrupted by a hand on my shoulder. I rolled on my back, all the better to see who occupied the space with me. But I knew who I would find before I even laid eyes him. Lattimer was propped up on his elbow behind me. His coal black hair spilled onto the floor around his elbow. He was stretched out parallel to me, wearing nothing but a pair of black pajama bottoms tied low on his hips. The light of the fire illuminated the smooth skin of his chest and stomach, adding radiance to his flesh, fueling my urge to touch him. His eyes daring me to resist only fed the desire.

CHAPTER THIRTEEN

Before I could give in to temptation, he reached toward me. His fingers delicately traced a line from the base of my neck to just below my navel, accentuating the fact that I lay naked before him. The desire his touch coaxed from within cancelled out the natural reaction of self–consciousness one would normally feel being so fully exposed. His hand retraced its path and continued on until his fingertips skimmed across my lips, eyes locked on mine the entire time his touch explored the curves of my skin. My body reacted to his touch instantly. Flesh tingled in anticipation, eagerly awaiting the gentle stroke of his fingertips once more. Staggered breaths announcing my arousal drew him closer, hovering above me until he straddled my naked body. Slowly, he lowered himself to me, bracing his upper body on his elbows, holding my head in his hands. His lips met mine tenderly at first, becoming more forceful when my hands slid around his waist. The unspoken consent of my actions encouraged him to act on his desires. He nipped playfully at my bottom lip and teased my tongue with his. The more we explored each other, the more he pushed the envelope. His hands clawed down my sides, the pain forcing a guttural moan between my clenched teeth. I could feel him hard against me. He kissed me deeply while my hands tugged at his pants, pushing them down his thighs. His lips left mine, making their way down my neck. I turned my head toward the fireplace, allowing him full access to the tender flesh below my ear his eager mouth was seeking.

Movement from the direction of the fire caught my attention. One by one, glowing hot embers rolled their way across the rug in our direction, fire spreading in their trail. Lattimer, unaware of the encroaching danger pressed between my thighs, more than ready to enter into much more intimate territory. The smoldering embers reached his hair, the fire spread instantly, bringing his actions to a halt. He shot to his feet, wailing in pain as the flames spread down his body and his hands franticly attempted to extinguish the blaze. I backed away screaming, watching in horror as he became completely engulfed in flames.

"Jacquelyn! Jax!"

A voice called to me. Even as I opened my eyes, my screams filled the room.

14

It took me a moment to come to my senses and find relief in my surroundings. But when I did, Collin sat facing me on the couch wearing a navy blue bath robe. Although he looked much better than the prior night, going unnoticed in a crowd was a stage he had not yet reached. His skin still looked red and raw. The worst of it where blackened flesh had once been, as if the healing worked on the most damaged parts first. I sat up, silently cursing myself for waking him.

"Collin, I'm so sorry," I said. My guilt only worsening when I realized his eyes were covered with an opaque fleshy membrane. He was still blind. "You need to be resting, not scrambling to answer false alarms."

"I was already awake," he said. His voice was back for the most part, it was the damaged flesh around his mouth that altered the familiar sound of his speech. Lips that normally move to help shape words were limited to the mobility his injuries would allow. The missing flesh of his cheek was covered over in the same opaque membrane as his eyes. "When Lisette left for the night, I came out here knowing how you tend to wake."

His attempt to make me feel better only made me feel worse. I slumped back into the couch with a groan.

"So glad I didn't disappoint," I mumbled. My miserable week blurred through my mind. "What is wrong with me? I don't know which is worse anymore, my dreams or my reality."

"You have been through a lot in a very short amount of time. I think you are holding up quite admirably."

"That makes one of us. Honestly, I feel like I'm going to have a complete nervous breakdown at any second."

"Do not be so hard on yourself," Collin said. "The first year is always the toughest."

"You mean I have eleven more months of this to look forward to?" I gasped. "You've got to be kidding me!"

Collin chuckled, "You will be fine. You are a tough one."

"Right," I muttered. "Look at me complaining to someone who almost died yesterday. Could I possibly be any more self-centered? How are you feeling today?"

"Awful—but much better than yesterday, thankfully. Nothing I cannot handle."

A knock at the door disrupted our conversation. Collin was about to get up when I stopped him.

"I got this, you relax."

Crossing to the door, I could only pick up a vaguely familiar sense of who lurked on the other side. Which meant it could be almost anyone. I really had to work on my basic immortal abilities. Maybe that would be my goal for the rest of the year. It would certainly give me something to focus on.

I opened the door to find Tatiana crushing out a cigarette with the toe of her red patent leather stiletto. She was dressed in a white satin nurse uniform, complete with hat fixed neatly in her blunt cut sable hair. The front of the dress was unbuttoned enough to reveal the red satin push-up bra she wore beneath and was short enough to expose the white garters holding up her white thigh high fishnet stockings. Her pale skin displayed the tattooed symbols of her human life in the Russian mob.

"Jacquelyn, good to see you again," she said in her thick Russian accent. "Petrus sent me to feed Collin."

I stepped back to invite her inside, "Good to see you, too." My response came more from common courtesy than anything, since she did scare the crap out of me. The irony of her outfit, however, brought a much needed smile to my face.

She approached the couch where Collin still sat and took the seat next to him.

"You look like shit," she informed Collin.

"Thanks, Tatiana. You, on the other hand, have never looked better," he replied.

Tatiana suddenly and unexpectedly broke into laughter, a sound I would never before have imagined coming from her. For a split second, she lost the lethal glimmer that resided in her hazel eyes and amusement softened the features of her heart shaped face.

"So says the blind man," she noted with the return of her normal demeanor. "I have client waiting. No time for jokes."

"I will leave you to Tatiana...unless you need me," I said. "The shower is calling my name."

"No, I will be fine," Collin replied. "But that reminds me, Lisette says you are more than welcome to her wardrobe if you would like."

Tatiana snorted, "I hope you are not allergic to latex."

Having seen the leather ensemble Lisette wore under her fur coat last night, I quickly became concerned for my options. Surely she had something a bit more casual in there? Maybe I should just plan on washing my own clothes.

The hot water cascaded down my body as I stood beneath the shower head. I closed my eyes, giving in to the gentle drumming of the water, the tension that gripped me melting away, if only temporarily. My thoughts drifted aimlessly, before my dream of Lattimer returned to claim my focus. I wondered if Lisette was right about Lattimer and the reason he tormented me. What would it be like to give in to him? Would it be like my dream? I could feel him all over again, my skin tingling under the spray of water. The taste of him returned as if it had been lingering there the whole time. His scent seemed to fill the air around me, clean and masculine. But something loitered in the background, becoming more intense. At first I couldn't place it until it almost became overwhelming. In my mind I saw Lattimer burning as he had in my dream.

My eyes opened, a heavy mist hung in the shower. I turned off the water and opened the shower door. The stale, smoky odor that clung to my clothes had been diffused into the steamy room. I toweled off and made use of the robe hanging on the bathroom door, determined to find a washing machine.

While my clothes were washing, I made my way to Lisette's closet. How bad could it possibly be, right? I wasn't sure what I was in for but when the doors opened, my jaw dropped. Before me stretched out a small boutique, the majority of its contents I wouldn't even attempt to try on. Tatiana wasn't lying about the latex, which was available in every garment imaginable. The only material that rivaled the latex was the leather. Not ready to give up hope, I headed for the drawers that lined the back wall. Lingerie, lingerie and more lingerie. If she did own a pair of jeans, they were probably hidden away somewhere under a layer of dust. Thankfully, my own clothes were probably ready for the dryer.

My clothes tumbled rhythmically in the machine as I headed back to sit with Collin. Settling in beside him, he spoke.

"Like a breath of fresh air," he said. "I would attempt a shower myself but I think each drop of water would feel like a needle."

"Well then I don't suggest it. At the rate you are healing, tomorrow may be a better option," I suggested.

"I have been looking forward to tomorrow ever since I woke up."

Poor Collin, I couldn't imagine what it's like to endure that amount of pain. I had a feeling at that moment he was worse off than he was willing to admit.

"Is there anything I can do for you?" I asked, trying not to feel completely worthless.

"Your presence is sufficient. Conversation makes for a good distraction, especially when it has nothing to do with how I am feeling," he stated, but I could hear the smile in his words.

"Ok then, we will find something else to talk about..."

"How did the meeting with Lattimer go?" he asked.

What felt like ages ago had only happened the prior night. I had spoken to Collin afterwards but, aside from letting him know I was staying at Claire's, we never did talk about my miserable night.

"Bad. I sort of lost my temper with him and he kicked me out."

"See, I told you."

"Told me what?"

"You are a tough one. Not many would dare to blatantly challenge him."

"He's a pretentious bastard," I said. "He used me like a puppet. There was no other motivation for what he did than to show me he could."

"Perhaps," Collin agreed. "He has a way of justifying his actions, if only to himself."

"Well, I felt like such an ass, somehow I convinced myself it would be a good idea to go apologize to Marco."

"For what?"

"Exactly. However, at the time, it felt like the right thing to do."

"And? How did that go?"

"Bad. I sort of lost my temper with him and he kicked me out."

"I see a reoccurring theme here."

"Yeah, it gets better," I added. "On the way out of Marco's, before he actually kicked me out, I had a run in with one of his staff members that got pretty ugly. In fact, it was bad enough for him to completely ban me and disable my building access code."

"Thus staying at Claire's that night," he concluded. "What on earth did you do to get banned?"

"He hired this new girl while we were still together that absolutely despised me. After we broke up he, apparently, didn't waste any time getting in her pants. On my way out on the night in question, she felt the need to share that information with me. Mind you, I had just stormed out of Marco's office and was absolutely fuming when I ran into her. She baited me into reading her thoughts and I was offered an uncensored replay of her little sexcapade with him. I didn't intend on breaking her nose, it just kinda happened."

Collin's head tilted to the side, "A human girl...with dark, curly hair?"

"Yes, you may have seen her around Marco's building."

"No, that is not where I have seen her," he commented absently as if trying to place her somewhere else as he spoke. "Before the fire, I was getting flashes in my mind of a girl with dark swollen circles under her eyes. She never got physically close enough to be perceived as a threat, especially since she was human." The familiar sinking sensation of dread crept into my stomach the more he spoke. I knew what this was coming to before he put it into words. "Jax, I think she caused the fire."

I arrived at Marco's building after making several failed attempts to contact him by cell phone. When I reached the code panel, I laid on the buzzer until my request could no longer be ignored.

"Can I help you with something?" Marco's question crackled through the speaker.

"Where is Lori?" I asked as calmly as I could.

"I could ask you the same thing," Marco replied suspiciously.

"Like I'm supposed to believe she isn't there?"

"She did not show up for work last night or tonight. Nor is there any sign of her in her room."

"Well then why don't you let me in so I can help you look for her?" I asked in a sickeningly sweet tone.

"Because I am not entirely sure you do not have something to do with her disappearance and I am not particularly in the mood for your company."

"You haven't even asked me why I'm looking for her. If you were really ignorant to her whereabouts, I would think you would want to know such information."

"Rumor has it Lattimer left town, so I assume you are lonely?" he replied.

My whole body tensed with anger. He was not going to blow me off this time.

"She tried to kill me, Marco! She burnt down my fuckin' house yesterday afternoon!"

"And yet you still live—good for you."

"Only because I wasn't there, but Collin was and he didn't fare so well."

"How sad. Is there anything else I cannot help you with?"

His cold indifference was like a slap in the face. I knew he and Collin weren't exactly buddies, but still.

"Marco, let me in. If you are protecting her, you may as well have helped her—"

"Good night, Jacquelyn."

"Dammit, Marco, let me in!" I yelled.

When I resorted to pounding on the buzzer with my fist, I could feel the stares of strangers passing by on the street and realized I was making a scene. I probably looked like a crazy person.

I closed my eyes, taking a deep breath in an attempt to pull myself together. He wasn't going to let me in, and acting like a fool would get me nowhere. Maybe he was telling the truth and she wasn't even there. Well, she couldn't hide forever.

CHAPTER FOURTEEN

Confident I was a little more collected, I turned to leave. Standing at the bottom of the steps staring up at me was an immortal male I had never seen before. His medium brown hair had been highlighted and cut in the latest style, adorning the men's magazines. The same magazines his designer outfit could be found in, no doubt.

"If you like, perhaps we can bust down the gate and take the castle by force?" he suggested with a prominent British accent.

I shook my head in embarrassment, knowing my assessment of my own behavior had been correct. I did look like a crazy person.

"No, that won't be necessary," I replied, descending the steps. "I wouldn't even know what to do if I did get in, quite frankly."

"Well, my mother would flail in her grave if I did not at least offer to help a maiden in distress," he said. His smile made his dark eyes sparkle, "I am Dorian, I do not believe we have ever met." He extended his hand toward me.

"Jacquelyn." I shook his hand.

"Now that I appear to be in cahoots with the enemy," Dorian said, nodding at the camera, "I suppose I will have to find another establishment for the evening. Would you care to join me?"

His charming façade should have warned me of his motives. The last thing I needed at the moment was another attempt at a relationship. Nor did I want to give the impression I was looking.

"Thanks but—"

Dorian's laughter cut me off before I could finish.

"Before you reject my offer, I should tell you that you are not my type," he said with a grin. "Although, I am actually quite flattered you perceived me to be so masculine. If anything you should be concerned that we may have the same taste in men."

"I'm sorry," I said, suddenly feeling a bit ridiculous, "seems like everybody around me has ulterior motives lately. It's not fair of me to project my paranoia onto you."

"Immortals are quite the conniving breed, are they not?" he replied with a sly smirk. "Regardless, I am going for a drink with or without you...so unless that was an example of your normal behavior, I assume you could use one too. You are more than welcome to join me."

That being said, he turned and started off down the street. With the events of the past couple weeks fresh in my mind, it didn't take much to remind me that I could use all the friends I could get. Perhaps I had reached a turning point in my new found life and things were about to change for the better. I just needed to take the first step.

"Wait!" I called after Dorian.

He stopped and turned to face me. When I caught up with him, he looked relieved.

"I had a feeling you were not that crazy."

"I try to save it for special occasions," I said. "So where are we headed?"

"A little place down the street, blessedly free of immortals."

"Sounds perfect."

15

The place Dorian took me was situated below street level. In fact, if you blinked in passing, the signage would certainly be missed. Before we even ventured inside, I was willing to bet on the fact that the original selling point for him was its subterranean location. Otherwise, I could see nothing about the place that would spark interest in anyone.

We found a vacant table tucked away in a dark corner. Dorian pulled out a chair for me, helping me out of my jacket before settling into his own seat. The stale air was laced with cheap perfume and sour beer. Nothing too overpowering, but it made its presence known. It wouldn't surprise me to find the place had been around since prohibition had been lifted. There was definitely a feeling of history to be found there.

"Now you know I am not trying to impress you," Dorian smiled, glancing around the room. "Granted, it is not the most polished night spot in the city but, like I said, it is refreshingly free of vampires."

"That much I will give you," I said, returning his smile.

Our waitress came for our drink orders. She looked as though she had better things to do and did not linger any longer than necessary. Her disinterest in us made me more aware of our surroundings. Dorian's stylish exterior stood out here but none of the other patrons seemed to notice. Some of them, however, kept darting glances my way. I leaned in closer to Dorian and whispered, "Why do they keep staring at me?"

He looked puzzled, "Make them stop."

I looked at the offenders who, for the most part, looked away, but didn't do much to curb further ogling. My attention returned to Dorian. Much to my dismay, I had to confess, "I don't know how."

He considered me for a moment, "When they make eye contact with you again, stare them directly in the eye and mentally request they stop."

Sure enough, it worked like a charm. So much so, I could have imagined their stares to begin with. I was smiling to myself, delighting in the success of my new found skill when our waitress returned with our drinks. She placed Dorian's martini on a napkin in front of him and my glass of merlot on a napkin in front of me.

With a grin, Dorian held his glass up toward me, "Here's to new things—may we never take them for granted."

I gave him a slight inclination of my head and tapped my glass against his. He took a sip of his drink before returning it to the napkin. I followed his lead. The cheap wine was tolerable, to say the least, even with my limited knowledge of wine, that was saying a lot. But it wasn't totally insufferable.

Dorian looked as if he had something he wanted to say but was talking himself out of it.

"What?" I asked, my curiosity getting the better of me.

"I do not want to pry."

CHAPTER FIFTEEN

"Yes you do. But you're struggling with your attempt to be polite," I replied honestly. My response brought a knowing grin to his face.

"I can see why your sire made you. We tend to be drawn to the audacious ones. They endure the trials of immortality better than most."

"Not necessarily, he actually made me because he felt he had no choice."

"Perhaps, but I am sure he had his sights on you before the choice had to be made," he said. I ran my finger around the rim of my glass, staring down into the wine. My time as a human with Trinnian came to mind, both the good and the bad. Dorian's assessment was spot on. Trinnian more than likely would have turned me regardless of the actual situation that forced his hand. "Please forgive me." I looked back at Dorian, his expression purely apologetic. "You are so young I had no idea this would be such a sensitive subject. Most of us take a much longer time to detest the one that made us," he added with an uncomfortable smile.

"How long did it take you?"

"Do you really want to get into this?" I thought about it for a second and shook my head. It would be nice to have someone that didn't know all the gory details of my short stint as a vampire. Not that I was the most tight lipped about it, perhaps I needed to change that? But if I asked him to share, he may expect me to do the same. "Before I drop the subject of our origins completely, there is one thing I must ask...do not fret, it is a simple yes or no question."

"Ok..."

"Are you completely alone or do you have other immortals, aside from your maker, you can turn to?"

Lattimer's comment about his rights to orphaned newborns came to mind. I suddenly found myself suspicious of my new found friend. What if he was working for Lattimer? Although I still wasn't convinced Lattimer wanted anything more to do with me, would a stunt like this be beneath him if Lisette was right? I would be the first to admit that I do tend to give in to paranoia but, really, what kind of question was that? Standing up, I grabbed my jacked off the back of the chair.

"I have a sick friend I should be with right now," I said, pulling on my jacket. "Thank you for the glass of wine."

I turned to leave, the legs of his chair scraped across the floor as he stood.

"Jacquelyn," he called to me but I ignored him.

Everybody was looking at me as I made my way to the door, except for the ones I had already dealt with. I didn't care anymore. Dorian called my name again as I passed through the door and ascended the steps. I had almost reached the top when I heard Dorian behind me.

"Jacquelyn, wait! What is wrong?" he asked.

I stopped, turning to face him, "Did he put you up to this?"

Dorian's shocked expression gave up little information. Either it meant he was completely innocent and was returning to his earlier suspicion that I was a crazy person. Or, I was right and he was caught off guard by my brilliant intuition.

"He who?"

I descended a couple steps in an effort to better read his expression, "You know exactly who—Lattimer."

Dorian's laughter echoed up the stairs, spilling onto the sidewalk. A few of the passersby half-heartedly looked to see what was happening without breaking stride.

CHAPTER FIFTEEN

"Really, Jacquelyn?" he asked incredulously. "I seriously doubt he even knows I exist and I would be more than happy to keep it that way."

"Don't gimme that crap, he knows about each and every one of us. He told me so himself."

"Is that what he told you? I cannot believe you fell for his lies," Dorian said, taking a step closer. "You honestly believe him?" I crossed my arms in front of me without answering his question. "You do!"

It wasn't really such a stretch to think that Lattimer could possibly know about every single immortal ever made, was it? My conviction was starting to waiver. He didn't sound like much of a fan of Lattimer. Maybe I was wrong? But what about that creepy question that started it all?

"So that's just something you would normally ask—whether or not a newborn was alone?"

"You openly cringe when you speak of your maker and cannot even influence the mind of a human, what am I supposed to think?" he asked. "At the very least you should know how to deal with humans. The only excuse for such lack of basic skills would be not having an immortal around to teach you. I was merely attempting to offer my help to you if you needed it."

I stared at him in silence. He was right. How must I look to others when I can't even perform basic immortal feats? I lowered myself to the steps and sat.

"I don't even know what to say at this point, except I'm sorry," I declared softly. "No point in trying to convince you I'm not a raving lunatic now, I suppose."

"I do not think you are a lunatic, but I do understand your opinion of immortals a little better—knowing you have had the pleasure of meeting Lattimer. Which also tells me you are not alone, else he would have snatched you up and shuffled you off to Canada with him."

"Yeah, he tried that the other day," I admitted.

"Ah, so you thought I was spying for him?" I responded with an embarrassed shrug. "That explains a lot then. Now I really do not blame you for your melt down. I would have been suspicious, too," Dorian said. "But these immortals you are surrounding yourself with...they need to step up and help you."

"I have only been with them for a few days. They aren't responsible for my lack of education."

"Well, if you like, I can help, too—that is if you do not think I am consorting with the enemy." He gave me a crafty smile, arching an eyebrow. I laughed quietly, shaking my head. He extended his hands to me. "Come back inside with me...you will certainly get to use your new found skill when we return together. Such scandal!"

I laughed and took his hands, allowing him to escort me back inside the bar.

Later, I returned to Lisette's apartment. Collin was resting in the guest room. Lisette was apparently still at work. I carefully sat on the bed next to Collin.

"I was starting to think you were taken prisoner," Collin said. "What happened?"

"Nothing. Marco claimed Lori wasn't even there and is missing," I replied. "In fact, he had the nerve to suggest I may have had something to do with her disappearance."

"What an ass. I still cannot believe you fell for that guy."

"I was in emotional turmoil at the time and he was there for me. Besides, you haven't seen him naked," I teased.

"Please do not feel the need to go into detail. You have heard that the other senses of the blind are heightened? I do not want to run the risk of my mind painting graphic pictures for me," he said with a wince.

"You sure? He has these really wicked looking scars—"

"Stop!" he pled, pretending to gag.

"Someone's feeling better."

"Actually, yes. Petrus has had a continuous parade of his lovely ladies dropping by to check on me and offering to feed me if I so desired."

"And here I felt bad for not rushing back," I said.

"What did take you so long, by the way? And don't think I did not notice the scent of cheap wine on you."

"I made a new friend. We went to have a drink together."

"Just what you need, another rebound guy. Good luck with that."

"Thanks so much for your faith in me, Collin. I am so fortunate to have such a good friend in you," I grumbled. "For your information, he is gay."

"Oh...ok. Anybody I know?"

"His name is Dorian."

"Nope, never heard of him."

"What a relief, since you're one of the few sane ones in my current circle of immortals," I said. "If you don't know him, the odds of him being decent aren't so bad."

My cell phone rang. I got up to go find it.

"Is that a compliment or the opposite?" Collin called after me as I left the room.

His comment made me laugh to myself while I dug the phone out of my jacket pocket. It was a number I didn't recognize. Against my better judgment, I answered it.

"Hello?"

"Jax, it's Diana," she said in a shaky voice.

"Hey, what's wrong?"

"I don't know what to do. Lori is gone. She has to be dead. It all makes sense to me now. I heard your conversation with Marco over the intercom and things that happened over the past few days started to fall into place. Especially when Julia started giving me the evil eye, I knew something bad—" she prattled on frantically.

"Diana, slow down and take a breath. Now tell me, what happened," I requested in a composed tone.

I heard Diana gulp air on the other end and exhale, "Ok, the night you broke Lori's nose I heard people talking in the hall just before dawn. I peeked out my door and saw Lori and Julia talking outside Lori's apartment. Sometime later that day...maybe around noon, I ran into Lori. She was all excited about something, saying she had an errand to run that would bring her immortality quicker than I would ever see it. She's such a liar, I just ignored her. I figured she was trying to get a rise out of me, like usual. Anyway, she returned shortly before sunset. I didn't think much of it until a little while later when Julia knocked on her door and they left together. Julia showed up after a couple hours at the bar while I was working but there was no sign of Lori. Today I saw no sign of Lori and she still didn't show up tonight. Next thing I know, you are at the bar looking for Lori. When you left, Marco and Julia got into it and she stormed out. But not before she ran into me and gave me the death stare. If I'm right, she put Lori up to burning your house down in hopes of killing you. I'm afraid that she knows I figured it out. So I snuck out. I can't stay there any longer. If I'm right, Julia will kill me."

My head spun with the onslaught of information. I knew in my gut Diana was right. I had to make sure she was safe.

"Diana, do you have some place safe you can go?"

"Um, yeah," she said in a trembling voice. "There is this vampire—"

"Don't tell me. It may not be safe to say. If you trust them then go," I told her, "I'm confident in your ability to read people well enough to feel you will be in good hands. When all this is sorted out I will find you."

"Thanks, Jax."

"Please take care of yourself, Diana."

The line went dead. All I could do was hope for her safety.

16

As per Alton's instruction, Dorian found himself in front of the second door on the right near the end of the long hallway. He knocked softly, knowing one never knew what they would walk into when Acacius lurked on the other side. Especially since Alton was kind enough to warn him Acacius was getting a massage. Waiting for the all clear, he impatiently tapped the folded newspaper he brought against the palm of his hand.

"Come," Acacius invited from within.

Dorian stepped into the room. Acacius lay on his stomach on a massage table, facing the door with his eyes closed. The towel that had been wrapped around his waist hung off either side of the table. A young, human female with honey colored hair kneaded his shoulders, offering Dorian a welcoming smile while she worked. Her pretty features were delicate, her smile was sweet. She wore a strappy, white cotton mini dress reminiscent of a goddess from the Roman Empire. The lights in the room were dimmed and ancient incense filled the air.

Stepping up to the table, Dorian slapped the newspaper down a few inches from Acacius's nose. His eyes shot open.

"Must you do that?" Acacius asked irritably.

"Do what? I brought you the paper as you requested," Dorian replied innocently.

"Took you long enough," Acacius grumbled as he sat up. "That will be all for now, Arielle."

The girl scurried off, exiting through the same door Dorian entered. Acacius picked up the newspaper, his eyes skimming the front page.

"You know it will not be long until they no longer print those." Dorian gestured to the paper. "There is this wonderful invention called the 'internet' that people rely on to get their news."

"Well, there is something to be said for the feel and the smell of a newspaper that will be sadly missed," Acacius scoffed. "Until that time comes, this is how I prefer to brush up on events in the outside world. But with the length of time it takes you to acquire them for me, this may be my last, apparently."

He eyed Dorian with displeasure as he dramatically opened the paper to examine the inside pages, creating a barrier between them.

"I am so sorry...but I thought you requested me to befriend the redhead?" Dorian asked.

The corner of the paper caved in as Acacius pulled the paper down in an effort to see Dorian's face. He studied him, trying to determine whether or not Dorian was pulling his leg.

"You are serious?" he asked, lowering the newspaper.

"I happened upon her assaulting Marco's building earlier tonight and invited her for a drink."

Acacius neatly folded his reading material, setting it to the side, "Judging from the length of time you were gone, I suppose it is safe to assume she was powerless to resist your elegant charm—being on the re-rebound and all..." A sinister glimmer lit up his eyes. "Did she lure you to the other side? Whatever will Alton do? He will be inconsolable. Tsk tsk tsk."

"Are you quite finished?" Dorian asked, not in the least bit amused. "I have actually obtained information that will be of interest to you." Acacius motioned for him to continue while trying to subdue the gratification found in Dorian's annoyance. "Our suspicions were correct. Lattimer attempted to take Jacquelyn back to Canada with him under the pretense that he thought her to be an orphaned newborn."

Acacius leapt off the table, grabbing Dorian by the shoulders, "I knew it! He wants her!"

"That would appear to be the case."

"How on earth did she manage to escape?" Acacius asked, grabbing his towel off the table and wrapping it around his waist.

"It seems she did have someone staying with her after all."

"Has she already taken another lover?" His astonishment changed his timbre as he eased back, leaning against the massage table.

"I do not think so. She refers to him as her friend," Dorian replied. "I heard her reference the name Collin when I encountered her at Marco's. That brings to mind only one immortal by that name that runs in her clique. The one sired by Trinnian Talbott a few centuries ago. Collin Edmonton, I believe is his name? He is tall, dark haired, muscular...you know, the quiet one."

CHAPTER SIXTEEN

"Hmmm...even with your drooling description, I cannot seem to place him. Do not look at me like that. In case you have forgotten, I am not Lattimer. I have better things to do than spend my waking moments penning lists of immortals in an attempt to convince myself I am in charge of something. Therefore, I cannot know all of them," Acacius stated.

"His companion is Olivia Langley."

"Oh yes, that one," Acacius said with renewed interest. "Does that mean Olivia is now without a companion? I would hate to think she is suffering somewhere out there dejected and alone."

"Perhaps, but she is still immortal, not exactly your usual cup of tea."

"Just because I prefer sex with humans does not mean I am completely opposed to the thought of sampling a female of our own kind. Especially one so exquisite as Olivia. I have been with immortal females before, you know."

"Anyway," Dorian said. His tone informing Acacius the conversation was getting back on topic. "For whatever reason, Collin was at Jacquelyn's house when an attempt was made on her life by a human female working for Marco. While Jacquelyn slept at her friend Claire's apartment the other day, the human burnt her house down."

"Sounds as if someone was jealous enough to make sure Jacquelyn and Marco did not try to resume their relationship," said Acacius. "Surely Julia caught wind of this? Did she say anything to you about it?"

"I have not spoken to her since we decided to make contact with Jacquelyn—which was one of the reasons I was at Marco's in the first place."

"So this Collin lives?"

"Yes, but he is badly injured."

"She has moved him to Claire's to nurse him back to health?"

"No, you will like this...they are staying with Petrus. I followed her after she left me for the night."

"This just keeps getting more and more interesting," Acacius said, as if deep in thought. "We have a girl working there, right?"

"We do. I have already taken the liberty of contacting her. She says Petrus has them on a feeding rotation. Her time had not come up yet but she promised to keep her eyes and ears open."

Acacius took on a satisfied expression, "Dorian, do I pay you?"

"Not enough, sir...not nearly enough."

"I shall have to consider giving you a raise." Acacius walked to the door. "When will you see the redhead again?"

"Tomorrow night, I am taking her to see Finn. He is in the city playing at a pub in mid town."

"Now there is a show. It has been ages since I have been to see him rile up the local Irish population with his arsenal of ancient songs."

"I do not think your presence would be the best idea. The object is not to chase her away, especially now that we have confirmed Lattimer's interest."

"I can be a perfect gentleman, you know."

"Well, I have yet to see it but I will take your word for it," Dorian said with a sly grin. "However, I request that you refrain from showing up."

"Only if it pleases thee."

Acacius exited the room, leaving Dorian to wonder what the following evening had in store.

CHAPTER SIXTEEN

*   *   *   *   *

When I woke the next evening, Collin was not watching over me. Although I didn't wake screaming, part of me still expected to find him there protecting me. Especially when you considered the fact that Julia wanted me dead, having him watching my back might not be a bad thing.

After we discussed my conversation with Diana the prior night, Collin thought it wouldn't be wise for me to confront Julia directly. She was much older than Violet and not so arrogant as to underestimate her enemy. I knew I'd gotten lucky in my fight with Violet and I didn't really need anybody to point that fact out. He felt that I would be safe staying in Petrus's building, surrounded by immortals we could trust. Provided we didn't let on that we knew Julia had been behind the attack, she would have no reason to blatantly come after me. But that didn't mean I could let my guard down when I left the building.

Lisette had already left for work but I could feel Collin was in the apartment. No sooner did I get up to search for him, I could make out the sound of the TV coming from the guest room. The door to the room was ajar but I still knocked.

"Come in, Jax."

I pushed the door open to reveal a most welcome sight. Collin propped up against the headboard of the bed watching TV, he was no longer blind. His skin lost the raw painful appearance for the most part. The worst of it remained in the areas that had suffered the most damage. Other than that, he appeared to have a very bad sunburn.

"Would you like to come in or would you rather stand in the doorway?"

151

The skin around his mouth had regained its mobility. He sounded exactly like his old self again.

"I wasn't expecting to see such progress...I can't believe how much better you look!" I said, pulling a chair up to the side of the bed. "How are you feeling?"

"Good enough to attempt a shower."

"That in itself is saying a lot."

"I am sure it still may not be the most comfortable thing, but I am ready. I was just waiting until you woke."

"Thanks for looking out for me," I said sincerely. "Honestly, I don't recall dreaming about anything." Did I ever really doubt he would have been there if I would have needed him? Regaining his ability to see apparently eliminated the need to sit with me while I slept. "How's your vision?"

"It is not exactly a hundred percent, but I can see, so I cannot really complain. Look at this," he said, turning so I could fully see the other side of his face. "My ear has almost completely grown back and my cheek is filling out. Maybe by tomorrow night I will be able to go hunt?"

"Looks like your little string of scantily clad visitors from yesterday really were in your best interest," I teased.

Collin looked at me suspiciously, "Do I detect a hint of jealousy?"

"What—no!" I gasped.

"You can lie to me if you like," he said, getting off the bed and heading for the bathroom. "But can you lie to yourself?" He laughed at my gaping wordless response. "In an attempt to remove temptation, I am going to lock the bathroom door."

He gave me a wink and shut the door, engaging the lock with a loud click. I threw a pillow at the door, knowing he heard the thud.

CHAPTER SIXTEEN

While on stand-by in case Collin needed me, I checked my phone for messages. My mother called earlier to see how I was doing. I tempted fate by returning her call, informing her I couldn't talk long. She asked about my non-existent job hunt. I lied, telling her it went well and left it at that. She then informed me that she had been looking into contractors to rebuild my house, claiming it was something she and dad wanted to do for me. Seeing no reason to argue, I thanked her and told her to keep me posted. Honestly, I hadn't even thought about that yet.

Much to my surprise, she ended the call saying she knew I had things going on and didn't want to keep me. Could vampires influence humans over the phone? Or was she just trying to keep from being the trigger for my complete mental breakdown? After all, in her eyes, I was unmarried, jobless and now homeless. By the time she was my age, she had all those things well taken care of. *And* she was pregnant with me on top of it all. From her perspective, I had no doubt my life looked pretty pathetic. I probably wouldn't be surprised if she emailed me the number for the suicide hotline. If she only knew the truth.

Once Collin was showered and settled back into the guest room, I hit the city streets on a mission. I desperately needed clothing. There were a few things I had been keeping at Claire's for emergencies but I had already dipped into that stash the other night when I stayed there. With the way my life was going, it would be to my advantage not to completely deplete my supply. Besides, I was going out with Dorian to see a friend of his sing and might want to look presentable. Having seen how Dorian dressed on an average night, I had to step up my idea of going out attire.

153

By the time I made it back to Lisette's I realized I didn't allow myself much time to get ready. Everything takes longer when you feel you have to keep looking over your shoulder. The further from Petrus's I got, the more I expected Julia to jump out of an alley and attack. Maybe I should have taken Collin's advice and asked one of the girls to go with me. But then I would have felt silly. Julia had no reason to suspect I knew anything. I was just letting paranoia get the best of me.

My getting ready time flew by. The time sucking culprit was not the shower, getting dressed or even hair styling. It was the make-up. There is a fine line between creating an evening look and looking like a five dollar hooker. Unfortunately for my hair, I decided to save it for last, forcing me to settle for smoothing it into the most sophisticated ponytail I could muster.

Men really don't understand how easy they have it. The time and effort women put into looking good enough to be able to leave the house can be mindboggling. Not that all my effort was in hopes of trying to gain the attention of any man. I had to agree with Collin there, a new man was the last thing I needed at the moment. Tonight, my efforts were as much for myself as for Dorian's sake. He struck me as the type of guy that took a great deal of pride in his appearance. Far be it for me to mar his reputation.

I made one last visit to Lisette's three-way mirror to make sure I was good to go. The form fitting knit dress wouldn't have been my first choice in my mortal life. But immortality does wonders for your physique. The required strength and speed needed for hunting tones muscle tissue better than any flavor of the month fitness fad. Thus allowing me to don the clingy, long sleeve, scoop neck fall version of the little black dress without giving it a second thought.

CHAPTER SIXTEEN

Pleased with the results of my work, I grabbed my clutch, dropped my lipstick inside and went to check on Collin.

"Hey Jax, Petrus has started sending his girls for my feeding already," Collin pretended to call to me as I stood in the doorway of the guestroom. "This one kind of looks like you...only hotter."

I planted my fists on my hips, "You're an ass."

Collin laughed, "I am only joking. Come closer, you are a bit blurry." I complied, receiving a whistle when stopped next to the bed. "I thought you said he was gay?"

"He is, and very fashion-forward, meaning I sadly have to abandon my jeans for the evening."

He eyed me up and down, "I see. Well I hope your coat is longer than that dress or Petrus may put you to work."

"Yes, Daddy," I replied. "It actually hits about mid calf. Is that sufficient? I was heartbroken to see they were fresh out of burqas all over the city."

"Ok, smart ass. As your friend, I am allowed to be a bit protective."

"Awwww...you said you were my friend!" I tried to dodge away unsuccessfully as his hand came down with a loud smack on my butt. "Ouch!"

"Just toughening it up for all the pinches it will surely receive in a crowded bar."

"You are too kind," I said, rubbing my stinging cheek. "I really gotta go. I still have to grab a bite before I meet Dorian."

"Ah, the vampire puns have started already. Nice to see you are finally embracing your new life," said Collin. "You do look amazing, by the way."

"Thanks, Collin," I said with a smile. "That almost makes up for smacking me."

He laughed, but his eyes took on the serious tone that used to always reside there, "Please be careful tonight."

"I will, I promise." A knock at the door broke up the somber moment. "Looks like room service has begun for the evening, I'd better go so you can enjoy your treats."

He shook his head, rolling his eyes as I turned, heading for the door. Thinking he was being cute, he starting making lewd noises while I walked. I ignored him, grabbing my coat and invited Collin's first guest of the night in.

"You must be Jacquelyn," said the cute, young, buxom blonde girl that stood before me. If she was sixteen that was a stretch, not that I was good with guessing age by any means, but still. "I'm Peyton, Petrus sent me to take care of Collin."

"I'm sure he did," I said with a smile before lowering my voice, "he did tell you Collin is gay, so a feeding is all you will be needed for?"

"Oh," murmured the petite vampire. "He didn't tell me that...but that's ok, I understand."

"Goodnight, Jax!" Collin growled from within the apartment.

I tried not to laugh, pointing Peyton in the direction of the guestroom and shutting the door behind me.

17

A jukebox played somewhere in the back of the bar. The place was packed for a Tuesday night, the draw undoubtedly the performer. Irish accents clung to the conversations all around me the further I ventured into the establishment, confirming my assumption. Mortals made up the majority of the crowd and the few immortals present were unknown to me. Dorian was nowhere to be seen.

I was about to turn and head toward the front when a door at the back opened and Dorian stepped through. *Really?* The expression of ironic disbelief was the first thought upon seeing him. His extremely dressed down outfit consisted of a weathered leather jacket, Led Zeppelin t-shirt and worn jeans with a hole in one knee. Even more strange was the fact that he still managed to look well put together. As soon as he saw me, he headed my direction.

"You made it. I was starting to think you were going to stand me up," he said. "Follow me, I have a table saved next to the stage."

He grabbed my hand, leading me through the crowd. The high top table was right up front against the wall, providing an unimpeded view of the stage. I unbuttoned my coat, feeling extremely overdressed. Not just because of Dorian's attire but the whole bar seemed to be out for a casual night. Dorian kindly pulled out a stool for me and helped me out of my coat. I wasn't oblivious to the attention my outfit was receiving, though I did my best to ignore it.

"You look absolutely stunning...very Audrey Hepburn," he gushed. "Please make sure you tend to the mortals eyeing you. I will have my hands full enough if I have to fight off the salivating immortal males."

"Oh stop!" I said, feeling self-conscious. "You make me want to go back home to change."

"I could say the same thing," he said. "Next to you, I look like a vagrant."

"Well honestly, my motivation for wearing this in the first place was to try to blend in with you."

"This is what I get for not asking for your phone number," he said with a grin as we settled into our seats.

Our waitress came for our orders as Finn took the stage, carrying a small red accordion. He was young when he was turned, perhaps seventeen. Of course, he too wore jeans and a t-shirt, which, I might add, proudly stated 'Made in Ireland'. His baby face was crowned with thick black curls that drew attention to his sea green eyes. He pulled one of the two wooden stools on the stage up to the microphone and sat. On the other stool perched a pint of dark ale.

The crowd that had started cheering with his arrival was being quieted with his simple gesture for silence. He adjusted the microphone and spoke.

"Thanks for coming out tonight," Finn said with a strong Irish lilt to the words. The crowd responded with cheers and whistles. His smile sparkled in his eyes as he surveyed the crowd, once again motioning for silence. "I see a lot of familiar faces but, for those who have not come to see me before, I would like to let you know what you are in for. My name is Finn. I travel the world to share long forgotten songs of my native Ireland with anyone willing to listen. My accumulation of songs has been passed down from generation to generation in an attempt to remind us where we come from and who we are." He paused to sip from his glass and return it to the stool next to him. "Let's start with one you may all know."

That being said, he adjusted his accordion and launched into the first song. His hands manipulated the instrument skillfully, making the music that emerged seem effortless. He had a beautiful singing voice and sang with what could only be described as passion. The whole pub practically joined in. They clapped along with the happy tune, singing and stomping their feet. It was contagious. Though I didn't know the words, I couldn't help clapping along with the crowd. Dorian was right there clapping with me, but he sang along as well.

The set flowed along, meandering through a variety of themes. Some of the songs were dark and brooding. But the happy outnumbered the somber, keeping up the energy and spirits of the audience. Never once did I hear a song I knew, but I enjoyed every tune, right there along with everyone else.

"Ok, one last song and I am going to take a break," Finn announced before jumping into the final song of the set.

About half way through, Dorian stopped singing and his attention shot toward the front of the bar before returning to the stage. He muttered something that I didn't quite catch over the noise of the crowd.

"What's wrong?" I asked, not seeing anything out of the ordinary.

"Nothing...just someone I was hoping to not have to deal with tonight."

I looked back toward the door to find an immortal male staring intently at me. Weaving through the crowd in our direction, his eyes never left mine. He was the kind of man that was offhandedly handsome. One of those that roll out of bed, grabbed clothes off the floor and didn't bother to run a comb through their hair but still managed to look as if they just stepped from a men's fashion magazine.

As he approached the table, his expression lost some of its intensity, but that intensity still lingered in his eyes. Shadowy stubble accentuating the angles of his jaw line only added to my initial assessment, especially when paired with the disarray of his dirty blonde hair. Just above his left eyebrow was a thin pale scar about an inch or so long that angled up toward his hairline. The little imperfection was powerless to distract from his effortless good looks. Perhaps if anything, it added a hint of bad boy to his borderline pretty boy face.

"Good evening, Dorian," the man said. "Still stalking Finn, I see."

"Something like that, I suppose," Dorian said in a sarcastic tone. "How on earth did you find this place?"

"Funny you should ask, it is called the 'internet'...people rely on it to get all their information these days," the man replied, very matter of fact, before turning his attention my way. "And who is this delectable auburn haired beauty?" he asked, making no effort to hide his examination of me. "I hope you did not get all fancied up for him," he said, leaning in as if to share a secret, "you do know he prefers the fellas."

CHAPTER SEVENTEEN

Finn's song finished and he thanked his applauding fans before exiting the stage. There was an awkward silence at our table before the jukebox started up.

Dorian turned his attention to me, "Please forgive him...he does not get out much. Believe it or not, he is actually an old friend of mine." His comment was more than likely an attempt to quell my offended expression. "Jacquelyn, this is—"

"Please, call me Roman," he said with a slight smile. "Do not take offense to our banter, it is the very nature of our relationship. Trust me, he gives back tenfold at times."

I looked to Dorian for corroboration and received a small nod. His initial reaction to Roman was beginning to make sense. My attention returned to our visitor. His gaze encompassed me. Rich, dark hazel eyes flecked with gold peered into mine, filling me with a growing sense of unease which I couldn't justify. Maybe unease was a bit strong of a word? Perhaps self-consciousness? Nervousness? I just couldn't seem to put my finger on it.

"Do you mind if I join you?" Roman asked me.

I looked to Dorian, who once again nodded.

"Sure," I answered.

"Alas, she speaks," Roman said in mock surprise.

His attitude caught me off guard, prompting me to speak, throwing manners to the wind.

"Yes, I do—and for your information, I also walk, chew gum—"

Roman's hand came down on the table so hard our drinks jumped. He leaned in toward me, his eyes taking on a lethal gleam.

"There are those among us that do not take kindly to such tones," he informed me in an agitated whisper. In that

161

second, I knew I'd done it again. Lattimer warned me to respect others. A mischievous smile spread across Roman's face before he once again sat up straight. "Thank God they are not here tonight, right?" he said laughing.

I wasn't sure how to respond. My first impression of being around Roman bore a stunning resemblance to riding on a roller coaster. Once again I looked to Dorian, in an attempt to gage how to react to his friend. He was chuckling to himself, shaking his head in embarrassment. It was as if he had taken me to dinner with his family and his senile grandfather just finished a rant about bodily functions and dating the Pope.

"I told you he does not get out much," Dorian said, trying to regain a semblance of normalcy to the table.

"So that's the story you're sticking with?" I asked.

Hearing Roman inhale deeply, I turned to find his face inches from my shoulder.

"You still have that 'new vampire' scent," he said, easing back in his stool. "How long have you walked among the immortals?" Fixed in his scrutinizing stare, I was speechless, still trying to make sense of him. Yet again I was about to turn to Dorian, looking for an escape. Roman grabbed my arm, fully commanding my attention. "Do you have to get approval from him for everything?"

Why did he have me so flustered? Sure, he was visually distracting, but there was much more to it than that. Although good looking men have always left me a bit frazzled, this was different.

I pulled my arm from his grip, "Um, no...it's just—"

"Dorian, how the hell are you?"

Finally relief came in the form of a man named Finn.

"Much better now, thank you..." Apparently Dorian needed a break from Roman as well. "Finn, this is my friend, Jacquelyn."

"I saw you clapping along, always a pleasure to see a new face enjoying the music," Finn said with a welcoming smile. He turned to Roman, "I have seen you a few times before but we have never met."

"Roman," he said, shaking Finn's hand. "I try to catch you when you come to the states, always a pleasure to hear the old songs."

"Thanks, I do my best...got to make my rounds, good to meet you. Jacquelyn. Roman."

With a nod he was off. Part of me wanted to beg him to stay. He had been a welcome distraction from Roman, if only momentarily.

"Well, Roman, thanks for stopping by but, if you do not mind, Jacquelyn and I had planned this night as a sort of 'get away from it all' time," Dorian said.

The look Roman shot him was tinged with acid. Apparently, he wasn't thrilled at being asked to leave.

"Of course, how rude of me," said Roman. He put on a smile, "Say no more, I shall leave you to it." A gorgeous brunette sauntered by the table. "Besides, I just realized I have plans for a late dinner." His eyes followed the woman. "Good to meet you, Jacquelyn."

Before I could respond he was off to intercept his prey. He said something to her in passing and she followed him out the door into the night. My head was still spinning from Roman's hit and run.

"Does he know her?" I asked.

"He will in a minute."

I glanced back toward the door, trying to digest all that had just happened. The process was diluted as Finn once again picked up his accordion, returning the majority of my attention to the stage. Although part of me was still attempting to puzzle through the phenomenon that was Roman.

At the end of the night, Dorian offered to walk me home. I saw no reason to object. He was fast becoming someone I enjoyed being around and trusted. When I stopped in front of Petrus's building, he turned to me, looking quite confused.

"This is where you live?"

"No, I'm just staying here until my friend gets better. Then I will probably stay at my friend Claire's place," I said.

"Oh," he replied, looking relieved. "For a minute I thought you were a working girl."

"Oh God no!" I gasped. "These were just friends of Collin's."

"Collin?"

I studied him for a moment, "Yeah, um, my sick friend."

"That is the first time you said his name," Dorian pointed out with a smile. "I think we have reached a new level of trust."

No sirens went off, no lights flashed, there wasn't even any recognition that went with the name. My newfound need for discretion hadn't been compromised. I actually even felt the tension lift a little in the aftermath of my slip.

"Maybe we have." I smiled in return. "So don't ruin it and keep that name to yourself, please."

He made a gesture as if pulling a zipper closed across his lips.

"Your words will never be repeated to another living soul."

The comfort I found in his sentiment was immeasurable. His friendship couldn't have come at a better time.

"Thanks for everything, Dorian. I had a wonderful time."

"Minus Roman?"

I shuddered, making a sound of vexation, "Yes, minus Roman!"

"Sorry about that."

"You can't be held accountable for the nature of others. But how the two of you are friends? I just can't see it."

"Time has an interesting influence on the way we perceive things just as it does for mortals. You spend long enough with someone and the initial circumstances tend to blur as the years pass. Before you know it, words like history and sentiment are being tossed about to describe a relationship that, in reality, may only be nothing more than habit," Dorian said as if he had pondered the possibility many times before. A warm smile touched his lips. "He is actually not that bad...but he does have his moments."

"Lucky me to have gotten one of his 'moments' as my first impression," I mumbled.

Dorian chuckled, "Goodnight, Jacquelyn."

18

Without bothering to knock, Dorian burst through the door and plowed past the curtains into the 'harem room', as he called it. Acacius fed from Giselle, cradling her in his arms. His head popped up from her throat. Blood dripped from Acacius's chin and ran down her neck.

"Roman?!" Dorian snapped.

Acacius stood, pulling Giselle to her feet. The sheer white gown she wore had been splattered with blood from the sudden interruption. Displeasure shadowed his features as he spoke.

"Go clean yourself up," Acacius grumbled at Giselle and wiped the blood off his chin with the back of his hand. "It seems Dorian has forgotten his manners." Giselle sped off as requested while Acacius licked the blood from his hand. "Might I suggest you take a moment to calm yourself down?"

Dorian took a moment but it did little to calm him.

"How shall I address thee in private, oh great one? Roman? Acacius?"

"I could not very well have her going around saying my name now, could I?" Acacius asked.

CHAPTER EIGHTEEN

"You would not have to worry about it if you would have refrained from showing up from the start!" Dorian replied, his frustration spilling over. "Bloody hell—you promised to stay away!"

"I did no such thing! You heard what you wanted to hear," Acacius said. "Besides, I do what I damn well please. You of all people should know that."

"To what end?" Dorian asked, descending the steps. "I did my best to try to convince her you are not completely mental or a bloody horse's arse but there is no telling what she will do if subjected to your company again."

Acacius approached Dorian, gaze narrowing, smile widening as if he had just solved a clever riddle.

"You have a soft spot for this female," he said.

"If you mean I enjoy her company, then yes, I do," confessed Dorian.

"While enjoying her company tonight, have you learned anything new?"

"Nothing of any use, really. However, I believe she is starting to trust me."

"Have you made plans to see her again?" Acacius asked.

"No."

He took a moment to mull over Dorian's answer, "Back away for a few days. I have no idea what is to come of this but I do not need things becoming muddy because you become all doe-eyed over her."

"And what if she wants to see me?"

"You are busy," Acacius stated. "Was that really so hard to figure out?"

"Fine."

"Have Alton send someone in to see me off to bed on your way out," said Acacius, settling back onto the sofa. "It is the very least you could do after ruining my pre–dawn snack— speaking of which, if you ever pull a stunt like that again, I will be sure to retire Alton for breeding. I can just imagine him curled up in the fetal position, crying in a corner after having been made to have sex with a woman."

The pleasure Acacius took in his own comment sickened Dorian. The elder immortal had a talent for cruelty and pain without even raising a hand. Which, often times, was more devastating than any physical wound.

Dorian left the room in silence, closing the door behind him. It had been years since Acacius had any reason to threaten him, but he knew from experience when Acacius resorted to such tactics, he was not joking. The ancient warrior never faded away, it lay dormant below the surface, skillfully kept at bay through a lifestyle of sensuality and decadence. Dorian did not want to be the one to wake the sleeping giant.

*   *   *   *   *

After being buzzed in, I made my way down the dreary gray hall to the only door. The process brought back less than fond memories of my time with Marco. Another buzz sounded, admitting me into what looked like a professional office. Dark stained, cherry furniture decorated the massive space that included a waiting room. The unexpected scenery did wonders to banish Marco from my mind.

To the right of a set of double doors, Lisette sat behind a huge desk with a phone to her ear, motioning me to take a seat in front of her. She wore a sheer white, sleeveless blouse unbuttoned just below the front of her white lacy bra. I silently wondered to myself what the bottom half of the outfit could possibly look like.

Unbuttoning my coat, I eased into the coffee brown leather chair as requested. She had just finished typing up something on her computer. Her eyes skimmed over the screen as she spoke.

"Ok, George, we will see you at 9pm tomorrow with Eden...Ok, you too, hon...bye," Lisette said, ending the call. She cradled the receiver and slumped back into her chair. Rubbing her temples, her eyes turned to me. "I need a day off," she sighed. "Not only do I have to cover Kayla's shifts—thanks to Petrus, but the closer we get to Halloween, the more freaks start to come out."

"I wondered why you haven't been home very much."

"Well, there you have it," she divulged. "I have become chained to my desk and not in a good way." Her defeated mood suddenly showing hope as she looked at me, "Would you by chance like a job?"

Her spur of the moment offer caught me off guard, "No...I couldn't—"

Before I could finish declining her offer, she interrupted me, "You would only have to do this," she said, gesturing to the desk. "Sit here, answer the phones, let the girls know when their appointments arrive and offer the clients beverages while they wait." My second attempt to turn down her offer never had a chance to escape my lips, dissolving on my tongue with her motion for silence as she stood. "Come here."

She stepped out from behind the desk, the theme of her outfit was finally revealed to me. Her blouse was tied in a knot below her ribcage, well above the short, pleated plaid school girl skirt that hung low on her hips. Knee-hi white socks and platform Mary Jane's rounded out the image, leaving me, with no doubt in my mind, this was not a job for me.

"Lisette, really, I appreciate the offer but—"

"Please? Just let me show you...then you can answer." Man, she was good. With a sigh, I got up. "Wait!" she said. "Take off your coat." Reluctantly, I slipped out of my coat and slung it over the chair. Her large, gray eyes seemed to glimmer with satisfaction. "Perfect! Ok, come here."

I rounded the desk, "Well?"

"Oh, do not be such a stick in the mud...sit," Lisette insisted, I complied. She returned to my side, putting her hand on the computer mouse. "See, that was not so difficult." She smirked before clicking through the screens. "Ok, here are the appointments for the current day. This is the calendar for the week, month, etc. Here are girl's availability schedules. This screen controls the cameras, as you can see the default is the front door cameras. They are, after all, the most important."

"Aha!" I interjected. "That alone should disqualify me, I would have no idea who to admit into the building and who to deny."

Lisette chuckled, "Ah, but see this?" She clicked on an icon. "Facial recognition software...and if for some reason that doesn't work, this button sends a snapshot to Petrus, or whoever is put in charge for the day, for their approval. The system is diligently maintained to offer up to the second information on anyone banned as well as new members." My deflated expression brought Lisette a new wave of amusement. "Did I mention it pays *really* well?"

I shook my head, "I don't know."

"You do not have to answer this second, take a few days to think about it." I looked from her face to her outfit, deep in thought. "Feel free to wear whatever you like. I just always figured, you know, 'when in Rome'..."

I got up, crossing to the chair to retrieve my coat.

"Did you have to use that as an example?" I asked, more to myself than anything. Her confused look let me know she heard my comment. "Sorry, I met Roman tonight. What a piece of work."

"Roman?" she muttered to herself. "Not sure I have had the honor."

"Honor is not exactly the term I would use."

She sat in her chair and started typing.

"Hmmm, not showing anyone...we also have an extensive database of immortals," she replied to my unspoken question.

"I met him through my new friend Dorian."

Again, Lisette's fingers went to work.

"Nope, not here. I do not think I have ever gotten two blanks in a row. This database is not only of our construction, it also contains information from Lattimer's. Strange..." she commented offhandedly before breaking into a smile. "Lattimer must be losing his touch."

"Obviously," I said, returning her smile. "Well, I am off to the apartment."

"Want me to call ahead? Roxanne was his last feeding of the night and I have not seen her yet. But, then again, she had no more appointments so she very well could have retired early."

"Don't be silly. Besides, if he's resting, I would hate to bother him."

"I understand," she said.

"What's the easiest way to get to your apartment from here?"

She sent me through a door off the right of her desk that I would've assumed was a closet. Behind it was a stairway that only went down one level and emptied out into the hall that led to her place. I quietly passed through the door to her apartment. The guestroom door was open and the light was on. I tossed my coat over the couch and went to see if Collin was indeed awake.

Perched on the edge of Collin's bed was a woman with vibrant red curls spilling down her back. Her cream colored peasant shirt billowed out of the top of a black leather corset. She was tugging on a black stiletto heeled boot and about to zipper it up when she noticed me.

"Oh! I didn't hear you come in," she said, offering me a friendly smile. Taking a second to pull up the zipper, she stood and approached me. Her eyes followed mine to the top two buttons of her black leather Daisy Duke's. "Oops!" She giggled as she buttoned them. "I'm Roxanne." She extended her hand to shake mine. "You must be Jacquelyn?"

I stared at her hand absently. It took me a second to take everything in. I could clearly hear the shower and sense Collin in the bathroom. Roxanne's hand dropped to her side and her smile started to melt away.

"Yes...I'm Jacquelyn," I finally replied, feeling more than a little awkward. "Sorry, but you weren't who I was expecting."

"No worries," Roxanne said with a nervous laugh. "I got to be heading out now...good to meet you."

She strode by me and out of the apartment. I stood in the doorway of the guestroom as if glued to the spot. At first I couldn't put my finger on what I was feeling. Then it hit me, I felt like I had been blindsided. As ridiculous as it sounded, that was precisely what it was. If Collin had the desire to bang every girl Petrus sent his way, why should it bother me? He was a grown man, able to think for himself. It wasn't like he was still with Olivia. So really, what did it matter? I was just being overprotective and selfish, that's all.

I wandered into Lisette's room, stripped down and got into the shower. The hot water would do me good. Besides, I needed to shake off the irrational mood brought on by Roxanne.

By the time I got out, dried off and slipped into my nightshirt, I was feeling better. Passing into the living room, I noticed the guestroom light was still on and the door was ajar. I knew Collin was out of the shower but I wasn't prepared to see him yet. Maybe he didn't hear me, I thought as I grabbed my coat off the couch and hung it up. I was about to start prepping the couch for sleep when he called my name.

"Jax? Is everything alright?"

My pre shower mood was trying to rear its ugly head again. I took a deep breath and headed for the guestroom.

"Yeah, I just got out of the shower."

"I do not particularly want to talk to you through the door, would you mind coming in?" he asked. I put on a smile and pushed the door open. "There she is...you sure you are ok?"

"I'm fine. Just a weird night," I replied. "You look better every time I see you."

"Why do I feel like you are trying to change the subject? What happened?" He laid the book he was reading on his lap and patted the spot on the bed next to him, so I sat. There was no way I was about to bring up Roxanne, instead I opted for sharing the Roman experience. "Nice friends Dorian keeps," Collin stated when I finished.

"That's one of the things I found odd...they are so different."

"Roman sounds like a moron. I do not recall ever meeting him."

"I'm sure you wouldn't have forgotten him," I said, getting up from the bed. "Well, I'm exhausted. I think I'll turn in early."

"Ok. Sleep well," he said, picking up his book. I made it to the door before he stopped me. "Are we still on to hunt tomorrow?"

"Sure—that is if you haven't made other plans."

No sooner did the comment pass my lips did I regret it.

"Right," he laughed, "you better go to sleep...you are becoming delirious."

Knowing I just got lucky, I smiled and left the room before any other stupid comment had a chance to slip out. One more odd remark and he would know my meeting Roman wasn't the only thing vexing my mind. Honestly, I had no desire to discover the grim details about his time with Roxanne.

19

"Why did you choose not to say anything about Roxanne?"

I had just reached the blissful floating state that precedes sleep when the question was posed to me. The verbal interruption was enough to rip me from the verge of unconsciousness and thrust me back into awareness. Collin loomed over me, patiently awaiting the answer to his inquiry. I propped myself up on my elbows and tried to decide whether or not to feign ignorance. That was, until I noticed the look on Collin's face letting me know evasion would get me nowhere.

"What difference does it make?" I asked in return.

"You think I could not tell it bothered you? Which, I might add, was not my intention. I did not realize how late it was at the time."

"As a grown man, you are free to do what you want," I stated. Pulling the blankets back up to my chin, I flopped over on my side to face the back of the couch. "I'm so glad we had this chat. Goodnight, Collin."

"I knew you were mad."

His ridiculous statement forced me to sit up. He was already headed back to the guestroom.

"I am not! You don't need my approval to have sex with anyone."

He stopped and turned. His expression was unreadable as he made his way back toward me.

"Do you honestly think that is what concerned me?"

"I don't know, Collin, you tell me, what am I supposed to think? You're the one that brought it up."

"I did not come out here to fight with you," he said. Motioning for me to slide over, he sat on the couch next to me. "The more I thought about it the more I found your silence on the matter troubling. I think I have spent enough time around you to confidently say you tend to speak your mind when something is bothering you."

"I wasn't bothered," I replied. Collin was obviously unconvinced. "I wasn't! Maybe...if anything...I was caught off guard. But, like I said, you can do what you like. Why does it matter so much anyway?"

"I thought my behavior offended you. It was evident you were reacting to the situation. Since you are one of the few people remaining in my life I consider a friend, I did not want to compromise that."

"You aren't going to lose me that easily," I said with a smile. "Men have needs. End of story." Collin studied me as if looking for any sign of contradiction. "I'm fine. Trust me. You'll be the first to know if I'm ever really mad at you!"

"I figured as much," he said.

"So, we're good? I can sleep now without you bothering me?" The look on his face resulting from my comment made me laugh. I leaned forward and wrapped my arms around him. "Just kidding, I'm lucky to have you."

CHAPTER NINETEEN

His arms encircled my shoulders as he hugged me in return. A feeling of content accompanied his gesture as if confirming the fact that I was right, I was lucky to have him. He was the one being in my life that was keeping me sane.

Perhaps it was his soothing embrace mingled with exhaustion but I found my mind wandering. The scent of his blood, so rich, so palpable it taunted me. I shamelessly wondered what he tasted like. When I closed my eyes, I could imagine my teeth breaking his flesh and his blood rushing into my mouth.

Caught up in my moment of blood lust, I didn't hear Lisette open the door.

"Whoa—I am sorry," she declared, her statement breaking me free from Collin's arms. "I did not mean to interrupt."

"No! Not at all," I exclaimed amid a short lived round of nervous laughter.

Collin stood, "I was just seeing Jax off to bed."

"No really, do not let me ruin the moment. I am exhausted," Lisette alleged with a forced yawn. She quickly crossed to her room. "Sleep well."

She wasted no time closing the door behind her, leaving me stranded in an awkward moment of silence with Collin. He was first to speak.

"I really should be getting to sleep myself," he said.

"Yeah, tomorrow is a big day for you," I agreed, relieved to have a new topic. "I'll bet you can't wait to get out."

"You think?"

He headed back to the guestroom. When he got to the door, he turned as if to say something, inner conflict shown on his face.

"What is it?" I asked.

"For what it is worth, Trinnian was a fool to walk away so easily," he replied. "I could never take what has come to pass between us for granted."

The heartfelt sentiment touched me so deeply, at first I wasn't sure what to say. In an effort to avoid rambling out of self-consciousness, I kept it simple.

"Thanks, Collin."

He turned and disappeared through the guest room door.

Once I was settled back in, ready for sleep, Collin drifted back into my thoughts. He was like an unexpected gift. I honestly don't know what I would have done without him. Even in the moments I was looking out for him, he was helping me. Strange and sad in the same thought.

It would be so easy to give myself over to more involved feelings for Collin than what I currently allowed, but there were so many reasons to keep anything more than friendship at bay. The one reason that outshined the rest was my recent track record with relationships. Losing his friendship by trying to make it more than what it might actually be would be a shame. That reasoning could only be rivaled by the weirdness of the 'wife swap' feel, which was made even more cringe worthy by the relationship developing between Trinnian and Olivia. And those were just the obvious reasons. It didn't take a therapist to see pursuing anything more than friendship with Collin would just be a really bad idea.

When I finally cleared my mind of anything that required active mental consideration, I started to relax. My subconscious took control and I drifted off to sleep.

The next evening I woke to an itinerary. Apparently Collin had been busy planning our night while I still slept. He followed me through the apartment into Lisette's bathroom, running down the list of things we needed to do while we were out. I allowed him to finish before I spoke.

"Can I please have a little privacy?"

"Oh, sorry," he said with a smile, closing the bathroom door behind him.

All that remained of his injuries was what mortals would take to be a mild sunburn. His hair was coming in nicely but still taking the longest to grow back, even his ear had already made a full recovery. Scientists would have a field day with the immortal healing process. Even the immortals themselves could not explain the phenomenon.

While I got ready for the night, I remembered fragments of the dream I had just woken from. I was in Lattimer's place in the city. But when I settled into the chair in front of the fireplace, it wasn't Lattimer sitting next to me, it was Diana. She was telling me she was safe and not to worry about her. Then she was asking me about immortality, what it was like and if there was anything I missed about being human. I was in the middle of speaking when the door opened. We both got up to see who it was but nobody was there. Diana told me she should be getting back, anyway, and started walking toward the door. I tried to ask her where she was going but she just kept walking until she vanished through the doorway.

All I could really chalk the dream up to was the fact that I had no idea what became of Diana and, whether or not I realized it, I was worried about her. Curiosity got the better of me. I picked up my cell and called the number she called me from the other day. An automated message informed me the number I had reached was no longer in service. What else could I do at the time? I had no idea how to find her. Maybe I should have let her tell me where she was going. After all, if a vampire was near her when she called me they could have plucked her intentions from her thoughts anyway. So really, there was no reason not to let her tell me. Too late now, she had simply vanished, just like in my dream. The one remaining hope rested on her finding me when the coast was clear. I slipped the phone in my pocket and headed for Collin's room.

The first stop on our list of errands was a trip down memory lane. Our hunt was to take place in the forgotten section of town where I took my first human. I followed Collin into the same building as before. There was a vast difference in the way I perceived my surroundings on this trip. The sounds in the building were sharper. Pungent odors of sweat, urine and other human byproducts hung in the air as a testament to the years of disrespect and vandalism inflicted on the forgotten structure.

Collin led the way upstairs and down the second floor hall. He stopped at a doorway halfway down on the left. Inside the wreckage of the abandoned apartment were two men huddled up against a wall. They were enjoying the spoils of their latest armed robbery, every cent of which went to the heroin they were shooting up. The larger of the two was slipping in and out of consciousness while the second was preparing to inject himself with a syringe. Preoccupied with his self medication, the man was unaware of Collin's presence until he was pinned to the wall. The man fought against him, punching and kicking in an attempt to free himself. His screams choked away to sputters as Collin's jaw compressed his throat, drawing the remaining blood from his jugular vein. The man was dead before he hit the floor.

With his first victim's blood fresh in his system, Collin turned his attention to the larger man. The struggle of the first

CHAPTER NINETEEN

man roused him enough to realize he was in danger. He was crawling toward me, pleading for help as I stood watching from the doorway. Collin latched on to him, hauling the man to his feet with little effort. By the time he could make sense of what was happening, his struggle started too late. He was already on the brink of death as Collin finished draining him.

On the third floor, Collin stood guard as I fed. My victim was a pedophile turned meth addict. He was a small, skinny man that got a bit feisty when I grabbed him. But I held my own, having to concentrate for fear the amount of adrenaline pumping through his system would hinder my self control. I have experienced the euphoric effect of adrenaline and certain drugs, like meth, can unleash heavy doses of adrenaline.

We made our way back to the heart of the city. Nothing quite compares to the feeling you have fresh from the hunt. All your senses are heightened. The slightest breeze dances on your skin like silk. The sounds of the city become as enchanting as a symphony. Every step you take feels buoyant, as if you have become light as a feather. Unless you have experienced it, understanding it is next to impossible. And once you have experienced it, you don't ever want to live without it.

Next on our 'to do' list was to get Collin a new phone. His was on the bed side stand at my house. Lucky for him his wallet was in the center console of the Range Rover. From what I have been told, getting new identification can be a bit of a hassle. Unless, of course, you deal directly with Lattimer, he seems to have the best connections. But that would require swallowing one's pride and asking him for help. Not exactly something I would want to do personally.

New phone in hand, we left the store. Collin was fidgeting with his new toy, trying to check his email.

"So how was Jamaica?" I asked sarcastically.

"What was I supposed to say?" he countered in defense. "No, this isn't sunburn. I almost burnt to death trying to escape the fury of a crazed arsonist?"

"Well no, but...it just sounded funny. That was the first time I have ever seen Collin charm at work."

"Collin charm?"

"You were flirting with that poor girl, she never had a chance," I giggled and elbowed him in the side.

"I was buying a phone. You are delusional."

"*Jamaica is beautiful in the fall, you should go sometime,*" I said in my best Collin impersonation. He stared ahead, his expression became serious. I didn't mean to piss him off. "I'm just messing with you, Collin."

"It's not that."

I looked up to find Roman staring at me. "Crap," I muttered to myself.

"What a small world," Roman said. He looked to Collin, "Who's your friend."

I figured if I kept it short maybe he would just go away.

"This is Collin," I said and looked to Collin. "Collin, this is Roman."

Collin's brow furrowed so minutely, it could have been missed.

He inclined his head slightly, "Roman."

"So nice to make your acquaintance, Collin," Roman said with a sly grin. "Jacquelyn, I must confess, I am so grateful to have run into you. I really wanted to apologize for my behavior last night."

"Really, it's fine."

"No, it is not. I was out of line and rude. You must let me make it up to you."

"No really, Roman—"

"I simply cannot accept 'no' for an answer. To have such a kind lady think of me as a dreadful oaf...well, I cannot allow that to happen."

Collin was about to say something until I laid my hand on his arm. Knowing how overprotective he can be, I really didn't want to know what it was he had the urge to say.

"Sure," I conceded, figuring giving in would be the best way to put an end to the encounter. "If there is anything I have learned recently, it is that sometimes people deserve a second take."

I looked at Collin to make sure he got the point, then back to Roman.

"Excellent!" Roman exclaimed. "Meet me at the pub where Finn played tomorrow at 8pm."

"Ok, I'll see you then."

"Good night, Jacquelyn...Collin."

Off he went, melting away into the crowd. I was replaying the odd encounter in my head when I felt Collin staring at me.

"What?"

"What do you mean what? You know exactly what," Collin stated.

"I got a second chance with you and see what good friends we have become."

"That's not the issue here...are you really going to meet with him—wait! That's not the issue either," he said, shaking his head. "Do you realize how old he is?"

"Ok, now I'm really confused," I replied. "Of everything you are worried about, it's his age?"

"You cannot tell me you do not feel that?"

"Feel what?"

"Is there anything about being in his presence that is reminiscent of being around Lattimer?"

I thought about it for a second. Lattimer always kind of unnerved me, so that wasn't a very fair comparison. Roman left me feeling scattered but, was it really the same?

"I don't know...maybe—"

"He is very, very old, Jax."

"So."

"Something's not right," Collin said suspiciously.

"Because men don't usually admit they are assholes?" I asked. "Yeah, you're right, I better think about this."

"No. That is not what I mean," he insisted. "Ones that old do not tend to cater to the feelings of newborns."

His conspiracy theory was starting to irritate me.

"I'm a grown woman. If I want to go have a drink with someone, I will. You really don't need to pull that overprotective crap with everyone you befriend."

"I am not being overprotective. You are too young to sense the strength of immortals and too stubborn to listen to one that can."

"Oh bullshit, Collin. You think that you're the only one that can enjoy the company of the opposite sex? God forbid a handsome guy asks me out," I growled.

"Handsome? That is what you consider handsome?" he countered. "But that is not even the point—"

"Oh no, I know the point. Maybe if I would have had sex with him the first time I laid eyes on him you would be fine with that."

"What?"

"Seemed to be acceptable for you and Roxanne."

CHAPTER NINETEEN

"Ok, now you are being ridiculous."

"Am I, Collin!?" I yelled.

I had nothing more to say, so I turned and stormed off in the opposite direction.

20

After putting a few blocks between me and Collin, the uncontrollable cussing subsided. I wasn't sure what pissed me off more, his hypocritical point of view or his compulsive mothering disorder. Perhaps I was angry at myself for thinking our time together had taught him how to lighten up a bit. I had gotten so used to who he had been while with me, I forgot how he was when we first met. The intolerant, self imposed bodyguard hadn't been completely abandoned. There just had been no reason for that side of him to come forward. That is until now, apparently.

What I needed was a distraction. I retrieved my cell phone, stepped out of the foot traffic and into a shop. My new surroundings gave me the perfect excuse to call Dorian. I wasn't really interested in rehashing my feud with Collin. Most of all, I just wanted to take my mind off him. Besides, shopping for some clothing may not be such a bad idea, since I essentially had none.

"Hello?"

"Hey handsome, what are you up to?" I asked, making a beeline for a rack of sweaters.

"Jacquelyn...I am actually taking care of some personal business," Dorian said. "What are you up to?"

"Shopping." I pulled an olive colored sweater off the rack, turning to find a mirror. "Would you like to join me?" I asked, holding the sweater up against me to assess its potential in the reflection, waiting for Dorian's response. It sounded like muffled voices on his end. "Hello?"

"Sorry...I dropped the phone," he responded. "Trust me, I would much rather be shopping than knee deep in obligation. However, it would seem the once avoided has now become the unavoidable."

"I understand," I said, returning the sweater to the rack.

"Everything alright?"

"Yeah."

"Liar," he responded. "Want to talk about it?"

"Collin's just being an ass and I'm just being a bitch, nothing that won't work itself out. Let me let you get back to your stuff."

"Alright, but if you need me..."

"Really, I'm fine. I'll call you tomorrow."

"Ok then, until tomorrow," Dorian agreed, ending the call.

Some alone time wouldn't kill me, I suppose. My first reaction anymore was to turn to someone at the first sign of crisis. I did point out to Collin the fact that I'm a grown woman, time to start acting like one. Sliding my phone back in my pocket, I returned my attention to acquiring a new wardrobe.

*　　*　　*　　*　　*

Dorian placed his cell phone on the end table next to the book he had been reading before Acacius showed up on his doorstep unannounced. Just as he answered the door, his phone rang, leaving him still ignorant to the reason for Acacius's presence.

"How rude, I just wanted to say hello," Acacius muttered, settling into an armchair, surveying the room.

"Me, rude? Find the section in any etiquette book about wrestling telephones out of someone's hand while they are speaking and I promise I will apologize."

"Good God, did Luis XV make you his sole heir?" he asked, scowling at Dorian's décor. "I do not think I have been here since your art deco phase. I miss it already."

Dorian returned to his spot on the sofa.

"You certainly did not come by to critique my interior design capabilities. Is there something you need?" Dorian asked.

"You are right. I actually came to gloat."

"About?"

"You will never guess who is meeting me for a drink tomorrow."

"Jacquelyn?"

"Yes!" Acacius leaned forward in his seat, "Did she mention something about it?"

"No, but I think I can figure out why Collin is upset with her now."

"Oh yes, him. He seems like great fun." His statement punctuated with a look negating his observation.

"I thought you were trying to be low key. You do realize that requires not drawing attention to yourself."

"Bah! He is just probably jealous she would prefer my company over his," Acacius stated. "Not much I can do about that. Can you blame her?"

"Not at all," Dorian mumbled.

"Very well then, I am off. Gloating was not quite as much fun as I imagined it would be," he said, heading for the door. "Be a dear and get me one of those mobile phones tonight. You know I am terrible with that sort of thing."

Without waiting for a response, Acacius let himself out. Dorian considered getting back to his book but decided against it. He knew the sooner he dealt with Acacius's request the better off he would be.

*　　　*　　　*　　　*　　　*

Shopped out for the night, I headed for Claire's apartment. I decided I would seek refuge from Collin there. The possibility of there being a round two between Collin and me wasn't much of a selling point for me to return to Lisette's.

I dropped my bags just inside the door and locked it behind me. Silence. Peace and quiet at last. There was only one thing that could make it even better. I set off to draw myself a bath. There would be bubbles, candles and a glass of wine in my near future. I could deal with the bags of clothing later, because I definitely was not leaving the apartment tonight.

Water crept up my skin as I slowly submerged myself into the tub. I leaned back until the bubbles tickled my chin. The flickering of the candles subsided when my motion no longer stirred the air. The restful atmosphere instantly started to chase away all the tension of the day. I took a sip of wine, thinking a call to my mother would be in order tomorrow when I woke. Whoever she found to build my house would definitely have to include a nice deep tub in the master bath—and a second bathroom for sure.

Speaking of my home, a thought suddenly occurred to me. If Lattimer was really keeping tabs on me, wouldn't he know that my house burnt down? Why hasn't he tried to contact me or even make another attempt to steal me away to Canada with him? I knew Lisette had gotten it all wrong. He was finished messing with me. That was all he wanted from the start. And I was fine with that. He got his chance to show the newbie how all powerful he was. Ok, point taken. It wasn't like Lisette's story did anything to sway my opinion. It just reinforced the reality that he was a narcissistic jerk. Anything that may have seemed to the contrary was certainly just her own adoration for him diluting the facts. Like the movie King Kong, everybody saw him as a beast, but the leading lady had a soft spot for him. In her mind she made exceptions for him even though—

A loud knock at the door brought all inner monologue to a halt. I stood so abruptly the water splashed over the sides of the tub. Toweling off as fast as I could, my mind ran through the list of possible callers. Lattimer? Had I discounted him too soon? Collin? Shouldn't he have enough sense to give a girl some space after infuriating her?

Stepping out of the tub, I pulled on Claire's red silk robe she bought in China. My reflection in the mirror called for immediate action. I rubbed away the smudged mascara beneath my eyes and freed my hair from the haphazard twist I had clipped it up in. Four more heavy knocks and I headed for the door.

CHAPTER TWENTY

I was halfway there when a new possibility offered itself to me. What if it was Julia? My stomach sank as my pace slowed. I did my best to try to sense who was on the other side of the door. It was someone I knew yet could not immediately identify. I tip toed up to the peep hole. All the air rushed out of me as if I had been punched in the gut.

"Jacquelyn, open the door," Trinnian said.

Against my better judgment, I complied. Trinnian was alone. He walked past me into the apartment. I shut the door, standing against it for fear my legs would give out. He turned to face me. I had forgotten how it was to be caught up in his gaze. His dark eyes fixed me there on the spot, peering into my soul. A twinge of sadness stirred in the wake of memories. I had gotten so used to adverse feelings for him, everything else had been discounted until once again, I found myself alone in his presence.

His attention broke away from me to the bags of clothes by the door. When his focus returned to me, his jaw clenched and he spoke.

"Why did you not tell us?" asked Trinnian.

How much did he know? Even though I was angry with Collin, I would never sell him out.

"Tell you what?"

He stabbed his finger at me, "Do not play with me."

"I'm not playing with you," I indignantly responded, crossing my arms in front of me. "There's a lot I haven't told you, so you need to be more specific."

In a few strides he was in my face, "You had no right to keep what happened to Collin from us." Cold, black fury glistened in his eyes.

"It was his choice and I respected his choice."

"That was not your decision to make," he snapped.

191

"What was I supposed to do? You weren't there. You don't know what we were going through. If he would have told me to call the Easter bunny, believe me, I would have. Because, quite frankly, I was terrified and had no idea what the hell I was supposed to do."

He considered my reasoning and eased back, giving me some room to breathe.

"So you wanted to call us but he would not allow it?"

"What difference does it make? It's over and he's almost completely healed."

"Because if you chose not to ask for our help out of your own distaste for me I would—"

"What?" I demanded, jumping on the defensive. "What would you do, Trinnian?"

His expression softened, "I would not be able to forgive myself." I was speechless. That was not the direction I was expecting. Having been the object of his disdain since he arrived, I just assumed my life was about to be threatened. "I know you detest me, and if that hatred—being the direct result of my actions—cost me the life of one so dear to me...I do not know how I could live with that."

"Well then, I guess you should start making better choices in your life," I remarked.

"You are too young to this existence to judge those who have endured centuries of regret. The closest you can even come to comparison in your life is but a few years of second guessing a decision, or even a lack there of. Now take that anguish and times it by a hundred, then tell me your verdict," he said.

"If you are referring to the Margaret incident, I think I actually came to understand your reasoning since I read your email. However, the grace your reaction lacked is what still gets me to this day," I pointed out. "Never once did you even bother to offer me an apology."

"I did not think you needed one since you had taken up with Marco so quickly. Being there to actually hear you tell him you loved him merely served to confirm my suspicion." He paused, taking in my reaction to his statement. "Oh, that's right...your back was to me. You had no idea I was standing in the doorway when Marco ran to the rescue...the night you killed Violet?" he prompted. I thought my knees felt week when I let him in, as he spoke I made my way to the couch. "I suppose I should have known by the baiting look he was giving me over your shoulder while professing his love for you that he would leave that bit of information out. For the record, it was me, not him, that cared enough about you to make sure Lattimer knew Violet's death was an act of self defense and not murder. Certainly he took credit for that."

I swallowed the lump forming in my throat, "No, he insinuated it was Augustine."

The strange moment replayed in my head. It was so obvious, in retrospect, that something was off with Marco's attempt to cover for Augustine. But I was so caught up in everything I had learned from Lattimer and his request, I didn't catch it at the moment.

Trinnian sat on the couch next to me. A conflicting mix of feelings were set off by his familiar scent. Part of me wanting to punch him, part of me wanting to hold him and the remaining part just wanted him to leave for fear one of the other parts would win.

"Jacquelyn," he took my hands, waiting to speak until I turned to him. "I know it is too late. But I am truly sorry for what I have put you through. You did nothing to deserve all the misery you have endured because of me."

I stood, rubbing my eyes, refusing to tear up in front of him, "Really, don't feel like you have to apologize to me. Especially since you didn't feel the need until I pointed out the fact that you hadn't. I'm fine."

"This is the first time I have had your undivided attention and even the hope that you would listen," he said. "You think I honestly never wanted to?"

"Actually, there is someone out there that is due an apology way more than I am. Or did you already take care of Collin and I was just next on the list."

He stood up, "I will not even attempt to defend myself to one that could never understand. That is between me and Collin," he said, striding toward the door. "Coming here was a mistake,"

"Now there's something we can agree on!" I exclaimed.

Grabbing the door knob, he turned back to me, "At least I can say I tried."

"Are you trying to convince yourself or me?" I asked.

With a grunt of frustration, he stomped into the hall, slamming the door behind him. I locked the door, mumbling curses under my breath—mumbling curses to myself being the theme of the day, so it seemed. I turned and almost stumbled over one of the bags of clothing left by the door from my shopping excursion.

In my aggravation, I kicked the offending bag out of my way. Beneath the bag was an envelope with my name written on the front. I must not have seen it when I put my bags down. The envelope was elegantly penned when I picked it up and examined it closer. There was a red wax seal on the back embossed with an image of a writing plume and ink well. I snapped the wax and opened the envelope. Inside was an equally elegant looking card that appeared to be streaked with dried blood. I slid the card out of the envelope and instantly understood, it was an invitation to a Halloween party. I was cordially invited to a party being held at Lattimer's Lake Winnipeg estate, Saturday, October thirty first. Guests were required to RSVP by October twenty–fifth to reserve overnight accommodations. Below the RSVP, the invitation specified, although it would be a black tie event, the guests were requested to wear a mask.

Shaking my head, I crumbled up the invitation. Really? He honestly thought I would attend his little get together, like nothing ever happened? I could only assume Lattimer and Trinnian were smoking the same thing because they both had lost their minds.

21

By the time I crawled in bed, it was less my choice and more the compulsion of the vampire I had become. Dawn was close and my body was shutting down. I lay in Claire's bed, trying not to think about all I had learned from Trinnian. But Marco's betrayal and lies haunted me. My eyelids grew leaden as I desperately tried to banish thoughts that would no doubt give way to nightmares. Last minute attempts at more pleasant thoughts and relaxing scenarios seemed too little too late as sleep took complete control.

The damp, heavy air saturated my flesh while the sharp scent of mold and mildew accompanied each breath. Gradually, another fragrance was coming into play until it could no longer be ignored. Immortal blood cut through the dank aroma that laid claim to the space for decades. I didn't need the mental pictures the combination conjured up to understand where the world of dreams had deposited me. Unable to break free from the grip of sleep, I reluctantly opened myself to explore the realm of my subconscious.

I sat on the floor in the basement of Claire's apartment building. The space slowly came into focus. Immediately, I became aware of where I had suddenly discovered myself. More specifically, at what point in the particular event that had transpired here I had been thrust in to. Violet lay dead in front of me in a puddle of her own blood. Her crushed skull and caved in face still lazily contributing the growing pool around her body. I looked down at my hands clutching the cell phone. The screen still illuminated from the disconnected call. Marco would be on his way.

No sooner did the thought cross my mind, I heard footsteps behind me. The phone slid from my grip and my fists clenched on my lap. I felt the strands of Violet's hair still tangled around my fingers. I looked down at my hands, relaxing them. Blood, scalp and hair still clung to my skin. The closer the foot fall, the more intent on picking the pieces of Violet from my hands I became. If I had any control over the matter, the way this memory played out would have a very different ending. Marco and his scheming was not about to manipulate me the way he had originally. I just needed a moment to decide how I chose to end it this time.

Still working at the strands woven around my fingers, the first view I caught of my alleged savior was his shoes as he stopped in front of me. Not bothering to look up at him, he knelt before me. I was still deciding whether to confront him verbally or to try to beat the crap out of him. Even though it was my dream, there was no guarantee I would win in a physical fight. That would suck about as bad as the original outcome. Caught up in the middle of making my decision, I heard my name but chose to ignore it. Just when I was trying to convince myself that at least attempting to kick his ass would be most satisfying, he grabbed hold of my wrist, stealing my focus.

"Jacquelyn, stop!" he said. Except it wasn't Marco, it was Lattimer. He clutched my wrist. My hand looked as if it were clawing the air between us. His silver gray eyes locked onto mine, holding me in place. "What is done is done. Violet is dead." His concerned expression, not to mention his presence, left me at a loss for words. "You did what you had to do. She would have killed you." In my confusion, all I could do was nod. A tiny smile touched his lips. "See, I told you that you are stronger than you think." He pulled me into his arms, whispering in my ear, "That is but one of the reasons I love you so much."

I took a deep breath, trying to sort out the drastic change in events. My senses were assaulted by his scent. It lingered in his hair like soft cologne. A current of pleasure slithered through my body as he held me close, stroking my hair. Recent fantasies of him flickered in my thoughts, denying any inclination to remove myself from his embrace.

Movement over his shoulder caught my eye. The incinerator door opened. Collin was inside.

"Something's not right, Jax. Ones that old do not usually cater to the feelings of newborns," Collin said.

Lattimer's lips brushed against my neck. In my mind I willed Collin to go away. Suddenly, the incinerator door slammed shut and ignited. From inside, I heard Collin groaning about how stubborn I was before the roar of the fire became too loud to hear him anymore.

Seductive kisses made their way to the front of my throat, fueling the arousal I had been subconsciously trying to fend off. There was still part of me lucid enough to realize that

CHAPTER TWENTY-ONE

I wouldn't just hand myself over to Lattimer so easily. However, that part was losing influence rapidly.

"Jacquelyn!"

A familiar voice called from behind me. Aggravation flared with yet another interruption. I turned to see Trinnian standing in the doorway. He shook his head desperately before fading away into a mist and dissipating into nothing.

I no longer wanted to restrain myself. Despite all the warnings, I turned back to Lattimer. The sinister glowering look in his eye summonsed forth an aching desire I had no intention of ignoring. I reached toward him, my hand slipping around his neck into his hair. Pulling him to me, I climbed onto his lap, kissing him hungrily, forcing him back to lie on the floor. He made no attempt to stop me, eagerly accommodating my wishes. Any clothing we had been wearing had vanished at some point unbeknownst to me. The delicious feel of his naked flesh against mine sparked a fresh wave of arousal with even his slightest motion beneath me.

He rolled on top, pinning me to the floor. Blood dripped from his hair and onto my body. At that point, I realized we were lying in Violet's blood. But for some reason, it didn't matter to me. He sat back, his blood soaked locks clung to his bare chest and shoulders. Crimson streaks ran down his stomach and arms. The scent of blood only adding to the frenzy I was building up to. Pushing his hair over his shoulder, he leaned forward to kiss me. It was soft at first, becoming more urgent. His fingers trailed down my side, pausing at my hip, before continuing down my thigh to grab behind my knee. He pulled my knee forward against his ribs, allowing him to push his body further between my legs. The feel of him pressing against me served to feed my ache for him until, at last, he slid inside. The sudden intrusion brought a gasp of pleasure from my lips. He rocked against me as I clung tighter to him, my nails clawing into the flesh of his back. I moved my hips against his, a low growl rumbled in his chest. Pleasure and pain embodied each thrust as he gripped me harder, holding me firm to his desired position.

I heard my name spoken in a whisper, it was not Lattimer. Trying to ignore it, I made an attempt to reclaim my focus. But once again, I clearly heard my name and this time the culprit tapped my shoulder. I looked toward the source of the interruption. Violet was propped up on her elbow beside me. Her mangled face inches from mine.

"Mind if I join you?" she whispered in her thick French accent.

My eyes shot open. I was alone in Claire's bed. With a sigh of relief, I sat up. At least I didn't wake screaming. Although, I had to admit, finishing the dream minus Violet may not have been so terrible...even if it was Lattimer. After all, it wasn't like he was hard on the eyes by any means. He was actually a very sexy man—in a forbidden, menacing kind of way. Provided the nature of the encounter was strictly sexual and there was no conversation to take place, it wouldn't be completely out of question. Like that would ever be possible?

The text alert of my cell phone sounded, presenting a welcome distraction to my lame attempt at justifying lusty feelings toward Lattimer to myself. It was Collin making sure I was ok. I simply told him yes and left it at that. Although I was just as tempted as I had been the prior night to ask him about his Trinnian encounter. Again, I managed to refrain. Certainly they had run into each other. How else would Trinnian have found out what had happened? If Collin wanted to talk about it he would when he was ready. Once again came the text alert.

CHAPTER TWENTY-ONE

This time Collin wanted to know if I was really going to meet up with Roman. I glanced at the time. Of course there was plenty of time to get ready to meet him at eight as planned. Honestly, I was curious. It would be in a public place. I typed in yes and hit send. Five minutes later, still no response. He was probably foaming at the mouth with anger, for some reason that gave me a twisted feeling of satisfaction. With a devious grin, I got up and headed to the bathroom to get ready for my meeting.

After each step in getting ready, I checked for a new text message from Collin. I took a shower, checked for a message. I blow dried my hair, checked for a message. I got dressed, checked for a message. Collin definitely had nothing to say. For the most part I was relieved. But the part of me that knew what that meant was bothered, because he had no right to be mad at me. I refused to let him think he could dictate who I spent my time with.

Dumping the contents of my makeup bag on the counter, my mascara rolled off onto the floor. I bent down to pick it up and saw Lattimer's invitation in the garbage. Ignoring it, I went about applying my makeup. But pretending the invitation didn't exist did nothing to stop my dream from replaying in my mind. Images and sensations from the memory faded in and out as I went about my routine. Finally, I applied my lipstick, thinking about how his lips felt on my skin. *This is pathetic*, I thought as I replaced the cap on the product and tossed it in the bag with all the rest. I blotted my lips with a piece of tissue and threw it in the trash...right on top of the invitation. Standing there frozen, I stared down into the small trash can. The only two items it contained were the freshly discarded scrap of tissue and the crumpled up invitation. *Nope, not gonna do it*, I said to myself and exited the room.

I made my way to the pub a few minutes later than I'd planned. Roman would just have to get over it if I was late. Halfway down the stairs of Claire's building, I turned around to retrieve the invitation, only to abandon the idea once I found myself hovering over the can again. I wasn't going to Lattimer's stupid party and that was final.

Roman was waiting outside the pub when I arrived. He was as casually dressed as I was, thankfully, he too opted for jeans and a sweater. The sweater, mostly obscured by a brown tweed jacket and lighter brown scarf, loosely hung around his neck. He grinned from ear to ear when he saw me.

"Jacquelyn, so good of you to come," he announced. "I was starting to think you only agreed to be rid of me."

"Actually, I did."

His bewilderment was powerless to erase his smile, "And yet you stand before me."

"Strange, isn't it?"

"Yes," he said, eyeing me suspiciously. "Shall we go inside so you can explain?"

"I don't think so."

His smile waivered, "I am afraid I do not understand."

I stepped toward him and spoke, lowering my voice, "Cut the crap, Roman."

He flinched, "Beg your pardon?"

Had I just seen his façade slip like I had once seen Lattimer's? Collin was right, something was not right with this. My new observation boosted my confidence. I crossed my arms in front of me and spoke.

"If I have learned anything in my short stint as an immortal, it is the ease with which others prey on trust and vulnerability of newborns," I admitted. "So if there is something you want, allow me to maintain some extent of dignity while at the same time retaining a bit of honor for yourself."

His expression went blank while he considered me. Either I had just screwed up big time or—

A smug grin turned up the corner of Roman's mouth, "As you wish—but, I will not speak here. You must trust me enough to let me take you somewhere."

Did he just call my bluff? I fought the urge to chew my lip as I debated whether or not I was willing to play his game of Truth or Dare. Collin knew who I was with and Roman knew that. He wouldn't try to hurt me, would he? What reason did he have to harm me period?

"Where?"

"Ah, that is where trust comes in," said Roman. A mischievous look altered his expression. "However, I will say, it is a beautiful night for a stroll in the garden."

He turned and headed off down the street. I watched him walking away, never once turning back. Collin was already pissed at me and, at this point, I couldn't have him confront me with nothing to show for it. Especially since I knew he was right. But most of all, I was beyond curious.

"I always liked the decisive ones," Roman said as I fell in step beside him.

"Now there's something I've never been accused of," I said.

He looked at me, "Immortality does strange things to people."

His smile touched his eyes, helping me to relax. But I still couldn't silence the old saying that played like a broken record in my head. 'Curiosity killed the cat.'

22

We made our way through the city. Roman gave me a guided tour while we headed toward our destination. Almost every block had historical significance, according to him anyway. There was no telling if anything he told me was true since most of it was unfit to ever have graced the pages of any history book. I had a sneaking suspicion that his tales were motivated more by his desire to control the conversation than to offer me an insider's history lesson. His accounts of prominent figures caught up in scandalous activities contained the perfect mix of probability and outrageous embellishment. The skill with which the stories were told entertained while, at the same time, forced the audience to contemplate the possibility of their integrity.

"Here we are," Roman announced.

I glanced up at the building, making a mental note of the address. A few of the windows were illuminated. He trotted up the steps of the apartment building—not much of a surprise there. Owning an apartment building in the city was not unusual for immortals of influence and power. I followed close on his heels, assuming he would be utilizing a keypad to gain entry. Not knowing what he was up to, I figured it would be to my advantage to capture his code should I need to escape at some point. Certainly immortals were just as lazy about changing pass codes as humans were. I pretended to check my phone for messages while he punched in his code. Either he had nothing to hide or was convinced I was preoccupied with my task since I easily made out the number combination he used. A familiar dull buzz signified the lock had been disengaged. Roman swung the door open, motioning for me to enter. This was it, last chance to abandon my poorly thought out plan. My hesitation was not lost on him. Arching an eyebrow, he spoke.

"Is it that obvious that I have nothing to say and merely plan to try to seduce you?" he teased. "I really must work on my acting skills. Or perhaps hone my powers of persuasion towards immortal females." Although he did not close the door, his stance relaxed while he awaited my decision. "I do not want to make you feel forced into doing anything." I was about to speak when he cut me off. "Although in my defense, I have been told I am an excellent lay."

His raunchy comment delivered in such a matter-of-fact way would have normally cracked me up, but this situation was not exactly a laughing matter. I looked back up at the building. Although lights were on, I couldn't sense anybody, mortal or immortal.

"Is anybody in there?"

He shook his head, "Nope. This is my own private space, for the time being. I keep the lights on a timer to avoid suspicion and would-be squatters."

I studied his face, as if I could tell he was lying or intended to do me harm. He acted as though he had nothing to hide.

"Why here?" I asked.

Some part of me thought that if I got an answer I could live with then we could proceed inside. Otherwise I would completely abort the mission.

"This is where my garden grows and I have not been to see it this week," he stated plainly. "Besides, its open air rooftop accommodations may put you at ease while ensuring our privacy."

Ok, I could live with that. Although, if anything bad did go down, open air or not, being on a roof didn't make for a quick exit. But until I got up there, I wouldn't know for sure, would I?

"After you, I insist," I requested with a smile.

Roman took a step toward me, keeping the door propped open with his hand. He smiled and touched the tip of my nose with his forefinger, "You are learning, little one."

I followed him inside, down the non-threatening earth tone hallway to the elevator. We took it all the way to the top, reaching our destination in silence. The doors opened to another hallway on the top floor. To our left, the wall was constructed completely from glass, and the wall to the right traveled the length of the hallway unbroken almost until the end. About midway down the hall, a panel was fixed to the glass. Roman hit a button, causing the slab of glass we stood in front of to slide behind its neighbor.

The lights beyond the glass gradually illuminated, as if to simulate daylight. A painstakingly manicured garden sprawled before us. The warm air that nurtured the vegetation seeped into the hall, heavy with the fragrance of flowers and earth. Roman stepped onto the cobblestone path, inviting me inside. I followed, taking in the beauty that surrounded us the deeper ventured. Not having a green thumb myself, the majority of the species of flora were unknown to me. I could pick out Oriental Lilies and Snapdragons but that was about the extent of my recognition.

The garden was laid out in a square, divided into four sections by the stone walkways. Well, five if you counted the center which hosted a sizable, round fountain. The focal point of the fountain was a stone statue of a woman draped in a flowing robe, pouring water from a seemingly bottomless urn.

In the remainder of the glass enclosed space, beyond the garden, was a wide lap pool beside a tasteful, modern seating area. Roman led me to the chairs where I assumed he would finally divulge my purpose in his world. He offered me a seat and took the one angled toward mine.

"I almost forgot. Would you like me to retract the outside walls?" he asked. "I do not want you to feel trapped."

Glancing back at the garden, I wondered if the chilly night air would harm the delicate blooms. Maybe I was being naive but I didn't feel I was in danger. So I saw no need to disrupt the fragile balance that kept the plant life flourishing here. I looked back at my host. He was patiently waiting for my decision, not at all bothered by having to take into account my comfort.

"That won't be necessary."

"Are you sure? I do not want your lover to feel the need to bust up my building in an attempt to rescue you."

"My lover?" I asked before it hit me who he could possibly mean. "Oh, Collin? He's just a good friend."

"Oh, I see," he said in a tone that implied much more than his actual comment.

"What?" I asked, a bit more forceful than intended.

"Then I fully understand the reason he is standing vigil in the alley across the street. That is just what friends do, I suppose."

I was mortified. Roman took in my expression and nodded toward the wall beside us. I got up and strode to the glass. Sure enough there was a figure in the shadows across the alley. Pulling my phone out of my pocket I sent him a text that simply read, 'Go away.' Seconds later, an object illuminated in the figure's hand and he vanished. I was furious. He had some nerve following me, especially when I was already mad at him.

"Do not be so hard on him. He is a tormented soul. This life is not easy for him, so he finds his purpose in protecting others."

I turned back to Roman. His comments were given as his own assessment, not to be taken in any other way. But still, I got a little defensive over his unrequested input, regardless of the truth behind the words.

"What gives you the right to profile someone you don't even know?" I asked, standing behind my chair, reevaluating my choice to stay.

The amusement my irritation gave Roman needled me. Apparently I was getting as protective as Collin.

"I have walked this earth a very long time. If I lacked the ability to assess immortals swiftly, I do not think I would still be here," he replied.

"Ok then, what do you make of me?"

Once again, no sooner did the query leave my lips, I regretted it. But it was too late to retract my question. I tried to appear self-assured as I reclaimed my seat. Even though I had a feeling he knew my confidence was all smoke and mirrors.

CHAPTER TWENTY-TWO

A sly smile crept across his lips, "One day...when you settle into your skin, I will tell you. That is if you still care to know. At the moment, I do not believe any opinion I have developed of you is relevant to who you truly are."

His revelation, or more realistically, his lack thereof came as a relief. Being in such a compromising situation, I really didn't need to know what a frail, insignificant being he thought me to be. The bleak notion only emphasized the fact that brushing off Collin's warning wasn't my best idea ever. But at that point, it was a little late for second guessing my decisions and showing uncertainty would only enforce any perception of weakness. The only remaining option was to do my best to maintain my confident exterior.

"Understandable...well then, shall we get to the reason you brought me here?"

His demeanor changed completely, becoming almost predatory. He leaned toward me as he spoke.

"So you would not believe it if I told you my sole purpose was to get you naked and roll around with you in the flowers?" he asked. I crossed my arms in front of me and gave him a look that said I was not amused. His brow rose unassumingly as he continued. "Not even a quick peek at your ample breasts?"

I got up, shaking my head, "What is it with you old vampires? You get a few centuries under your belts and you think you can treat others like toys? Do you think we exist exclusively for your amusement? I honestly don't know what I expected from you tonight...but it wasn't this."

I headed toward the hallway, down the cobblestone path toward the fountain. Roman's laughter was closing in on me. I felt his hand on my wrist, the unyielding grip stopping me before I could even make it to the fountain.

"You have an awful long life ahead of you to be so damn uptight," Roman stated, his amusement tapered off and he released my wrist. "If you promise to come back, I promise to behave."

Turning to face him, I studied his expression. I had no doubt in my mind that those puppy dog eyes worked like a charm on many women. No matter how handsome he was, I would not allow him to use me for his own personal entertainment. Nor was I going to set myself up to become another of his conquests—if that was really his goal, because I was starting to wonder if that really was all he had in mind. Maybe his lewd comments were not just comments? One would think that beings so old would have more important things to do than torment newborns.

"For some reason I don't think you can," I confessed. "Goodnight, Roman."

Making my way around the fountain, I was expecting the door to the hall to close. It was all I could do not to run for it for fear he would trap me inside.

"If you have not figured it out yet, my name is not Roman."

Even though I could have easily made it through the door, my forward progress ceased. Was I really that naïve? Obviously some part of me figured out that if established immortals didn't recognize his name, something was amiss? But that wasn't the case. Certainly if I'd have known his age before the prior night I would have wondered how nobody had ever heard of him. But without that little piece of information, I never really questioned it. Why would I? Even Lattimer couldn't possibly know every single immortal that roamed the earth.

CHAPTER TWENTY-TWO

His proximity shattered my train of thought. He stood behind me, for what I could only assume was waiting for me to ask the only other relevant question left.

"Ok, so what is your real name?"

"Acacius."

The name dissolved into the air with no fan fare attached. Although it was unique and sounded ancient enough, it prompted no recognition. So, really, what was the big deal? If he was someone to be feared, wouldn't I know about it? But then again, I didn't know anything about my new culture, past or present for that matter.

"No offence, but I haven't heard of you before."

"None taken. I was actually more concerned about the ones that have."

"Because?"

"Like Dorian said, I do not get out much."

"Ok, I am already bored with this," I said as I took a step. But then something occurred to me. I turned to face Acacius, trying my best to ignore the sinking feeling in my stomach. "Dorian called you Roman the night I met you," I said. "He's part of this game of yours too?" I took a step backward toward the hall.

"This is not a game—"

"You set me up!" I took another step back. "You used him to make contact with me. That was no chance meeting the night I met him, was it?"

"I am sorry but I had to."

"So I'm right, it was all planned out."

"Well...not entirely." He scrambled to save face in light of my indignant reaction. "I had no idea we would ever come here," he said, gesturing to the garden.

I stared at him, unwilling to hide my repulsion before swiftly heading toward the elevator. Stepping inside, I smashed the first floor button with my fist. I looked up in time to see him heading toward me.

"No!" I yelled, hitting the button to close the doors. "Don't you dare!"

Ignoring my demands, he wedged himself between the closing doors into the elevator and stood next to me.

"You cannot tell me you are not curious in the least," he suggested, reaching for my hand.

I swatted his hand away, backing up until I hit the wall, "No, I'm not!"

Why did I tell Collin to go away? The question gnawed at my brain as I suddenly became furious with myself.

Acacius approached me, attempting to look into my eyes as I stared down at the floor, "Yes, you are."

Examining my shoes, refusing to make eye contact with him, I felt like a child. He wouldn't persuade me into being his puppet anymore. No matter how juvenile I felt.

The car came to a sudden halt. Acacius had attempted to open the elevator doors while it was still in motion. The between floor stop would not set off any alarms like the stop button would, one of the many reasons for call buttons in older elevators. With the outside set of doors still shut, he had essentially trapped us inside the car on purpose. My knee jerk reaction altered my stance, preparing to defend myself. But he didn't even seem to notice, not perceiving me as a threat.

"Ok, fine. I need your help," he desperately stated, flinging his hands in the air in resignation. "I have been watching you—no, more precisely, I have been watching Lattimer."

I was more confused than ever. My stance relaxed as I spoke.

"I don't understand."

He sighed and leaned against the wall beside me.

"The past two times Lattimer has come into the city was to see you. There is something about you that peaks his interest."

For the first time since I came to the building with Acacius, I was concerned for my own safety. A chill ran through me as I spoke.

"You plan to use me as leverage for something?"

Acacius appeared confused, then thoughtful.

"I could, I suppose...but kidnapping would negate the peaceful offer I plan to impose. So thanks for offering, but the answer is no."

"I wasn't really offering—"

"Oh...right...uh, of course not."

The hatch above us taunted me. There was no way I could make it through without him overtaking me. I rubbed my temples in effort to remain calm, returning to the moment.

"Then what could I possibly do for you?"

"Funny you should ask, I would like you to appeal to his gentle nature on our behalf," said Acacius.

"Um...you say that like you are sure he has one."

"Well, if I am correct in thinking Lattimer would like to impress you. Then, yes, he has one."

"Ok. Since I am apparently your prisoner at the moment, could you explain yourself? Not that I am really that interested, more than anything, I feel if I allow you to hash out your plan, I may be released before dawn."

He looked at his watch, "I think that can be arranged."

I slid down the wall and hugged my legs to my chest. *Might as well get comfortable*, I thought, this was about to be a long night.

23

"We can return to the garden, if you would like?" Acacius suggested, staring down at me.

"This is just as good a place as any."

"As you wish," he said and reluctantly sat across from me.

Looking around at the floor, he muttered something about having the cleaners come by as he wiped his hands on his jeans.

"It's fine, really," I said. "Just because I requested to be finished by dawn, doesn't mean I wouldn't prefer to be done sooner."

He assessed me before speaking, "So sorry to be keeping you from bickering at Collin but there are things about your new life that you should know."

"I wouldn't be bickering at Collin if I wasn't here—" At least I didn't think I would be.

"And you would not be pleasuring him either, which tells me that being with me is the most interesting option you have."

"Oh please," I gasped. "There are things I could be doing...you don't know me..."

He had a point. I really had nothing better to do. More accurately, I had no life at the moment. No job, no man...I didn't even have Claire. She was one of those friends that disappeared for a few months every time she fell in with a new love. Provided she and Augustine were still in the initial stages of slobbering bliss, my phone would remain silent. But once the newness wore off, she'd be back with a vengeance. In other words, Acacius's observation was spot on. However, he didn't need to know that.

"You are correct there. I do not know you. How ungrateful am I to assume your time is mine to waste?"

"Thank you. That is the first selfless statement you made tonight."

"I was not finished," he responded flatly.

"Please forgive me, your highness...continue."

Acacius chuckled to himself, shaking his head.

"I knew I was right."

"About?" I asked.

"He likes the infuriating ones."

There was no need to ask which 'he' Acacius referred to. Lisette once offered a similar description of Lattimer's taste in women.

"I'm so sorry that being held prisoner tends to bring out the worst in me. You should try it sometime then maybe you'll understand."

"I have been trying all evening..."

"Wrong 'it'. I meant being someone's prisoner," I growled. If I had ever met a man with more of a one track mind, I couldn't recall. "You promised to behave."

"If you sat with me in the garden—I never said anything about the elevator," he grinned. "However, I have been someone's prisoner. In fact, fortunately for you, that brings me to the point of why I brought you here."

"Oh thank God. Can we please get this over with?"

My exaggerated display of relief was taken seriously. Acacius sat up straight and spoke.

"I spent fifty years in Lattimer's dungeons." His words echoed in my mind as I studied his face. He told the truth. No amusement lingered as he spoke. "You do not have the slightest clue what it is like to be someone's prisoner." He looked around the elevator before his eyes returned to mine. "Actually, I would like to return to the garden."

I made no protest while he fixed the doors, resuming function to the car and returned us to his rooftop, Eden. We rounded the fountain and returned to the seating area. Reclaiming our chairs, he glanced up toward the lights, squinting.

"I cannot recall what it feels like to walk in the sun," he said, looking at me. A sad smile touched his lips, "With that in mind, being here feels real to me. Perhaps that is why I enjoy having such a place as this at my disposal."

"Actually, if I don't look at the lights, I wouldn't know the difference," I said. The more I thought about it, the more I felt I was right. Or maybe the more I convinced myself I was right.

"You are kind to lie. I have given you no reason to show me any compassion, yet it is in your nature. Humanity still influences you and, for that, I will tell you how I have come to this moment."

His words stopped me from speaking, thankfully. If he thought my good intentions enough reason to be honest, why would I want to retract any prior comments?

"There was a time when I stood beside Lattimer," stated Acacius. He was staring off into the garden, but then his attention returned to me. "He was the man who would lead a species into the new millennia. Me, I would be his second in command, the one that would protect him and fight for him selflessly. Not to mention for the greater good of our followers. When I came to this life, I was a soldier, a warrior. I fought for empires ruled by great men. Naturally, the place at Lattimer's side held a comforting sense of belonging to me...a perfect fit. Not that he had ever been a great man until immortality happened upon him. But, none the less, it had been the company he kept in his mortal life that groomed him for the position."

Acacius stared back off toward the garden. The look in his eyes intensified. He could have been trapped in a place in time I could never know. I had no desire to rip him away from whatever it was that stole his focus.

"It did not take long before our views began to conflict on how the social order we governed needed to be run. Him taking the stricter road while I trusted our choices in the beings we gave immortality to allow for a more relaxed society. But ultimately, the great divider was when I came to the conclusion that we did not need to kill to survive."

I may have made some noise revealing my surprise but, for whatever reason, I suddenly became the center of his attention.

"Then you can understand my reaction when I, the cold blooded killer—by today's standard's anyway—the once revered soldier who thought nothing of taking another life once the order was given, discovered this little fact. If I drank from multiple humans, no one had to die. I no longer had the desire to take any life needlessly. Remember how I said immortality does strange things to people? Well, there you have it." He snorted ironically. "Lattimer thought me to have gone mad at the time. After all, to him, having the authority to give life or death was what placed us above all other species. He completely turned his back on me, disassociating himself with me entirely."

His expression turned dark, "That was until I started making my own immortals. Instilling in them the same ideas I gradually came to live by. It took Lattimer a few centuries to become concerned with what was happening. But when he did...everything changed.

"I managed to evade him for quite some time, continuing on as I was until I started to gain defectors from his empire. That was when all hell broke loose. He put a bounty on my head, promising high standing to anyone that would bring me to him. When he found that being a part of his noble stance lacked the motivation he thought it would, he made a new offer in exchange for me on a leash. He offered a pardon to anyone whom he hunted for their crimes at the time. It was then he achieved the fervor he had originally intended. Every hooligan that had dodged from shadow to shadow in effort to avoid Lattimer's attention came forward to find me."

I was missing something. Acacius read my expression and paused for my question.

"I'm sorry...if you were only trying to live a more peaceful existence, why would he hunt you down?" I asked.

A smile crept across his face, "Because he fears me—even to this day."

"But he had the power...all the followers, why would he fear you?"

Acacius laughed. It was a dark, chilling sound.

"Because the first time our paths crossed, I was human...he had the privilege of taking a brief glimpse into my soul. What he saw there terrified him. The blackened heart of a warrior whose sole purpose was to protect and serve as requested at any cost. Living only for the love of the empire he defended. Lattimer knew nothing of such selfless devotion except that it was exactly what he needed for himself."

"So he was afraid you would turn on him?" I reasoned.

"Basically, yes. Why do you think he surrounds himself with huge bodyguards?" Acacius pointed out. "He is still afraid I will leap from the shadows and extinguish him. You know Petrus, do you think he turned him for his intellect?" he chuckled at the thought. "But you see Petrus grew tired of Lattimer's ways, too. Thus the reason he no longer subjects himself to Lattimer's company on a daily basis.

"Anyway, where was I? Oh, yes, Lattimer gave incentive to the criminals to find me. But the lack of results only served to further infuriate him. I managed to stay a step ahead of them through my own craftiness and the help of my followers. My elusive existence became a slap in the face to Lattimer, ever preoccupied with maintaining an image of control and supremacy. He became desperate, opting for underhanded and dirty tactics. He had my immortals hunted down and killed. The newborns were targeted because they were the easiest to prey upon. My followers became fearful, begging me to figure out how to put his wrathful tyranny to an end."

Looking back to the garden, Acacius became silent. His expression was blank, not unreadable but...helpless? Perhaps he was reevaluating the time he spoke of. Wondering if he could have prevented what happened? Maybe mourning those lost to Lattimer's battle? Whatever the case, his silence was torturing me. I had to know what happened.

"What did you do?" I asked cautiously.

His attention returned to the present. He looked at me as if suddenly uncertain he should be telling me any of this.

"The only thing I could do. I turned to Anath, my second in command...so to speak, and asked her to take our people underground. The earth would conceal them until they could one day roam free again. She knew instantly what I was up to, only because she knew me so well."

"You were going to surrender yourself to Lattimer," I asserted.

"Yes, but only if he agreed to put an end to his extermination of my followers."

"Did he?" I inquired.

"He agreed, imposing a stipulation of his own. Only if they did not cross his path," Acacius replied. "Even after I was released, the condition held firm. Thus, the reason we still reside underground."

"Does he still enforce his decision to this very day?"

"We do not extend him the opportunity," he said. "But I have no doubt in my mind he would. He has in the past."

"Have you tried to communicate with him? Maybe he has lightened up over time? If you have gone this long without trying to harm him—I'm assuming you haven't, that is, perhaps he is no longer so paranoid about it?" I suggested.

"You cannot even begin to understand how long this has been going on, Jacquelyn," Acacius insisted. "Can you fathom the concept of a thousand years? Because it has been more than that."

A thousand years? How old were they, for crying out loud? Honestly, I was having trouble imagining fifty years imprisonment. Now this? What did Acacius seriously think I could do to 'appeal to Lattimer's gentle nature' that could release a population that had been repressed for over a thousand years? I wish I had that kind of power!

"Acacius, I don't know what magical incantations you think I possess—"

"I am not requesting you to perform magical feats or anything outrageous on our behalf. All I want from you is to ask him to allow us to once again roam above ground without being put to death for the privilege," he pled.

Here I was again, being asked to perform a task for a powerful man. Was this my newfound purpose? Being stuck in the middle of ancient immortal situations like some sort of supernatural mediator? At least this time it had nothing to do with me whatsoever. I could walk away and lose nothing. No one would have to be the wiser.

But, of course, I would be. I would know that there was a population of immortals sentenced to dwell underground because they chose to follow the wrong leader. A group denied freedom because of another man's insecurity. What if all it took to give them back that freedom was asking? Was that really so unreasonable a request? But would Lattimer listen to me? That was really my only argument left. Even though the others seem to think I have captured his adoration, I think they are mistaking his interest in me for his attempts to figure out how to kill me without looking like a complete douchebag.

"Why me? Contrary to popular belief, the man hates me."

"I do not believe he hates you or I would not be wasting my time. To answer your question, you are the most logical choice. Your status as a newborn means any affiliations you have at this point have been bestowed upon you. The passing of time has not worked its influence to turn you to one group or another. Your impressions are purely your own and not tainted by years of others' opinions infecting your judgment," he explained. "In other words, you have nothing to lose, or to gain, by speaking for any particular group."

His disclosure made sense. Not that it made me any more confident about relaying the message to Lattimer. But at least it felt more reasonable.

"How exactly do you expect me to relay the request?"

"Every year Lattimer hosts a Halloween party—what?"

Apparently my maniacal laughter disrupted his plan. He looked at me as if I were a lunatic.

"You have got to be kidding me...I just can't show up at his party and toss this out there."

"Sure you can, you do not need an invitation."

I couldn't help laughing, "That's not what I meant. Somebody's party is not exactly the best time to gain their undivided attention—which this sort of thing is going to require," I contended. "But, ironically, I actually have an invitation."

"See! It is a sign!" he exclaimed, sitting on the edge of his chair.

I considered him for a moment, "I will think about it."

"Alright," he replied. "That is something."

"I really must get home."

He stood, "Of course."

Motioning for me to lead the way, he followed me to the hall. I continued on to the elevator alone and pressed the down button. While I waited for the doors to open a thought occurred to me. I turned to see him watching me from the glass doorway.

"What happened to Anath?"

It was like the curtain dropped. The change in him was instant. His demeanor turned somber.

"She crossed Lattimer's path," he replied.

The answer struck a chord with me. To see the once ill-mannered man's façade give way to someone capable of compassion and depth, I knew in that instant I would help him.

24

Little by little, Claire's room came into view. I didn't wake screaming but, then again, I couldn't recall having dreamt about anything. Despite my lack of nightmares, I felt mentally exhausted. The past few days were definitely taking a toll on my brain. If my argument with Collin, or even my spat with Trinnian, weren't enough, having to remain composed around Acacius would've been sufficient to sap my energy. It did become easier while he gave me the brief overview of his situation, since it offered me something other than my own nerves to focus on. Maybe if I would've fed before our meeting I would've fared better? The answer to that would forever remain a mystery.

Speaking of feeding, that would undoubtedly have to find a spot on my evening to do list. I rolled over to look at the time. There, on the bedside stand lay Lattimer's invitation. Propping myself up on my elbow, I picked up the wrinkled card. As much as I didn't want to attend his little shindig, it really wasn't my choice. There was a group of immortals depending upon me to do the right thing.

I was reading over the RSVP instructions when interrupted by a knock at the door. Still wearing my clothes from the previous night, I had no excuse not to answer. In my defense, the day crept up on me with the dawn.

With an irritated grunt, I went to see who it was. The peep hole confirmed what I sensed, the caller was Collin. My head hit the door with a dull thud. Certainly I was about to be reprimanded on the dangers of ancient immortals. Against my better judgment, I opened the door.

Collin took in my attire as he passed by me into the living room. Was it my imagination or did he inhale as he passed? I closed the door and followed him into the apartment.

"Someone had a long night," he said.

"Someone needs a hobby," I returned, settling into the couch, ready for my reprimanding.

He stood before me. I was expecting him to take a seat. When he didn't, I started to feel a bit uncomfortable. The last time I felt this way, it was my father looming over me the one and only time I broke my curfew. Was Collin about to ground me? The thought of him sending me to Claire's room with no supper made me smirk.

"I am glad you find your reckless adventures amusing," he noted. "Because I do not."

"I wasn't...never mind," I said, abandoning any attempt to explain my misunderstood amusement to him. Surely the joke would be lost to the generation gap. "Apparently you didn't come to apologize for being a jerk. So I will assume you came to chastise me for behaving like an insolent child. Go on, get it all out of your system."

"That was not my motivation to come here. Despite my personal opinions of your actions, you are absolutely correct, you are a grown woman. This gives you the freedom to associate with whomever you choose in any manner you wish."

The approach in which he recounted my own words made me suspicious. I thought about the true meaning behind his observation. He thought I had sex with Acacius. It wasn't my imagination, he did take a whiff of me in passing. This new passive aggressive tactic may be more annoying than his usual outright blatant style.

"Well I hate to disappoint but the most contact he had with me was touching my arm."

"Do you honestly think I wanted him to have anything more?" he asked. The hurt in his tone was obvious. "I wouldn't have wasted my time—" He stopped mid thought. "Jax, I have a flight to catch. I do not have the time for this."

A flight? I was at a loss.

"You didn't mention this before."

"I booked it last night after deciding I need to get away for a while."

"Oh," I said.

It was all I could say at the time.

He looked at me, a mix of sadness and frustration shown on his face.

"It is not you, per say, it is the events of the past week that have decided for me."

"I understand."

At least I thought I did. Trinnian and Olivia, near death experience. I could see his reasoning. It was a lot to happen in a short amount of time. But it still hurt, especially since it was so spur of the moment. How could I not feel like it had something to do with me? Especially since I wasn't part of the decision making process. I felt the cold trail of a tear rolling down my cheek.

He took a seat next to me and brushed away the tears that began to fall liberally.

"Ok, maybe part of it is because of you. But not for the reasons you think. I am becoming accustomed to your thoughtless and stubborn antics," Collin said with a slight smile.

If that was his attempt to lighten the mood, it wasn't working. My silence made my opinion of his comments clear. He turned, sitting closer to me. His tone became sincere.

"I am afraid of my motivations when it comes to you," he whispered.

"Why?"

"Last night when I got back to Lisette's, I had a lot of time to think. The things that have happened to me recently need to be dealt with. I have not had the time to properly come to terms with the drastic changes that have occurred in my life." I attempted to speak but he stopped me with a slight motion of his hand. "The night you discovered me at your house could be viewed as the start of a friendship between us. But it was not so innocent. I am not denying the fact that I consider you a friend or that you feel the same for me...or at least you did."

"I still do," I said, wiping away tears. "You know I do."

"What I am saying is the moment we came together that night, it was out of need. We both needed someone at that moment. The friendship that has arisen from that need has helped me as much as it has helped you. But a friendship founded on such things can cause confusion between the heart and mind." Collin paused, pushing a stray lock of hair over my shoulder. "But there is so much more to it for me. It started when you found me, hidden away beneath the remains of your home. You became more than just my friend. You became my protector, my provider and my inspiration. The role you have come to play in my life deserves proper defining."

"Then why are you leaving me?" I sobbed.

"Because I do not know what to do with it, and being in your presence does nothing to help me figure it out. When I am around you, I am convinced it is one thing. But when I am alone, it is possible it all becomes something else. I need some time away so I can make sense of everything for myself. This is the one thing in my life I need to understand and be certain of, because it is one of the few things I have left. Right now, the boundary lines have become so blurry—"

He shook his head. It was as if he lost the words to explain. I stared at him in fear of what he may say next and in fear of what he wouldn't say next. He sat before me like the forbidden fruit. I knew exactly what he was going through, because I thought about it, too. The warning flags still waved in my head, attempting to stifle what I had already labeled as a terrible idea. But his admission was testing my resolve. Where was my notorious stubborn side when I needed it?

Collin's dark eyes peered into my thoughts, or so it seemed, because without warning, he leaned forward and kissed me. His fingertips gently tilting up my chin while his lips caressed mine, rendering me unwilling to resist kissing him in return. He kissed me harder, pulling me closer. I held onto him in return for fear if I let go, he would leave. The very thought frightened me enough to ignore my own warnings and give in to his desires. Not that I didn't want him. That was not the case at all. My biggest fear was what would happen if I did give in, which apparently was still not enough to stop me. His hands slid into my hair, holding me closer with the growing intensity of his kiss. He teased my mouth with his tongue. I shuddered with pleasure, encouraging his sensual exploration. This was quickly getting to the point of no return. But I did nothing to stop it. Instead, I mirrored his hunger, spurring him on.

His lips abandoned mine, making their way to my neck. He tormented my skin with his mouth, kissing and nipping at the sensitive spot below my jaw. It was all I could do not to squirm under the relentless assault. I heard him breathe deep, taking in my scent. His teeth grazed my flesh but didn't draw blood. A deep rumble sounded in his chest as he took another deep breath, hovering just over my throat. I slid my hand into his hair, pulling him closer and purred into his ear, "I don't want you to stop."

The breath held, rushed out of his trembling body. Collin sat back, rubbing his face in his hands. I sat up, smoothing out my sweater and running my hands through my hair, taking an unanticipated stab at composure. He was leaning forward with his elbows on his knees. When at last he looked at me, it was with shame in his eyes.

"I am sorry. That really did not help things."

"It wasn't all you, Collin," I tried to assure him. "I could have said no—I mean I should have said no."

He stood, "I need to leave."

"No...no you don't." The tears started fresh. He said nothing as he stood before me, staring at the floor. I got up from the couch, "Collin, please, look at me." He reluctantly did as requested. Everything else aside, first and foremost, he was my friend and I wasn't ready to say good-bye to him. I didn't know what I planned to say or what I needed to say, so I just spoke in hopes it would all make sense. "We can take a day or two and...and...I don't know, maybe not see each other until—"

"Until what, Jax?" he growled. "Until I can decide whether or not what I feel for you is real. Not just leftover feelings from a centuries old illusion I lived with Olivia? I cannot do that. Not to myself and not to you. You know from experience what I mean. Remember how things worked out for you and Marco?"

"That's not fair."

"But it is."

"I knew the difference in my feelings," I exclaimed.

"Well then you are better than me. Because what just happened there..." he stated, stabbing a finger at the couch before his words dissolved into the air.

"Go on, please, don't stop now that you're on a roll."

His expression turned dark, "What happened just then? I heard your voice, but all I could see in my mind was Olivia." The words stung, he may as well have slapped me in the face. What could I say, I asked for it. Regret clouded his eyes, "I am truly sorry. I never intended to hurt you."

"I know." I made my best effort to appear as if I was going to be ok. But it wouldn't hold long, so at least there was some relief to be found in his having to leave. "Don't miss your flight." He stared at me, perhaps trying to find something to say. Instead, he nodded and turned for the door. "Where are you going, if I may ask?"

"I am meeting up with Augustine and Claire in Germany."

"How much do they know?"

"Nothing. I just told them I wanted to get away for a little and they did not press the issue."

"What are you going to tell them?" I asked.

"I had not really thought about it. But eventually I will tell them the truth, I suppose. They are bound to find out eventually," he said, opening the door. "Take care of yourself."

My lip quivered as another tear fell, "Yeah, you too."

I sat on the couch for about an hour staring at the door. Surely Collin would come back. I could imagine him coming through the door with some fantastic plan of how we could make things work out. How the feelings we felt for one another were genuine and safe to act upon. How we were both being too cautious, when in fact we were probably denying ourselves something wonderful for no real reason.

But I knew in my heart that wasn't the case. His feelings for me were straight up residual from Olivia. My feelings for him were a mish mash of leftover Trinnian and Marco. I had known already it was a bad idea, why I even let myself entertain the prospect is beyond me. Collin just swept me up in his own wave of hopeful possibility and I allowed it, against my better judgment.

It was actually a shame he left. I deserve the awkward moments with him in the aftermath of the train wreck. Strange run-ins where neither of us know where to look or what to say but feel obligated to acknowledge each other. Wait a second, no I didn't. I was being ridiculous. What I did need was to feed, not sit around wallowing in self-pity. Would it be such a stretch to think vampires could suffer from lack of feeding like humans do low blood sugar? Before I could talk myself out of it, I grabbed my coat and left the apartment.

The night's hunt was way too easy. I came across a pimp dumping the body of one of his girls in the Hudson River. He was much larger than I would normally attempt on my own, but I had the element of surprise on my side. Besides, I had a reputation for reckless adventures to maintain. Whatever.

I wandered the streets looking for something to keep my mind occupied. Out of habit I reached for my cell thinking I would call Dorian. Great, something else I wasn't quite sure what to do with. I suppose I couldn't be mad at him and not at Acacius, could I? Yet another item to add to my 'deal with another day' list, because I wasn't in the mood for thinking. What I needed was a place to be alone and keep me from my own misery. One place came to mind instantly and, without further thought, I set out for the garden.

Using the code Acacius carelessly let me observe, within minutes I stepped off the elevator on the top floor. I opened the glass door to the garden and the space illuminated just as it had before. Taking full advantage of my solitude, I strolled leisurely along the walkways. My mind opened up to the onslaught of aromas and colors that surrounded me, the placid sound of the fountain instilling a much needed serenity.

A vibrant orange bloom caught my eye. I plucked the flower from its stem. It reminded me of Hawaii for some reason, I thought as I placed it behind my ear. In an effort to keep up my newfound theme, I headed for the pool. Tempted as I was to strip down and swim, I couldn't shake the possibility of Acacius showing up or if he had cameras monitoring his building. Glancing around I saw no signs of being filmed but, just in case, I limited my swim to taking off my shoes, rolling up my jeans and dunking in my feet. I lounged back, propped up on my elbows and closed my eyes. Acacius definitely had something here.

A cool breeze danced across my skin and, even with my eyes closed, I would swear the lights lowered. I opened my eyes to see every other glass panel sliding open. It was almost completely dark as the chilly night air forced out the warm air that had only moments ago filled the space. I got up, looking around me to see if I hit a button by accident as I slipped into my shoes and unrolled my jeans. There was nothing near me.

It was then that I sensed I was not alone. An immortal was in the hall outside the garden, blocking the only way out. And it wasn't Acacius.

25

Using the fountain for concealment, I crept up the center path of the garden. When I reached the wall of the fountain, I ducked down as far as I could and peeked around the side of the statue. A figure stepped into the doorway, scanning the area. The slight, delicate frame was enough to fill me with dread, even before she spoke.

"Hello, Jacquelyn," Julia said. "If you think you can slither your way around the fountain and slip through the door, you are sadly mistaken. Why not just come out from there so we can have a little chat?"

I stood up, knowing there wasn't much else I could do. A disturbing smile spread across her lips as she casually approached me. The girl I once thought to be hauntingly adorable reemerged, more like a menacing threat. So much for first impressions.

"How did you find me?"

"Actually, I have been watching you for days. But tonight was my best opportunity to approach, thus far." She started to round the fountain, forcing me to move in the opposite direction in an attempt to keep the barrier between us. "Where are you going?" she inquired, switching direction. "I just want to talk to you."

"Then talk," I responded, changing direction in turn.

She stopped and sat on the edge of the fountain quartered to me. I knew it was more than coincidence that she situated herself in a direct line between me and the door. Muttering a curse under my breath, I sat on the edge closest to me.

"See, that was not so difficult, now was it?" she asked.

"No, it wasn't," I conceded.

Folding my hands on my lap in an attempt to seem more at ease, I waited for her to say what she had to say. In the meantime, my mind scrambled desperately to figure a way out. There were no roofs close enough to jump to from my vantage point, as if I would even really attempt such a stunt. No makeshift weapons lay about for me to defend myself, should it come to that. Who was I kidding? There was no doubt in my mind this meeting would end in a physical altercation. But there was always a slim chance she really did just want to talk, right? Maybe if I filtered my words carefully enough, I could make it out unscathed.

"That's better," she said. "You should know that what I want to tell you is for your own benefit."

I resisted the urge to ask her when she started caring about my well being for two reasons. First, that would negate the non-confrontational façade I struggled to maintain. Second, if I took that road, I would be putting Diana at risk, divulging things only she could know to the enemy. Not having the luxury of knowing what had become of Diana, it wouldn't be wise to gamble with her safety.

"Please, continue," I requested in a pleasant tone.

CHAPTER TWENTY-FIVE

"Thank you," Julia responded with a slight inclination of her head. "If you have not figured it out yet, you have been a pawn to the immortals since you took your last mortal breath. Silas to Trinnian, out of revenge. Marco to Trinnian because of his connection to Lattimer. Then, of course, Lattimer to Marco, in attempt to keep him in check. But now? The granddaddy of them all, Acacius to Lattimer." She took in my reaction, which I fought to keep level. But when it was laid out like that, I couldn't help feeling like a tool. "I have to know, what exactly did Acacius want from you?"

"I don't know what you mean," I answered, feigning innocence.

Before I had time to even flinch, she sat next to me. Settling into her new seat before the drops of water flung into the air with the speed of her crossing returned to the fountain.

"I should have known Dorian's interest in you came from Acacius. Dorian can barely bathe himself without seeking approval from him. If I would have been paying attention, my first clue would have been Dorian's sudden interest in a female. After all, his sexual preference is no secret. Even his prying questions about your ties to Lattimer did not alert me. I feel like such a fool." She grabbed a fistful of my hair, pulling me harshly within inches of her face. "Now tell me, what does Acacius want from you?" she demanded.

The pain shot through me and suddenly I saw no reason to withhold his request from her. If I gave her what she wanted, maybe she would let me go...in more ways than one.

"Alright! Alright!" I shrieked, prying at her hand. She let go, brushing a few of my auburn strands of hair from her hand. I rubbed the spot the hair had been torn from my scalp. "He asked me to attend Lattimer's Halloween party on behalf of him and his people."

My answer brought a curious grin to her face, "For what purpose?"

"To ask Lattimer's permission to roam free above ground without fear of retribution."

Her brow rose, accentuating her incredulous expression. She studied me as if baffled by my very existence.

"Are you really that stupid?" she pondered aloud.

Biting one's tongue to avoid confrontation was one thing but being manhandled and insulted for the effort was intolerable.

I stood up, backing away.

"What am I supposed to think? What else could he possibly want from me?" I argued.

She rose from her seat, "He wants you to start a war." Taking a step toward me, she forced me to step backward. "Human nature dissipates quickly for our kind. Acacius preyed upon your lingering desire to help your fellow man and you reacted as predicted. So, I guess stupid was a bit harsh, gullible would have been more accurate."

"Why would that start a war?" I asked, ignoring the rest.

"Because your decision to speak for Acacius means he has succeeded in capturing your allegiance. Under the assumption Lattimer has his own agenda for you, what an insult that would be. Think of it like two emperors playing capture the flag...and you are the flag."

Julia stopped in the middle of the path as if deep in thought.

"Acacius claimed I would be there with him when he set things in motion. He told me if I was loyal to him, I would finally get my revenge on Lattimer. Obviously he had a change of strategy that no longer involved me. That would also explain his silence." She looked around the garden, then back at me. "I never even knew this place existed, yet he claimed I was a part of his inner circle."

"He told me nobody else knew about it," I added, aiming to quell her increasing agitation. It seemed like the only logical tactic I had.

"Who are you to try to defend him?" she spat at me in disgust. "You mean nothing to Acacius and I plan to make sure that does not change. I knew you were a problem when you revived the tension between Marco and Lattimer. Unfortunately, I relied upon a spineless human to remove you from the equation. This time I will rely upon my own bare hands."

She lunged at me. I tripped over a cobblestone, falling back into a flower bed. Julia dropped into a crouch, her hand latched onto my ankle, pulling me through the dirt into her reach. With all my might, I kicked her in the face. The force of the blow knocked her backward, hitting her head on the side of the fountain.

"You killed Lori before her thoughts could reveal your involvement in the effort to kill me, didn't you?"

"Was it that obvious? Or did your little friend Diana tell you?" she asked, wincing as she attempted to get up.

"Did you kill her, too?" I asked, despite the fear I had for her answer.

Taking advantage of her disorientation, I scrambled to my feet and made a break for the hall. Less than two strides from the doorway, her hand closed on my neck. She pulled me into her grasp, lips brushing my ear as she answered my query through gritted teeth.

"I guess you will never know," she growled, throwing me back into the room.

The rectangular footstool of the seating area toppled over beneath me, breaking my fall. I looked up to see the space where a thick glass panel once stood between the garden and a bone crushing drop. Hearing Julia approaching from behind, I knew I had to move or risk being tossed out the window.

I was going to push off the footstool, using it to help me stand. But when I did, the downward force caused the lid to flop open. Stowed away inside were a few gardening tools. I grabbed a set of large pruning shears. Holding them firmly, I was getting to my feet as I turned to face my attacker. From her point of view, Julia was oblivious to what I was doing as she ran at me. She was so intent on shoving me off the roof that, by the time she saw the weapon, she was already impaling herself on it. The blades of the shears slid into the base of her throat with ease.

Her momentum knocked me backward, over the footstool. I rolled to a stop at the base of the low guardrail bordering the roof. Julia was not so fortunate. Blindsided by the sudden change in events, she pitched headlong over the rail and fell to the alley below.

Pushing myself to my knees, I looked over the railing. Julia lay behind a dumpster, obscured from the street. The position of her motionless body confirmed the devastation of the impact. Blood was spreading fluidly across the front of her crème colored sweater. The shears lay next to her on the pavement. She stared up at me, unblinking. As much as the thought did not appeal to me, I knew I had to get down there.

The elevator ride took an eternity. I fidgeted with the zipper of my jacket, wishing I would've grabbed a weapon from the remaining gardening tools, just in case. But judging from the grotesque angles of her broken body, even if she was not dead, she would not be getting up.

I caught my reflection in the door as I was about to step outside. Dirt and broken vegetation hung from my hair. Blood seeped from a cut on my forehead. I shook the debris from my hair, wiped the blood from my face and stepped out of the building. Confident nobody was paying attention to me, I turned into the alley.

It took me a moment to talk myself into walking behind the dumpster. Years of scary movies were trying to convince me Julia would be gone. But while I stood, baffled by her sudden absence, she would appear behind me, ready to exact revenge.

Of course, when I finally found myself on the other side, there she lay. The blood no longer flowed but oozed as her reserve dwindled to an end. My hand clamped over my mouth when I noticed her head angled toward me and her lips started moving. The urgent whispers made no sense, but one thing was certain, she was not dead.

"Oh my God, oh my God, oh my God," I muttered to myself, pacing back and forth, wringing my hands.

What was I supposed to do now? It was her fault this happened. She attacked me! I had to defend myself. Like I could have just sat there and let her kill me? All I wanted to do was find a place where I could be alone and think. How was I to know she had been stalking me?

Choking sputters reclaimed my attention. She was coughing up blood in her attempt to speak. Not all of it had poured out of the hole in her throat, some of it leaked inside. The coughs were getting louder. I had to do something. Crouching down beside her, I put my hand over her mouth and fished out my cell phone. Petrus would know what to do.

I sat next to Julia, waiting for Petrus. Minutes felt like hours while I kept an eye out for my help to arrive. Much to my relief, she eventually stopped spitting up blood. I was wiping the blood off my hand onto her sweater when Petrus stepped into the alley with one of his girls. I had met the girl before. She had been on the feeding rotation for Collin.

As soon as Julia came into view, the girl gasped in horror. Petrus came to a stop at Julia's side and squatted down next to her for a better look. Julia's eyes flickered as if trying to focus on his face. Petrus rubbed the top of his head, exhaled hard and looked at me.

"This is bad," he said, shaking his head.

"But you can fix her? Like you once told me, it is our amazing ability to heal that defines us as immortals, right?" I reminded him.

Petrus stood. From the grave look on his face I knew the news wasn't going to be good.

"Not everything can be healed. I have seen this before. The spine has been severed at the base of the neck. The only thing keeping her alive is what little blood remains still flowing to the brain. You cannot heal such an injury. Once the head is parted from the spine···" he looked back down at Julia, "there is no mending the damage to such a complex part of the anatomy."

"So what are you saying?" I asked, even though I already knew the answer.

"You have to put her out of her misery," he stated, returning his attention to me. "Showing her mercy will be to your advantage."

"What do you mean, to my advantage?"

CHAPTER TWENTY-FIVE

"When I said this is bad, I was referring to the fact that Lattimer is her maker and I knew the moment I saw her you would have to kill her."

26

"This infuriating thing!" Acacius shouted when Dorian entered the harem room.

He barely made it through the curtains into the space when the cell phone Acacius requested from him was sailing through the air in his direction. Thankful he took the urgency of Acacius's summons seriously, his heightened state of awareness allowed him to catch the phone with ease.

"What seems to be the problem?" inquired Dorian.

He automatically started examining the phone for noticeable damage, knowing that Acacius had little patience, especially for any sort of technology.

"It kept chiming. While I was trying to figure out what the damn noise meant, the screen turned black," he responded, glaring at the device in Dorian's hands.

When Dorian attempted to power it on, the cause of the problem became obvious.

"Have you charged it since I gave it to you?" The blank look he received was about what he expected. He scanned the room for the box he gave Acacius with the phone. There it sat on the table closest to the door in the exact spot

Acacius had originally set it down. Dorian retrieved the box. "Remember, I told you when I gave you all of this that the charger was in the box and you would need to charge it daily, perhaps more often depending on use. That was two days ago."

"I have been busy," Acacius said dismissively. He watched closely as Dorian removed the cord from the box and went about setting the phone up to charge. "How long will it take until we find out what all the noise meant?"

Dorian turned the screen to face him. It was illuminated as if nothing had ever happened.

"Now," Dorian said, navigating to the message screen. "You have four texts from Peyton."

Acacius was looming over his shoulder instantly, "What do they say?"

Both sets of eyes were glued to the screen as the messages opened.

Julia is dead. She attacked Jacquelyn and was thrown off a roof in self defense.

The damage to Julia was so extensive, Petrus informed Jacquelyn her best option was to put Julia out of her misery.

The whole way back to our place, Petrus was attempting to remain calm. But I do not think he realized he was muttering to himself.

If Petrus is concerned, this cannot be good. Is there anything I should be doing?

Acacius stepped away, consumed by his thoughts, staring off into the room.

"Would you like me to reply?" asked Dorian.

Acacius returned his attention to Dorian but didn't immediately answer. It was as if he expected the solution to everything may appear at any moment in the air between them.

"Tell her to do nothing," he finally replied. "Her disclosure was more than enough for now."

While Dorian responded to Peyton, Acacius stormed off toward the door.

"Where are you going?" Dorian asked.

"This unfortunate incident will more than likely change everything. I need to find out what Julia told Jacquelyn."

*　　　*　　　*　　　*　　　*

The steaming hot water surrounding me couldn't chase away the icy chill that clutched my heart. I hugged my knees to my chest, sitting in the middle of the bathtub at Claire's place. Bits of garden debris floated in and out of my line of vision while I stared absently into the bath water.

In my mind, I could still see Julia's lost gaze and hear the scrape of bone against the blades as I closed the garden shears, removing her head. Petrus was kind enough to pack up the body in garbage bags and stow it away in his trunk. I could recall watching him close the trunk after tossing the shears inside, wondering how many bodies had found their way inside there.

When he dropped me off at Claire's building, Petrus assured me that he would properly dispose of Julia's remains. He told me that if I needed anything at all to call him. I was not to worry, he would handle everything. I couldn't help asking if that included Lattimer. He nodded, stating with confidence that his very long history with Lattimer afforded him a certain level of concession the majority lacked. In other words, I was left with no other option than to trust his reasoning.

Lowering my forehead to my knees, I started to sob. It was more than just the uncertainty of Lattimer's reaction. The past two months flickered through my head. Julia's assessment of my time as an immortal was hard to deny. Did all my anguish really stem from others' need for vengeance, spite and control? It made sense, if only because I could come up with nothing to combat her logic.

The realization came with a hollow feeling, emphasizing my loneliness. A void in me that Collin had filled once again made its presence known. In his absence, it felt deeper and colder than ever. Maybe it was because I had no doubt in my mind about the motivation behind his connection to me. His friendship was pure, not inspired by what his association with me would reap. A decree of morality few could attest to.

Perhaps I should just turn myself in to Lattimer? Tell him I lied about killing Julia in self defense and the truth was I killed her because I didn't like her face. My blatant disregard for the lives of others undoubtedly made me a danger to everyone, locking me up would be the only way to guarantee their safety. At least tucked away in a dungeon I would no longer be of use to anyone. By the time I emerged, the humanity they all preyed upon would be gone and I could exist in peace.

Absorbed in my pity party, I wasn't immediately aware that an immortal was in the apartment. I turned my head to discover Acacius standing in the doorway. How I didn't notice the onset of nervous energy that came with his presence was beyond me. Once I saw him, I couldn't ignore it. My forehead returned to rest on my knees.

"Go away," I muttered.

I felt him draw near until he stood next to the tub.

His hand stroked my head, "Are you alright? What happened?"

I smacked his hand away and looked up at him.

"No, I'm not alright. Marco's sex buddy, or should I say your little double agent Julia, tried to kill me...again."

"Again?"

"The first time she had a human set my house on fire during the day. But that's a whole nother story."

"Why would she want to kill you?"

"Oh, I don't know...because she's insane? Spiteful? Jealous? You know her, feel free to jump in anytime."

"In the tub?" The exasperated look he received in response got him back on topic quickly. "For what it is worth, Julia is not one of mine," he said.

"Whatever, just leave. I don't have the strength to play these games anymore," I confessed.

"I am not playing games."

"If you don't claim her, then it shouldn't bother you that she's dead, should it?"

He shook his head, "No, it does not." Searching my expression, which I could only assume was unconvinced, he explained himself. "Julia came to me after she left Marco. She claimed to not be affiliated with anyone and wanted to become a part of our society. I felt sorry for her, offering her a home among us. Shortly after, her true motivation started to shine through. She wanted us to bring down Lattimer and destroy Marco as well. I wanted nothing to do with her insane fantasy, evicting her from our ranks immediately. From what I understood, she ran back to Marco. Dorian spoke to her a few times afterward against my wishes. He felt I was too hostile toward her and took it upon himself to befriend her. That was the last I even heard her name mentioned."

"That's odd, she was under the impression that Dorian's interest in me stemmed from you."

"I have already confessed I had been watching you. When I asked Dorian to find out what he could, I never specified from where," Acacius admitted.

He had a point there. But I had no desire to discuss his stalking methods.

I sighed, "Why are you here?"

"I went to my garden and it had been destroyed. The scent of immortal blood hung in the air," he explained. "Since you were the only immortal I have ever taken there, I naturally assumed it was you. I wanted to make sure you were alright. Now it all makes sense."

I wasn't sure what to think anymore, was he lying about all of it, some of it or none of it. If he was, what did it even matter? It wasn't like I could do anything about it at the time.

"Here," he said, offering me a towel. "You must feel a bit awkward having a conversation with a man you barely know while in such a vulnerable position. With your consent, I need only a little more of your time and then I will leave you for the night. There is something I would like to discuss with you. I will be in the other room waiting...unless, of course, you really do want me to go now." Taking the towel, I considered him briefly and shook my head. "Very well then, I shall leave you to it."

The door closed behind him. I got up, toweling off, half expecting him to pop his head back in to ogle me. Should I have expected any less judging from prior experiences? But the door remained closed. I pulled on Claire's robe and ran a comb through my hair, making no effort to figure out what he could possibly have to say. I figured I would smile and nod and it would all be over soon enough.

Acacius sat on the couch when I emerged. Part of me expected to find him lounging on Claire's bed. Thankfully for me, that wasn't the case. Maybe he could behave without having to be asked?

"Red is such a sensual color," he grinned, his eyes slithering over me.

I suppose I should have known better.

"I'm gonna stop you right there," I proclaimed. "I can retract your invitation to stay at any minute."

"That will not be necessary, I can behave. That much I have proven to you."

"True." Although, thus far, only by request. Therefore, in effort to remove temptation, I sat in the chair across from him. "Ok, what do you want?"

"Alright, straight to the point then?" I nodded and he continued, "It was not fair of me to ask you to speak on our behalf to Lattimer."

"Why the change of heart?" I asked suspiciously.

"Because this has nothing to do with you, and my dragging you into it under false pretenses makes me look even worse. I downplayed the risk factor. You have every right to know Lattimer could very well view even the most benign contact from me as a threat."

"Starting a war," I said, repeating Julia's accusation.

"Yes," he paused. "Especially for choosing you to be my messenger."

"Julia said starting a war was exactly what you were trying to do."

"Only because she knew it was a possibility. It was not my goal. But her sharing that would serve to discredit me in your eyes. I trust I was not the only one you know she slandered in attempt to weaken your defenses."

"No...there were others," I confirmed.

I would take more comfort in his guess if her statements were a tad more coincidental. But they weren't, so I didn't.

"Besides, think about it, what could I possibly gain from starting a war? Such antics could spiral out of control quickly and would no doubt expose us to the mortals." He leaned toward me, his expression became morose. "We have been hunted by mortals before. If it was ugly in the dark ages, imagine how horrifying it would be with modern technology."

I conjured up a scenario of soldiers busting into known vampire establishments during the day. Sunlight engulfing immortals in flames before the armed forces could even fire off a round. Civilians acquiring night vision goggles in their own effort to eradicate the threat, sweeping basements and other underground hideouts. The grim reality of exposure horrified me. I forced the images from my mind with a shiver.

"Ok then," I said, standing abruptly. "I won't relay any messages to Lattimer on your behalf."

Acacius reluctantly took his cue from me, getting to his feet. I motioned to the door, taking little comfort in the thought of him behind me. A slight grin crossed his lips, as if he'd read my mind. He passed me, heading for the door and I followed. Just short of the threshold, he turned back to me so quickly I almost ran into him.

"Why were you crying when I arrived?" he asked. "It was not for Julia."

I thought about my answer and saw no reason to lie.

"Immortality has not been kind to me."

"I think you just started off with the wrong crowd. My immortals are not so vindictive to one another," he said. "You are more than welcome to join us, if you like."

"It's always good to have options," I replied pleasantly.

"No better time than the present. You do realize Julia was transformed by Lattimer," he said. I felt the smile disappear from my lips. "Coming with me tonight would allow you to avoid any future inquisition."

I contemplated his offer. As appealing as hiding away sounded, I trusted Petrus to be able to sort things out. No matter how misguided that may be, he was my best chance. Running would do nothing to prove my innocence. Talk about starting a war, joining camp Acacius after killing Julia would definitely provoke the worst case scenario from Lattimer.

"I appreciate your concern, but defecting at this point would only make matters worse. Besides, I did nothing wrong. She attacked me," I affirmed.

The comfort I took in knowing from experience that Lattimer accepted self-defense as an adequate plea was immeasurable.

A warm smile crept across his face, "Of course." He took me into his arms, hugging me. His scent infused the air with an exotic mix of incense and spices. "If you should change your mind, let me know."

The suggestion was barely more than a whisper in my ear before he released me. His eyes bore the sincerity of his proposal.

"Goodnight, Acacius."

"I can stay if you like," he offered. "Perhaps you should not be alone tonight?"

CHAPTER TWENTY-SIX

I should've known his good behavior wouldn't last. Planting my fists on my hips, I informed him, "That won't be necessary."

He smiled, opening the door, "I am shocked you thought I meant that with any sort of disrespect. For that, I retract my gracious proposal and bid you goodnight."

Acacius theatrically stalked off down the hall, as if offended. I smiled, closing the door, and made sure I locked it this time. As much as I hated to admit it, I didn't feel as dismal as I did before he showed up. Maybe I believed what he told me and found comfort that someone was finally honest with me. Or maybe I knew he was lying like all the others and my boost came from his comical exit. Whatever the case may have been, I hoped the change in mood was enough to keep the nightmares away.

But as I prepared for sleep, I couldn't shake the feeling I got in Acacius's arms. It was like a subliminal awareness that floated in the background. Between his gentle embrace and the look in his eyes that followed, I couldn't help but feel as if he were saying good-bye.

27

The Irish Sea crashed against the cliffs below, mirroring Owen's own turmoil. He sought out the solitude of his ancient Welsh cottage but it did little to ease the tension that utterly possessed him. The breeze off the angry sea ran through his golden blonde hair like a lover's caress, helpless to melt away the tightness at his temples. The cadence of the crashing waves falling in step with the throbbing in his head. His dark cobalt blue eyes turned to the glass in his hand. The fine crystal held the last swallow of his vodka. He gave the liquid a swirl and downed it. He had not fed in...had it really been almost two weeks? The spirits were starting to touch him, taking advantage of his diminished strength.

He turned his back on the sea, heading back to the cottage to refill his glass. The fire in the hearth was calling to him through the open door. Topping off his glass, he settled in to the stout leather chair next to the crackling flames. The hypnotic dance of the flames claimed his focus. Not quite entrancing enough to clear his mind.

It had been weeks since his fight with Trinnian. The altercation stuck in his head as if it happened only yesterday. How dare Trinnian accuse the one that made him of such malicious treachery, much less raise a hand to him. Trinnian's desperate attempt to cover for his own failures somehow manifesting themselves in his mind as Owen's doing. Having the audacity to attack him in Lattimer's house was nothing short of an outrage. Certainly Trinnian was aware of how lucky he was that Joel showed up when he did. A minute sooner and Lattimer would have been notified. Trinnian would have faced punishment for his blatant disrespect for Lattimer's home—not to mention assaulting his sire. The need for retaliation stirred in Owen's gut. He would not be dishonored by one he made.

The glass once again found his lips, its contents drained in one swift move. He stood to refill his glass, but stopped dead in his tracks. Olivia stood in the door of the cottage. Her expression was troubled. The sadness in her eyes was so uncharacteristic. Had Trinnian sent her to find him? He could sense she was alone. Yet another oddity, rarely did she leave New York, much less unescorted.

"He sent you to find me?"

Owen walked past her to the bottle on the counter, pouring a healthy shot into the glass.

"No one sent me. I had no idea you would be here."

Eyeing her suspiciously, he tossed back the shot.

"What brings you to Wales then?"

"I had to leave. I could not bear being there any longer," Olivia whispered, tears welling up in her eyes.

"Did Collin hurt you?" Alarm suddenly gripped him completely.

She shook her head, her beautiful features twisting in anguish. Burying her face in her hands, she wept.

Owen abandoned his glass and went to her, wrapping an arm around her shoulder, he walked her to the chair by the fire. She dropped down into the seat as Owen crouched before her.

"Was it Trinnian," he asked, the question tinged with anger. "What has he done to you?"

Her hands dropped to her lap and her eyes met his, "Oh Owen. I do not even know what to say."

She stared off into the fire. Her bottom lip quivered as she spoke, "Collin almost died...because of me."

Tears ran down her cheeks. Owen brushed them away, turning her chin back toward him.

"What happened?" His pause gave her time to collect herself.

Olivia's head tilted up and she scrubbed at her eyes with the heels of her hands. Returning her attention to him, she finally spoke.

"Trinnian came home. Collin was in the city hunting..." She swallowed and looked down at the floor. "Owen, you know how I have always felt about Trinnian."

She did not need to elaborate. He knew exactly what happened. Anger surged through him but he refused to let Olivia see it. She was so fragile, so defeated.

"How did Collin find out?"

"We...we told him."

Owen's eyes pinched shut. He ran his hands through his hair and down his face, "Did Collin attempt to take his own life?"

"No! Not at all. He left the manor and was staying at Jacquelyn's place. Her house burnt down during the day—" she explained, her voice thick with sorrow. "He barely made it to the basement."

A fresh round of tears welled up in her eyes. Owen stood and turned away, knowing he could not mask the rage consuming him.

"Is Collin alright?"

"Yes," she whispered. "He has healed."

CHAPTER TWENTY-SEVEN

"Jacquelyn?"

"She was not home."

Yet another Trinnian catastrophe, no surprise Jacquelyn found her way into the situation as well. Those two deserved each other in Owen's opinion. Trinnian certainly did not deserve someone like Olivia. She was of royal blood, her beauty and charm were—

Olivia's hand between his shoulder blades abruptly ended his thought.

"Owen, please do not hate me...I never intended to hurt him."

Slowly he turned to face Olivia, her pale green eyes begging for forgiveness. No, Trinnian did not deserve her and he would make sure he did not have her.

Pulling Olivia into his arms, he whispered into her ear, "I could never hate you, you know that."

Her arms encircled his waist, her head snuggled into his chest as he stroked her hair. The sweet perfume of her diffusing into the air, along with the rich, vibrant aroma of her blood. His hunger lunged to the surface, unwilling to be ignored. His hands started to tremble, he had to concentrate to keep them steady.

"What is wrong with me? I have ruined everything."

Pulling away, Owen held her face in his hands. His thumbs smoothing away traces of tears on her cheeks, "There is nothing wrong with you. You just need a little time to figure it out. Stay here as long as you like. I will leave if you wish so you can have the space you intended to find here."

"No, no. Please stay...I am actually glad you are here." Olivia's gaze narrowed on his face. "Owen, when is the last time you fed?"

He backed away, breaking eye contact.

"A few days."

"Why?"

"Just makes hunting that much sweeter sometimes."

"Liar."

"Believe what you will—"

"Use me, you need blood," She approached him, pushing her hair over her shoulder. Her scent seemed to fill the room. "Drink."

"No, really, I—" His mouth clamped shut on the words. The sound of her blood pulsing beneath her flesh silenced him, his focus stolen by its rhythmic flow. The blood itself seemed to sing to him, begging to be released.

"You are starving yourself and I cannot allow that to happen. Now drink." Olivia insisted. Hunger got the better of him. He reached for her with shaking hands. "My God, look at you. Why have you done this?"

To avoid answering, he grabbed her by the shoulders, burying his head in the crook of her neck. His teeth sank into her flesh, her blood ran over his tongue as he took the first pull. Olivia gasped at the urgency of his mouth. His eyes closed, body swaying in the rush of blood filling him after having gone too long without.

Lifting his mouth from her neck, he gasped, "I need more."

"Take what you need, I will be fine."

"Thank you," he whispered. His eyes locked on hers, the hunger possessing his gaze caused her body to tense slightly, until his mouth returned to her throat. She cradled his head, encouraging him to feed. His hands slipped over her hips, pulling her closer. The taste of her and the feel of her body was almost too much. Owen moaned, doubling his hold. Her hand gently stoked his hair, the gesture meant to sooth, stoking the arousal that grew inside. Strength washed over him, mingling with the effects of the vodka he had consumed, gradually working to cleanse the alcohol from his system.

A moment of clarity came to him amid all the sensations he was experiencing. He knew how to put Trinnian back in his place.

His lips left her throat and he rested his forehead on Olivia's shoulder, still holding her tight to his body.

"I need to lie down," Owen whispered.

"Here, let me help into the room."

He let her escort him into the bedroom. When they got to the edge of the bed, she started to turn him so he could sit. Owen slid his arms around her waist, he peered deep into her eyes. The act caught her off guard for a split second. Her reaction brought a smile to his lips.

"Why are you looking at me like that?" Olivia asked.

The smile he wore melted away, Owen knew without a doubt, Olivia was the key to dealing with Trinnian.

*　　*　　*　　*　　*

"What do you mean you can't publish the article? I worked my ass off on that and quite frankly, I think it is one of my best—in my humble opinion," Claire said, trying to defend the piece she had come to Germany to write. But her magazine's Editor in Chief was not budging.

"Claire, I'm not arguing that it is well written. You've definitely pegged German nightlife. All I am saying is that I don't think it is exactly travel material."

"I don't get what you mean, Ross. If it's well written and gives an accurate picture of what I was trying to capture, then what's wrong?"

"Well, how do I say this politely?"

Claire's grip tightened on the cell phone, "Oh for Christ's sake, ya just say it!"

"Fine. I felt like I was reading a serial killer novel."

Laughter burst from Claire, rendering her unable to speak. The line was silent when her chuckling tapered off.

"Where the hell do you get that?"

"Shall I read you a sample? Oh, here's a good one...'From the shadows on the edge of the dance floor, one feels almost like a voyeur, transfixed by the seductive movement of the crowd seemingly on the verge of sexual indulgence at any given moment. A sea of glistening flesh adorned with little more than sequins and leather, their pulses throbbing to the same bass encouraging the vulgar motion of their bodies.' What is that, Claire? Were you on drugs?"

"No!" Claire gasped incredulously. "In fact, I hadn't even had a drink at that point."

That came shortly after in the back alley, she thought to herself with a giggle.

"This isn't funny, Claire. If this is honestly the article you were planning to submit, I'm going have to reject it— hopefully giving you enough time to write something worth printing. Mind you, we already have a night life writer, we don't need another."

"What the fuck? Are you kidding me?"

"No, no I'm not. You have 24hrs to submit something worth my time."

With an irritated snort, Claire ended the call.

Augustine looked up at her from the bed. His sultry hazel eyes studied her for a moment before falling victim to the grin creeping across his face.

"It's not funny," Claire informed him.

"I told you he would not like it. But you insist to know him so well. Eh, what can I say?"

CHAPTER TWENTY-SEVEN

"Well when you are finished reveling in your 'I told you so' victory, I need some peace and quiet to rewrite an article he will submit. Oh, and I have 24 hours to do so," Claire stated, her fists balling up at her sides.

"Tisk, tisk, tisk. You should work out that aggression first, *amore mio.* One should not write such important things with pent up frustration," he purred in his velvety Italian accent.

Claire's anger melted away instantly, her eyes roaming his body shamelessly.

"Well, I'm sure it couldn't hurt," she concurred, sliding into the bed with her lover.

*   *   *   *   *

The heavy door of the manor house closed behind Trinnian, echoing through the emptiness surrounding him. He could not recall a time when his home felt so hollow and abandoned. Olivia had not returned. He strode across the foyer, removing his coat and draping it over the railing before sitting on the stairs. The cell phone in his pocket remained silent. Tempted as he was to call Olivia again, he was not willing to deal with the disappointment that accompanied his attempts at communication going straight to voice mail.

It was not as if he felt no guilt over what had happened to Collin. That was purely coincidental and Collin was almost completely healed. He may as well have put a torch to Collin himself for the way Olivia regarded him before running off. It was the manifestation of her own guilt she had to deal with. Maybe she just needed her space. She would come around once she thought about things logically. After all, she was a level headed female, one driven by reason and logic, normally.

His cell phone rang, echoing through the foyer like a siren. It was Olivia. Another ring peeled through the silence before he answered.

"Where are you? I have been worried sick!"

"Trinnian?" His name was barely a whisper.

"I'm here. Are you alright? Where are you?"

"I am at the cottage in Wales...please...please come help me." Her voice sounded rough and unsteady.

"Are you alright, what—"

The call disconnected on her end. He grabbed his coat, bolting into the night.

28

When my eyes opened the following night, it was in the wake of a disturbing dream. My subconscious had been cruel enough to make me relive the incident with Julia. But there was a sickening twist to the ending.

Petrus had just opened the trunk of his car. However, when he turned back around, my perspective changed. I viewed his actions from ground level looking up and it was no longer Petrus. It was Lattimer. He crouched down next to me, my eyes following him. It became difficult to see what he was doing, for some reason my point of view was limited. That was until he started to rise. There, cradled in his arms was my decapitated body, which he gently placed into the trunk. It took him a moment to situate my torso and limbs to his liking before he turned back to retrieve the remainder. He reached toward me, placing a hand over each ear and picked up my head.

The look Lattimer wore was an unsettling mix of pity and adoration. His face was all I had to focus on as he moved me toward the trunk. I felt as if I lacked the ability to close my eyes. All I could do was watch as he placed my head in the trunk beside my body, more specifically in the crook of my arm. That I could tell from my peripheral vision. Not exactly a perspective of myself I ever thought I would see. With my body neatly packed away, he took a handkerchief out of his pocket and wiped the blood from his hands. He tossed the soiled cloth into the space with me and shut the trunk. That is when I woke.

I lay in bed staring at the ceiling. The confidence I clung to the prior night in Petrus and his ability to deal with Lattimer no longer comforted me. The only thing that had changed was the dream and its implications. Lattimer's complete control over me was obvious, not to mention the fact that it could be interpreted in ways I would rather not contemplate at the moment. There was but one way to quell the rising panic wrought by the dream. I had to call Petrus.

He answered on the second ring, greeting me as if the prior night never happened.

"Jacquelyn, good evening."

"Hey...I wasn't sure if I was supposed to call you or if you were planning to call me after you spoke to Lattimer."

"I spoke to him last night."

"Oh, ok. So that's it. Everything is ok?"

"Well..."

My stomach sank, "Well what?"

"He is coming to the city, if he is not already here. You should be hearing from him."

"Petrus! Why didn't you tell me?"

"Oh, it is nothing. He just needs to sort out the details. He did not seem to be too upset."

"Why am I not comforted by that?"

Laughter sounded on the other end, "Because you worry too much. Relax. Everything is going to be fine."

Easy for him to say, I wasn't so confident he'd feel the same in my shoes.

CHAPTER TWENTY-EIGHT

"Great, I feel better already. I'm so glad I called," I replied dryly.

"Good, I am glad I could put you at ease."

"That was sarcasm."

"Oh."

"Well, thanks again for all your help, Petrus. I'm sorry to have to keep putting you into such situations."

"Anytime, Jacquelyn. It keeps life interesting, anyway."

Ending the call, I sat up, dangling my feet over the edge of the bed. I decided I would get ready for the evening and hunt. If for no other reason, I may need some strength later.

While I showered, I tried to think about what to wear. What exactly does one wear to an inquisition? Something non-threatening and demure? Feminine attire may plead to his masculine side. If I looked like a delicate flower, he wouldn't try to treat me like a thug, would he? My offhand idea from the previous night came back, if he locked me up, nobody could mess with me anymore. That school of thought was quickly abandoned with the knowledge of his impending visit. Yeah, that was just 'woe is me' at its worst. I really had no desire to be locked away for fifty years by anybody.

I took a little more time to get ready than normal. My auburn hair was dried section by section with a large round brush, making the ends hug my shoulders gently. Makeup was chosen for its enhancing abilities, not to draw attention or dramatically play up features. The outfit stuck to the idea that the key to the treatment I would receive lay in portraying myself in the most ladylike way as possible. I chose an emerald green cardigan and a paisley skirt infused with shades of green, blue and black. My suede pumps were a gorgeous navy, purchased for a particular outfit last year and forgotten at

Claire's until that night. At least my luck wasn't all bad, I suppose.

Coat in hand, I locked the apartment door behind me. If I wasn't ready at this point, I never would be. One last moment to gather my wits, I headed toward the exit and onto the city streets.

Try as I might, I couldn't seem to stay focused on the hunt. More than anything, I wandered aimlessly through the city. My thoughts diverting to Lattimer and what would happen to me. As much as I tried to regain control, it kept straying just out of reach.

The approach of an immortal stopped me instantly. I searched the oncoming crowd for the familiar signature and, sure enough, Marco was heading toward me. Surely he couldn't have found out about Julia already? That was the moment I realized, I just passed his building. I was merely in his path.

Not bothering to pause, he acknowledged me with a stiff nod in passing.

"Marco, wait."

He continued on ignoring my request. I followed him up the steps to the door of his building. He rounded on me.

"No, I still have not seen Lori," he stated, clearly annoyed with my presence. "If you will excuse me, I have a business to run."

Quickly utilizing his code, he passed into the building. I followed close, making it through the door before it closed.

"Marco," I said, he turned to face me. His expression proof he wasn't expecting me to follow. "I need to talk to you."

He scowled at me, "Please make it quick. I am in a bit of a hurry."

"Fine, although I'm not quite sure why I feel compelled to tell you anything. Having found out about all of the lies our relationship was—"

"Jacquelyn, I really do not have time. I am three employees down in the past week alone."

"Well then, let me get to it. Lori is dead. She was killed by Julia for fear anyone would find out about her involvement in Lori's attempt to kill me." I now had his attention. "Diana is gone because Julia suspected she figured it all out. When Diana called me in hysterics fearing for her life, I told her to find somewhere safe to go and she did. At least I think. Julia never did respond to my question."

"You have spoken to Julia?" He looked confused. "I have not seen her since the night you came looking for Lori."

"I saw her last night," I said. Suddenly, the words didn't want to flow so easily. "She had been stalking me. That's what she told me, biding her time, waiting to get me alone. Somehow she had convinced herself I had to be taken out of the picture. She...she attacked me."

His expression went blank, "You killed her."

"I had no choice."

Running his hands through his hair until they came to a rest on the back of his neck, he looked down at the floor.

"That is why Lattimer is here." Now that, I wasn't ready for, the comment left me completely speechless. Marco looked up at me. "Please leave. I do not want him coming here looking for you."

He headed off toward the elevator. I watched him walk away, wondering why I felt the need to tell him anything. Maybe I felt I ran into him for a reason and letting him find out any other way wasn't right. Whatever, my spur of the moment confession did little to ease my mind.

No sooner did I step out of the building, my phone rang. Looking at the screen, I knew my time was up. Von was calling. As much as I wanted to hit 'ignore', it really wasn't an option.

"Hello," I said.

"Jacquelyn Livingston?"

"Yes, Von, it's me."

"Lattimer would like to see you as soon as possible at his place in Manhattan. Would you like me to send Nikos to pick you up?"

"No, that won't be necessary. I'm not too far from there."

"Excellent. I will let him know you are on your way."

Without another word, he hung up. I descended the steps to Marco's building and headed to meet Lattimer.

When I arrived at the building, Von was there to escort me up to Lattimer's place. He silently navigated me through to the threshold of the usual meeting room. The door opened and Nikos came out, gesturing me inside.

Once I was inside, Nikos backed out of the room, closing the door behind me. I could sense Lattimer ahead of me, sitting in his usual chair. The short walk to my seat felt much longer on wobbly knees. The warmth radiating from the fireplace did little to combat the chill of fear growing inside me.

When Lattimer finally came into view, I was ill prepared for my own reaction. I had been so wrapped up in the repercussions of Julia's death, everything else was forgotten. The instant I saw him, mental images of erotic encounters surfaced. Although only the product of dreams, I felt his naked flesh and could even taste him on my lips. I didn't realize I was chewing my bottom lip until he spoke.

CHAPTER TWENTY-EIGHT

"There is no need to be so frightened. Please, sit," he said, gesturing to the vacant chair next to his.

I did as I was told and tried to focus, ridding my mind of any less than ladylike thoughts. Settling back into my chair, I studied him for any trace of anger. But I saw nothing. In fact, he looked at ease, wearing a black suit with the jacket unbuttoned. His long, black hair pulled back from his face. He openly looked me over, but not in the same lascivious manner as Acacius.

"You look lovely this evening. I hate to think I ruined any plans you may have had."

His comment lacked the sincerity of one truly apologetic for their intrusion.

"No, not at all."

"Still, I would like to get straight to the point, if you do not mind. I would like to return to Canada as soon as possible."

Fighting the urge to take a deep breath, I answered, "Please do."

That didn't come out right but, thankfully, he didn't notice.

"Petrus tells me Julia was to blame for yesterday's confrontation," he announced. "Do you agree?"

"Yes, she was jealous of my involvement with Marco and..." I paused. His look prompting me to continue, did I really almost say Acacius? Mentioning his name at this point would not be to my benefit. "And you."

"Me?"

"She had this crazy idea that you wanted me for your own."

"She always was a jealous woman, so that does not surprise me in the least," Lattimer said. "Therefore her solution was to remove you entirely?"

"That is exactly what happened."

"Petrus also told me that in your attempt to defend yourself, Julia had been thrown from a roof. The fall injuring her so badly you had no choice but to 'put her out of her misery' as they say?" he asked.

"Yes."

He stood and turned to me, "Jacquelyn, I am sorry you had to be the object of someone's delusions of jealousy yet again. It is especially bothersome coming from one that I created."

I followed his lead, getting to my feet, amazed things turned out much better than I had anticipated.

"It's not your fault, she—"

"Where are you going?" he asked, looking at me as if I were insane.

"Oh, I thought we were finished," I replied, resuming my seat.

"I am afraid I just cannot let you leave," he stated, his matter-of-fact comment instantly making me nauseous. "How would I look to the others if I let a newborn with a penchant for murdering immortals loose to roam the streets?"

"I'm not a murderer!" I exclaimed, getting to my feet.

"Two corpses in as many months? That does not look good," he noted, shaking his head.

"They attacked me!"

"I understand, but it is this second murder that will raise suspicion amongst the others."

"Why?" I asked, desperately looking for a way out.

"This one you committed as an orphan."

He knew Collin left and I was alone. I had to think of something, anything that would gain my freedom.

"I was offered a job—working for Petrus. I decided to take it and move into his building," I claimed.

CHAPTER TWENTY-EIGHT

"Jacquelyn, we both know you are lying. What Petrus does there..." Once again he looked me over. "It is not you."

He took a step toward me.

"Please, don't do this," I whispered, shaking my head as tears welled up and spilled down my cheeks. "You don't have to do this."

"It is for your own good. You will understand one day," he said, taking me into his arms.

I knew what he was about to do, I was told once how vampires were subdued for imprisonment. They were drained of blood to keep them weak. I tried to push against his chest, struggling against his hold. But it was like being bound by steel, my pathetic attempt at freedom was pointless. There was no point in fighting against one as strong as Lattimer. I just closed my eyes, my hands clenched into fists at my sides as his teeth sunk into the crook of my neck.

*   *   *   *   *

"Lattimer has taken Jacquelyn!" exclaimed Dorian, storming uninvited into the harem room. "I saw his Neanderthals put her into the limousine."

"I know," Acacius replied, turning the page of his newspaper.

Dorian lunged at the paper, ripping it from Acacius's grip and tossing it to the floor.

"You knew Lattimer would take her, yet you did nothing to stop it?"

"Might I suggest you change your tone?" Acacius countered. "The only thing keeping me seated comfortably at this point is the fact that I understand you feel a fondness for her. I believe by restricting you from seeing Jacquelyn, I have only added to your romantic notion of the connection you may or may not share—thus, triggering this foolish, melodramatic outburst."

Taking a second to calm himself, Dorian rephrased his question, "Why did you let this happen?"

"I suppose I could have carted her off by force but everybody involved would take that the wrong way, aside from you and me, that is."

"If you would have told her he would take her I am confident she would have come on her own free will."

Acacius stood, bringing the two of them face to face. He gently patted Dorian on the cheek.

"Ah, my old friend, you see I did offer her refuge. But, when she is not blinded by her trusting nature, she is quite clever. In her own words, she conceded that avoiding Lattimer would only make matters worse," Acacius said, motioning to the newspaper scattered across the floor.

Dorian's brow furrowed in thought as he stooped to gather up the pages, stacking them neatly in order. He stood, handing the paper to Acacius.

"You did not just hand her over to Lattimer wrapped in a bow. There is something in this for you."

Acacius's eyes lit up with joy, "I knew you would piece it together!" He smiled, "That is why I chose you above all the others to be my confidant."

"The fact that your motivation in most things is for selfish reasons made this one pretty obvious."

"Oh Dorian, do not be so modest," he responded, tossing the paper down on the couch. "As much as you hate to admit, we do think alike. Your only set back is your conscience. In my position, I do not have the luxury of entertaining principles. The fate of those that follow me rely on my ability to do whatever it takes to survive."

CHAPTER TWENTY-EIGHT

"And how exactly does Jacquelyn fit into that?" Dorian asked.

"If I would have taken her outright, it would have forced Lattimer's hand. The blatant insult would have set forth retaliation on a scale never before witnessed. Centuries of tension between us finally come to a head," Acacius replied. "I would be forever known as the instigator, the one that brought the immortals to war."

"So you let her go because you are worried about what history would say about you?"

"No, that is not the point. More than anything I need the guise of innocence to acquire defectors. If it looks as if Lattimer attacked for no good reason, I will gain the loyalty of those on the fence. The ones that claim independence," Acacius said.

"But you have not given him reason to attack."

Acacius grabbed Dorian by the shoulders, his expression devious, "Ah! But I have. You see, Jacquelyn knows of our plight. She is sympathetic to our existence. I have managed to plant the seed while removing myself from the equation. How long do you think she will be able to hold her tongue while such knowledge tugs at her heartstrings?"

"What have you done?" Dorian breathed, backing away from Acacius.

"I have successfully launched a grenade into Lattimer's house..." A look of vexation came over him. "I just wish it had more of a predictable timer."

"You would sacrifice our people to this...this need for revenge? How many will die because of your ego?"

Acacius glared at Dorian. The cold stare broke off as he walked away from Dorian toward the couch.

"Our people?" Acacius stood, staring at the ancient Roman swords that adorned the wall above the seat. "In case you need reminding, they are not 'our' people," Acacius stated, removing a gladius from the wall and turning to face Dorian. Before his eyes, the warrior Acacius had once been emerged. "What have you had to sacrifice for them? Nothing. Do you understand what I have sacrificed for them?" Dorian backed toward the exit until his heel hit the bottom step. "Do you?!"

"Yes," Dorian answered. His trembling response did nothing to ease the anger that twisted his superior's face. Stumbling back onto the steps in his attempt to put space between them, Dorian fell. "You know I do."

"I have lost everything for my followers. EVERYTHING!" Acacius wailed, hovering over Dorian. "I lost my home. My freedom. My companion." Tears of anger and sorrow filled his eyes as he spoke. "You speak as if my hatred toward Lattimer were petty and selfish. Your ignorance comes from your lack of sacrifice." Acacius fell to his knees, straddling Dorian and raised the blade in both hands, "You need to know what sacrifice is like."

The gladius came down.

Epilogue

The salty ocean breeze swirled through the stone hallway, courtesy of the open windows at either end. Sheer curtains framing them rose and fell lazily on the gentle wind. A piano played a delicate tune, providing the music for their subtle dance.

As much as Ruthie hated to admit, it felt good to be home. She missed the distant sound of the waves crashing on the shore and the air heavy with the scent of the ocean. The city had kept her away too long.

Having reached her destination, she knocked on the door. Before the echo of her request dissipated, an answer came from within the chamber.

"Come in."

Ruthie entered the room. A human male played the piano in the corner. His complexion was tan, emphasized by the gauzy white shirt he wore. Platinum highlights from the sun shimmered in his short light brown hair. He gave Ruthie a warm smile that lingered while he played his tune.

"Almost finished," said the woman sitting at a desk with her back to the door. The desk was positioned in front of an open window facing the ocean. Pale blonde hair fell to the small of her back, shifting every so often with the breeze. "There we go." She got up, setting down her pen and turned to Ruthie, arms wide. Her willowy frame was draped in a white cotton sundress. "My Ruthie," she said, beaming.

Ruthie stepped into the woman's embrace, returning the gesture with sincerity.

"I cannot thank you enough," she whispered into the woman's ear.

"Anything to see you smile again." The woman held Ruthie at arm's length, admiring her as one might a rare painting. Her dark sapphire eyes glistened with tears. "It is so good to have you home."

Ruthie smiled, "It is good to be home...but, please do not cry. You have already made me feel bad enough for staying away so long."

"It is the music," the woman said, with a wink. "Ethan, that will be all for now. Would you mind drawing me a bath?"

Ethan rose from the bench, abruptly ending the music, "Not at all, Genesia."

Watching Ethan pass through the door, Ruthie could not help but notice how his khaki shorts accentuated his toned butt. He was not her type but she was not ignorant to the attributes of a fine male specimen when she saw one. She returned her attention to Genesia.

"You sure you are not—"

"Ruthie! I told you, I raised that boy," Genesia said, a look of disapproval touched her features. "See, that is how long you have been gone—and then some."

"He adores you," she noted.

"As a son should adore his mother," Genesia stated firmly. "Now, what can I do for you?"

"I have something of a huge favor to ask of you."

"Anything for you, all you have to do is ask." Ruthie's weight shifted on her feet uncomfortably. Genesia's expression became concerned, "Is something wrong with Diana?"

"No—no, not at all. Again, I cannot thank you enough for agreeing to transform her for me. She has been such a joy to my existence since the first night I met her..."

"Here, sit," Genesia offered, motioning to the chair next to her desk. Ruthie shook her head. "What is it, my child?"

"There is someone I have never met that I owe for Diana seeking refuge with me."

Genesia's face relaxed, her relief was almost tangible, "Absolutely, you tell me what it will take to repay them—"

Ruthie buried her face in her hands, "I am sorry, I cannot believe I am asking you to do this."

"You are starting to worry me," Genesia said, taking Ruthie's hands into hers. "I am not willing to lose you again. You mean way too much to me to endure that heartbreak again."

Ruthie pulled her hands back, crossing her arms, "You see, I know that and that is why I am struggling with this so."

"What?" Genesia implored.

"Lattimer has wrongly imprisoned this person for murder." Genesia's demeanor completely changed. Her stance becoming stiff as Ruthie continued. "She is being held in his dungeons in Canada."

The only sound in the room was the crash of the waves filtering through the open window.

Genesia turned, walking toward the door. She exhaled loudly, shaking her head, "I do not even know what to say."

Hope was not lost to Ruthie. She planted herself in front of Genesia to lay out her plan.

"We can do this!" she said, optimistically. "I have it all figured out."

"You have no idea who you are dealing with. The few times you have met Lattimer, he has been pleasant. You do not know him like I do."

"That is why I am relying on you to help," Ruthie pled. "All I am asking you to do is to go to his Halloween party. Your presence there after so many decades will catch him off guard enough for me, Diana and a few of the others to make the grab and be gone before he even suspects anything."

"Ruthie...I—"

"You always said he owed you one for stealing Augustine."

Genesia planted her hands on her hips, her expression indignant, "That was a totally different situation!"

"Maybe, but you have yet to repay him..." Ruthie's eyes glinted with mischief, mirroring Genesia's stance. "You are afraid of him!"

Gasping incredulously, she responded, "Do not be absurd, child. He would never dare threaten me."

"Well then?"

Standing her ground under Genesia's scrutiny, Ruthie waited for an answer. The longer it took, the more confident she felt. As much as she hated to take advantage of her maker's adoration of her, Ruthie's desire to make Diana happy outweighed anything else.

"Halloween is fast approaching. Iron out your plan and get back to me. There cannot be any chance for failure."

Squealing with excitement, Ruthie latched onto Genesia, "Thank you so much!"

"I hope this...what is her name?"

"Jacquelyn."

"I can only hope she knows what we are risking to save her."

"I trust Diana's judgment," Ruthie said from the doorway. "Your bath is getting cold." Flashing a victorious grin, she closed the door.

Acknowledgements

಄ಞಛ಄ಞಛ

I would like to thank my family for encouraging me. I love you all dearly.

Of course, it wasn't just family spurring me on. I would also like to thank Caleb Cornwell, Kristin Burns, Berni Stevens, AJ Skinner, Grayson Copeland, Debra Johnson, Lori Stevens, Mel Jokanovic, Lauren Coombs, Mazzadonna, Hannah Rowe, Olivia Mistretta, Anna Haller, Becky Voie, Kassidy Anderson, Justine Maxwell, Kathryn Klepper, Abigail Entrican, Dan R. Wakefield, Sharon Worsley and last, but definitely not least, Tamara Williams.

Finally, a special thanks to St. John's Pub for providing me a quiet spot to finish my final novel review. If I missed anyone, I'll catch you next time!

www.ingramcontent.com/pod-product-compliance
Lightning Source LLC
Chambersburg PA
CBHW020259200626
46816CB00001BA/372